SUNDOG

HIGHWAY

To Dan & Carol –
A little remembrance
from Saskatchewan.
Love,
Tracy & Trev.

April 2001.

SUNDOG

WRITING FROM SASKATCHEWAN

HIGHWAY

GENERAL EDITOR: LARRY WARWARUK

COTEAU BOOKS

TWENTY-FIVE YEARS

General editor, Larry Warwaruk. Editor for the press, Geoffrey Ursell.

Cover photo, "Aegean Grass Sea; camera motion on windswept grass, near Central Butte, Saskatchewan, 1983" by Courtney Milne. Cover and book design by Duncan Campbell.

Printed and bound in Canada at Houghton Boston Lithographers, Saskatoon.

Canadian Cataloguing in Publication Data

Main entry under title

Sundog highway: writing from Saskatchewan
ISBN: 1-55050-167-4

1. Canadian literature (English) – Saskatchewan.*
2. Canadian literature (English) – 20TH Century.*
3. Art, Canadian – Saskatchewan.*
4. Art, Modern –

20TH century – Saskatchewan, 1. Warwaruk, Larry, 1943-

NX513.A3 S38 2000   C810.8'097124 C00-920162-9

10 9 8 7 6 5 4 3 2 1

COTEAU BOOKS
401-2206 Dewdney Ave.
Regina, Saskatchewan
Canada   S4R 1H3

AVAILABLE IN THE US FROM
General Distribution Services
4500 Witmer Industrial Estates
Niagara Falls, NY, 14305-1386

This publication has been produced with the assistance, including financial support, of Saskatchewan Education, and the financial support of SaskTel Pioneers. The publisher gratefully acknowledges the financial assistance of the Saskatchewan Arts Board, the Canada Council for the Arts, the Government of Canada through the Book Publishing Industry Development Program (BPIDP), and the City of Regina Arts Commission, for its publishing program.

SUNDOG HIGHWAY

Batoche, Molly Lenhardt

Oil on canvas board, 45.7 cm x 60.9 cm, 1982

Contents

INTRODUCTION

"People are made of places," says poet Elizabeth Brewster. And Cree people say, "The people do not make the land; it's the land that makes the people."

Sundog Highway is a look at the people and places of Saskatchewan. It explores the diversity of our many landscapes – from the dry and rolling hills of the southwest to the central prairie to the northern woodlands – and the diversity of our many cultures through the eyes and hearts of our writers.

Sundog Highway reflects a phenomenal growth in Saskatchewan writing over the last few decades, in which a new range of voices is being heard. This is most evident in the strong presence of First Nations and Metis writers such as Louise Bernice Halfe, Randy Lundy, Rita Bouvier, and Janice Acoose. Writers like Lorna Crozier, Maria Campbell, Ken Mitchell, and Guy Vanderhaeghe are also receiving national and international acclaim.

Sundog Highway also works as an imaginative history of this province. The pioneer struggle to survive in a new land is balanced by First Nations viewpoints about what the arrival of Europeans meant to them. All of the writers here bring useful and challenging perspectives.

Understanding where we've come from can help us think about where we're going. No one can predict the future, but Doug Cuthand offers an intriguing vision of a time without racism, when cultures will be more balanced and mutually tolerant.

Welcome to this journey through time and space, where you can experience the ideas of our writers and their passion for our unique landscape and heritage. And where you can consider the sometimes difficult questions they ask about our future.

– *Larry Warwaruk*

I. HOME PLACE

Near Big Muddy, Don Hall.
Silver print, 22.8 x 30.4 cm, 1980

A pair of aces spans a dirt road leading to a home far off in the distance. As the photographer, Don Hall, says, he was struck by "the humour of the playing card images – the uncertainty, the 'gambling,' of trying to make a living from the land." Prairie agriculture has always been a gamble. Maybe it's a gamble that's now being lost, when "Thousands of people, rural for generations, have been driven off it," as Sharon Butala says. And there are ongoing conflicts to deal with, as, for example in Barbara Sapergia's play, about the roles of men and women. Or the rights of First Nations people that Doug Cuthand discusses. He says, "I don't like to rant about the past, preferring to emphasize positive changes, but sometimes we must remind the public where our roots lie and that the mistakes of the past are the reason for our present situation." Guy Vanderhaeghe says about the passing on of the land in his story that "Gil MacLean is prepared to sacrifice his son for the sake of the land, and Ronald is ready to despoil the land as a way of injuring his father." How can all these conflicts be resolved? Can changing demographics and choices in agriculture bring new opportunities and a new vision for the land? Or is it true, as Barbara Sapergia says, that, "We've had so many farm crises that sometimes it seems people have stopped listening"?

HOME

SHARON BUTALA

During the years that I was beating my way through the thickets of self-delusion, the world around me was not static. In fact, the agricultural world was facing a growing crisis too, a crisis of such huge proportions and breadth that everybody around me was eventually affected by it to some degree. One major factor was drought.

From my journal:

June 29, 1984: 11:10 a.m. It is 91 degrees F. and the wind must be blowing up to 50 mph. That hot wind and lack of moisture (last July we had a three-day rain and virtually nothing since) is ruining the hay and the grain crops. Even my vegetable and flower gardens won't grow. The sky is a pale, dusty blue at the horizon, and higher up where the dust doesn't reach it, it is the usual bright blue of summer. Anxiety Butte is faded by the haze of dust in the air. The hay crop is short and thin and burning at the bottom and the crested wheat grass in the yard has whitish tips and is pale dun below. The road is crumbling to dust. Everything looks white, even the air, even the grass and trees that have been watered and are green, and the earth between the back door and the caragana hedge is blown bare and is white and cracking. People who are overextended are worried sick.

1:20 p.m.: 98 degrees F.

2:00 p.m.: 101 degrees F. in the shade of the deck. Still blowing.

5:30 p.m.: A dust storm. For some time, clouds — normal thunderclouds, not very serious-looking — had been coming from the south and there had been thunder occasionally for about an hour. I looked up and a dust storm was on us from the southwest. Everything was obliterated by the fine brown air. It lasted only ten minutes or so and then vanished and a hard rain came down briefly. In those moments the temperature fell 20 degrees to 75 degrees F., but the wind never stopped.

July 16, 1984: All the cattle have been sent out of the PFRA pasture three months early because all the water holes have dried up. The constant sound of wind in your ears.

September 1, 1984: We're almost out of water here. The river is barely flowing.

July 29, 1985: Our grain crop has been writtten off 100% in all fields.

The summer of 1984 we set records for heat every day from July first to the eleventh. Peter reported that the hay crop was the worst since he'd taken over the hay farm in 1965 and young grasshoppers were detected everywhere in the grass. Farmers in Saskatchewan, the worst hit by the drought, began to hold the first of the drought meetings trying to get help from the government, and everybody scrambled to pull in any slack, while those in the most precarious financial position began to lose their farms. But, for the most part, people believed this was just another drought in the relatively predictable cycle of droughts, and that those who could had only to wait it out and prosperity would soon return.

I had a roof over my head and three square meals a day because Peter raised cattle for market and sold them, because he had some farmland (farmed by others), and whether it rained or not or the winds blew too hard or spring was early or late or the winter colder or warmer than usual with more or less snow were matters of importance to me as they were to the people in whose midst I was living. Hardly noticing I had, I'd begun to watch the sky for signs of rain, for cold fronts moving in, for approaching storms, or blessed Chinooks and to study cloud formations and sunsets for clues as to the next day's weather. In the early eighties when the rain began to fail, the drought was of grave interest to me for more than its sociological effects.

One major consequence was that we had to sell a liner-load of cows and calves, unheard of on the Butala ranch and which might be compared to starting to live off the capital instead of the interest from your trust fund, or like selling off parcels of your land. Peter took this step because the drought had meant there was no hay crop with which to feed them in the winter, and because no grass had grown there was no grazing either, with the result that we had to buy a lot of expensive feed. For the first time in quite a while people with cattle had an edge on those who raised only grain, because we could at least sell cattle, while people with only grain to sell, what there was of it, were encountering additional problems having nothing to do with drought.

Other factors, too, were at work which hadn't been foreseen by most farmers during the good times. Overall, farm input costs – chemical fertilizer, herbicides and pesticides, machinery and fuel – went up about three hundred percent in that ten-year period from the time the cash from the huge crops of the last half of the seventies hit the farm economy, into the early eighties when the bonanza began to dry up.

As if drought and the increase in input costs weren't bad enough, bank interest rates hit an astonishing high – up to twenty-four percent on borrowed money, and since nearly everybody ran their farms or ranches on operating loans, the fiscal system itself began to put people out of business, regardless of their continued ability to grow grain or raise livestock. By 1989, in most places, the drought had ended, but it no longer mattered whether we could grow grain or not, because increasingly either we couldn't sell it or the prices we could get for it were below what it cost to produce it.

For the first time, farmers had to face the fact that stiff competition in grain markets wasn't something they were going to be able to beat. Countries which had bought Canadian grain had now become exporters themselves, while others became at least self-sufficient, and as buyers became fewer, the sellers began to compete even harder and grain prices fell to lows unheard of for the generation currently on the farms. There was constant talk about the greenhouse effect – global warming – which would ruin the western climate for grain farming. And nobody was admitting it, but in parts of the Palliser Triangle the land was dying as a consequence of its being marginal farmland in the first place, of which too much had been asked for too long. It wasn't that the present was bad and growing more desperate, it was also that the future had suddenly turned from apparently limitless to a brick wall.

I was privy to the endless conversations about the situation when Peter's friends dropped in for coffee or we dropped in to their kitchens. I heard the amazement, the anger, the bitterness, the sadness, the "if" talk and the potential solutions dreamt up by this one or that one. If I was surprised at anything it was at how civilized everybody managed to be, no matter how bad his/her situation. People seemed to feel helpless to force out of the powers that be whatever changes were needed to save farms and farmers. I have the impression that most people were coming to see that no government had a clue what to do – or that governments knew what to do, but refused for political reasons to do them. There were meetings and protests, but compared to the rage of, for example, the rioters of Los Angeles, who in an orgy of violence burned, looted, and otherwise destroyed in response to the racism which blighted their lives, or even the vocal militance of farmers in France, the protests of prairie farmers, whose lives were also being broken in a way apparently impossible for city dwellers to imagine, seemed to me to be surprisingly muted.

But then, I think there was a part of most agricultural people which remained disbelieving, which did not fully realize the extent and apparent irreversibility of the catastrophe. Raised for at least two generations on the myth that we were "the breadbasket of the world," we didn't find it easy to look in the eye so basic a belief, the framework on which three generations had build their lives and a whole society, and see that this was no longer true and, in fact, probably never had been. If the agricultural people's fatal flaw had been hubris, and I believe it was, they had been led into it by shortsighted governments and the so-called experts who were themselves only the common people with degrees, and by agricultural corporations and financial institutions whose only mandate or interest was to make as much money as possible out of the work, the hardship, of others.

All of this has been documented in countless magazine articles, radio broadcasts, and television specials, and somewhere, no doubt, somebody is writing the definitive book about the end of the family farm on the Canadian Prairies. Nothing was the way it had been ten years earlier. Wherever necessity dictated and there were jobs to be found, farm people went to work off the farm. Women who had always been available to help with farm work at home and to drive kids to after-school activities were suddenly at work in the bank, the credit union, the grocery store, school, hospital or senior citizens' lodge, jobs which might help keep body and soul together, but which had little or nothing to do with self-fulfillment, and which took women away from the satisfaction of spending the day in the midst of natural beauty. As a result of economic stress, rural life was changing so quickly that the old "traditional" life was getting harder and harder to find. I had moved from the city into a world I thought was in some ways idyllic and now, with truly breathtaking rapidity, it seemed it was dying.

I began to see the lives of the people around me as not merely picturesque, interesting, or beautiful (and therefore as removed from me), but as *real*. It wasn't just that their losses were real in terms of real pain, real suffering, but that it was coming clear to me that the grain farmers of Western Canada had built the world out of their own sweat and muscle-power and bank of knowledge handed down from generation to generation – they and the members of my own family had spent their lives doing hard work with small rewards. If I found it hard to lose what I had had for such a short time – the wide, wild fields around me, the animals, the slower and more meaningful pace of life – how much harder for those who had never known any other life, nor their parents and sometimes their grandparents before them.

At the same time, I was beginning to get phone calls from magazine, newspaper, and radio editors and researchers who wanted someone with a proven record as a writer, who actually lived in the midst of the crisis and was directly affected by it, to write about it. This too forced me into looking at its genesis and history in a more comprehensive and fundamental way. I had to study the situation as a scholar would, with the additional advantage of having a good measure of skepticism at anything that smacked of conventional wisdom. (For the first time since I'd left the university, I found myself grateful for the training in research I'd received in grad school.) I had around me the evidence of my eyes, my own family history as westerners behind me, and the stories of the families in the Palliser Triangle, all things which most scholars and most journalists who came from Vancouver and Toronto to report on what was going on in Saskatchewan lacked.

And I had Peter, an unconventional thinker if ever there was one, clever, patient, and in whose long silences a lot of cogitation had gone on over the years. He had some clear ideas about what had gone wrong, and more, about what really mattered, what losses counted in the ongoing stream of life, and what didn't, out of which I might discern what the essence of rural life really is.

I thought of Thomas Hardy's account of the agricultural workers of late-nineteenth-century England in *Tess of the D'Urbervilles*, of Tolstoy in *Anna Karenina* writing about the Russian peasants at work on the land, of Knut Hamsun in *The Wayfarers* chronicling the lives of the working poor of Norway. I thought of Patrick White's magnificent *The Tree of Life*, and much later, of Olive Schreiner's *The Story of an African Farm*. I remembered my first attempt at writing a novel seven or eight years earlier, how it was to have been about the life of an urban, academic, single parent, how I thought I had nothing else of interest to write about. Now I saw how insular and blind I had been.

I had come to know my way around the countryside, I had stood in the midst of a field of our ruined wheat that was singing with grasshoppers, I had climbed the fence and stood with my husband in what was left after it had been destroyed by hail, I had helped pull calves in the spring, I had sat proudly in the sale ring while the auctioneer sold our big steers, and held the twitch while the vet cut out a growth on a horse's face. And I used all of this, every incident, every – to me – astonishing detail of my new life, in my writing. If I could do nothing more, I told myself, I could pay intense and precise attention, I could at least make a detailed, accurate record of life here and what had happened to it that wouldn't be the self-serving version of those who had made it happen, but would be told from the point of view of the people who had lived it and suffered it.

As I write this we are calving. In the past two weeks I've been present at the births of five or six calves, running to get equipment, helping get the heifer into the barn or corral, on one occasion narrowly escaping being flattened by a cow who'd decided to leave through a gate I was standing at, not yet having made up my mind whether to go in or stay out. Peter teased me about it, saying he didn't know I could still move that fast. I never get over the excitement of seeing that calf emerge, at that moment when it opens its eyes and blinks and its sides tremble with its first breaths of air. "It's alive!" I always catch myself saying in astonishment and joy, and "Welcome to the world!" to the little creature. If the grim inevitability of death is always present in rural life, so is the never-ending surprise and joy at the birth of new life.

I don't go out every day with Peter to help him any more. We agree that my writing is more important. I am no longer as curious as I once was, nor am I as young. He has responded to this, as most people in the business have to the lack of help, by mechanizing as far as possible. I sometimes regret this, but I know now that I would never be as content, even as happy, as some of my friends and neighbours seem to be checking pregnant heifers with a flashlight in the middle of the night, pulling calves, driving tractors, balers, or combines, pickling and canning and freezing food, and in the evening playing cards or making quilts or crocheting or knitting or just visiting. I envy those who find contentment in these things, because in them, it seems to me, there is a calm, a sense of peace and of the simple rightness of existence from which, for whatever reason, I have been forever barred. Nonetheless, through working with Peter all these years and sharing in the joys and the trials of this ranching life, I had been gathering another, deeper kind of understanding about rural life.

The circumstances of our neighbours and acquaintances grew more and more critical and the talk everywhere – on the streets, on coffee row, at dances and family gatherings – grew more and more despairing. Loss was everywhere around me, fear, anger, and an omnipresent, inexorable sadness at the destruction of a way of life several generations old and of the dream of the future that had proven to be unattainable. In the midst of the confusion and chaos and contradictory ideas going on around me, I tried to make sense out of the desperation of farm families to stay on their farms no matter what the price. I tried to see beyond the reasons they gave when asked: because they were too old to start a new life somewhere else, or because they knew how to do nothing else, or because they knew the virtual impossibility of finding work in towns or cities in the midst of a general recession, even beyond those who called on a moral right – this was my father's and my grandfather's place and nobody is putting me off it.

Clearly there was more to this need to stay on the farm than what was being said, no matter how true these reasons were. The more I thought about it, the more I lived the life myself, the more it seemed to me that the roots of the profound sorrow and genuine desperation of farm people lay in something deeper than these things. Because I had finally come to know a life lived in Nature myself, I began to believe that, at root, the basic loss to farm people was greater even than a loss of livelihood or a familiar way of life, as hard as these things would be to endure. The greatest loss, it seemed to me, was the loss of constant contact with Nature and of all that implied.

I didn't believe the hopeful prophecies that salvation was just around the corner and that soon everything would go back to the way it had been in the late seventies. When I heard experts prophesy about even bigger and better technologies which would save us, I shuddered, since it seemed to me that it was technology run rampant that had brought on the disaster in the first place. When I heard about corporate farms I saw only a modern-day feudal system where people would work the land for the profit of landowners whose faces they would never even see. When I heard about any ideas for saving the place which involved moving people off their farms, I saw only unlivable, dangerous megalopoli full of the poor and homeless – and an empty landscape.

North America, obsessed with the notion of progress and the technological means to achieve it, and increasingly urbanized, has failed to make a place for people on the land. Thousands of people, rural for generations, have been driven off it. We have raped our natural resources and despoiled them, overused pesticides, insecticides, chemical fertilizers and huge machinery to subdue Nature, and devalued the rural person and his/her way of life along with rural culture.

It seems to me unavoidably true that the plight of the farmers is directly related to the question of our need as a species to come back to Nature. If we abandon farms and farmers as we have known them for the last ten thousand years, we abandon our best hope for redefining ourselves as children of Nature and for reclaiming our lost souls, for what other sizable body of people exists in North America with their knowledge? There are only Native people left who have been speaking to deaf ears since their conquest from five hundred to a hundred years ago. We may at last be ready to listen to them, but the cultural differences – in particular, religion – make it difficult for many non-Natives to hear what Natives are saying. Increasingly we know in our hearts they are right, have been right all along, but we can't seem to find a way of implementing their knowledge, of blending it with our own beliefs into a workable salvation both for the land and for all of us as a species.

At the simplest level is the fact that all the values we cherish and that we consider to be the basis of our culture as a whole, and that provide for its continuity but that are difficult to keep alive in cities, live on in the country: tightly knit extended families and small communities, where the loss of any one member leaves a gap, but where deviance is tolerated and doesn't mean a life on the streets, where interdependence is clear and cooperation thus a way of life, but without destroying self-reliance essential for survival in a sparsely populated countryside and in a harsh climate.

Country people understand how the world was built; it didn't appear whole and shiny the morning they were born; their fathers and mothers built it step-by-step each day. With only the most fragile and minimal of support systems rural people have learned to do everything for themselves: to build roads and houses and machinery and to grow crops to feed thousands as well as their own families. Even more precisely, each individual farmer knows his acres of land intimately, knows the weather patterns over it, knows what grows best where and why, and he knows intimately what the minute variations in the colour of his crop or the way it stands mean and what he must do to rectify problems. No society can afford to wipe out the whole class of people in whom the practical knowledge laboriously passed down by generations remains alive.

Though we can't all live on the land, we have to keep a substantial proportion of us on it in order to re-establish and maintain our connection with Nature. Further, these people have to live on the land for a long time, they need a lot of time to come into tune with it, and to do so it is vital that they not be driven only by the need to feed their families and themselves, which always results in their disregarding what they know very well about the needs of the land, and to overwork it or overstock it with animals, or to plow up marginal land – that is, to exploit Nature instead of nurturing her.

It is unbelievable to me that futurists and experts at universities and in government don't see how important it is to all of us that a stable body of people remain in intimate touch with the land, and include it in their equations about the future. So far there has been no concerted effort that I know of by governments at any level to address the issue of rural depopulation in a creative way. Any efforts have so far been based on the unexamined belief that rural life and farming or ranching must be synonymous. As long as we pursue reasoning from this narrow foundation, given current market conditions and the prospect of more and more countries becoming self-sufficient or exporters of food, we are unlikely ever to find a solution that allows for a considerable, stable body of rural people.

Years ago an old man who had farmed and raised cattle on this land all his life, when we were speculating about the future for people out here given financial disaster and rapid depopulation, remarked that he thought one day there would be people on every quarter again as it had been during his childhood. I asked him how he thought this would come about. He had no answer, not conceiving of a mechanism that would produce this result, but when I asked he looked not at me but into the distance and repeated his belief. I couldn't forget what he'd said, because it seemed so clearly a visionary moment to me, beyond reason, beyond the facts. I thought he had seen something that was more than a dream, even if he had no logic with which to defend it.

Ideas for a new life out here are beginning to be heard: small, highly specific farms, medium-sized farms with a high rate of diversification, a buffalo commons with no farms at all, advanced, amazing new technology doing what we can't imagine, on enormous tracts of land, partnerships between urban families and farm families to produce food for a specific, small population, and numerous other vague and mostly unsatisfactory notions.

Much of this land, that which should never have been broken because of its marginal agricultural value, needs to be put back into grass and to do so will require money, time, and a love of grasslands for themselves. Because of the extreme fragility of this landscape, any such project would require many years, probably more than one lifetime. I have no doubt that there are many people, from former farmers driven off their land to people aching to get out of the city, who would be overjoyed, if given a salary, good advice, and equipment, to move onto quarters or half-sections in need of reseeding and/or nurturing, and to devote their lives to this project as stewards of the land.

I don't think the repopulation of the Great Plains will be easy, nor do I claim to have a clear notion of how to do it. But any such repopulation has to be based on a belief in what I have been saying, that in a renewed relationship with Nature as a people, and in a flourishing rural life, lies the salvation and the foundation of our nation. First we have to begin with the vision and with the desire; we do not lack the wit to bring it about; what we require is leadership.

Most environmentalists tend to be urban, and as Neil Evernden has shown in *The Natural Alien*, the only way they have known how to fight the corporate world and governments has been to put Nature in their terms, as manageable, sustainable resources, withholding the designation of value of another kind – its innate value – as the primary issue. This seems to me the same kind of mistake farmers made when they asked to be taken seriously by urban people by saying that farming was a business like any other business and that farm life was just like city life, except that it took place outside of cities. Those who genuinely saw it (as distinct from those who merely paid lip service to the idea) as such destroyed it. Farm life is overwhelmingly unlike city life in most ways, despite the presence of microwave ovens, dishwashers, and even the occasional swimming pool by farmhouses. True family farming has never been a business like any other business and ought never to be seen as such. What is best in farming and farm life is that it takes place, day in and day out, in the bosom of Nature.

I think of that old man's vision of a countryside dotted with houses and houses filled with families, children in small country schools, churches filled again on Sundays, weekend dances and entertainments, well-travelled roads, a vibrant, living culture flourishing far from cities. In his vision he sees this place as it was sixty or seventy years ago; I see it too, but I see a people with a different ethic than those of his childhood had.

I see them less poverty-stricken, less driven by the simple need for survival. I see them as aware of themselves as vital to the human community in providing the direct link to Nature our species must maintain. I see them as the preservers of a body of knowledge thousands of years old, as caretakers, stewards of the land, and maybe even, in a much better world than this one, as the wise men and women to whom others will turn for guidance and healing.

My mother's golden memories of life on the farm, where she had lived till she was fourteen when her father lost it to drought, and my father's lifelong but hopeless dream of going back to the farm, neither of which I had paid much attention to when I was growing up, came back to me now. Now I saw that this was where I had come from; these were my people, too, whether they accepted me or not, whether I felt fully at home among them or not.

I began to feel, with the immediacy of a blow to the stomach, not only what all of us would lose, but more particularly what I would lose if Peter fell victim to the crisis too. Every blade of grass, every trill from a red-winged blackbird, every sparkle of sun on the Frenchman River that trickled past our house at the hay farm, seemed more precious. It seemed I had discovered a good place, a good life, just in time to lose it.

In the city for short visits now I studied people's houses, or the rows of condominiums or the new apartment buildings, assessing how close they were to each other, how big their yards were, what their occupants had for views, trying to imagine how I would live again in the city and what arrangement might be acceptable should something happen to Peter, or to the ranch. At home walking in the hills or down narrow country roads, I tried to imagine life without this space, this welcome, close presence of grass and sky. My dream of the blossoming twig took on new meaning. For without my realizing it, instead of being unable to imagine spending the rest of my life in the country, I found to my surprise that now I couldn't imagine how I might survive if I had to leave it to go back to the city to live.

NATIVE PEOPLE FINALLY CLAIM THEIR FUTURE

DOUG CUTHAND

Our history in this country has always lacked a vision of the future. We were always assumed to be a people who had none.

In the early 1900s, things were just moving right along, the boarding schools were operating at full capacity, and Indian land was fair game for speculators and governments.

The Indian Act of the period had lots of provisions concerning the sale and disposal of Indian land but nothing existed for additions to reserves. The Act was clear on enfranchisement or loss of Indian status, but vague on the creation of new band members other than those born into that status.

We were considered a vanishing race, and government policy reflected that notion.

In the course of about three decades, more than 300,000 acres of Indian land was confiscated and sold. Some was done "legally" by using the Indian Act and the Soldier Settlement Act. Other land was taken through questionable means by land speculators and their co-conspirators in government.

Because Indian people needed a pass to travel off the reserve, they did not use some of their land and it fell into a surplus category. For example, the Last Mountain Reserve had been established for the bands in the Treaty Four territory as a hunting reserve. However, when nobody was allowed to travel, it fell into disuse and was sold off.

At one time, there were small parcels of reserve land down the eastern shore of Last Mountain Lake. These reserves had been established to serve as camping areas while the people exercised their fishing rights. Again, because nobody could travel freely, the land was declared surplus.

In the Battlefords area, Father Delmas had a dream of a Catholic colony made up of settlers from Quebec. He found some beautiful land west of the Battlefords that suited his purposes. But, unfortunately, it was home to the Thunderchild and Moosomin First Nations.

Delmas nagged and threatened the chiefs until they finally agreed to hold a vote, sell, and move to a new area. The vote was questionable and close, but Delmas got his way and the two bands were relocated to inferior land farther north. Today, the town of Delmas sits on the old Thunderchild reserve.

After the first wave of settlement, the province was filling up and all that "unused" reserve land was too good to resist. Land speculators moved in and worked in collusion with the Department of the Interior and the minister, Clifford Sifton, in particular.

Sifton had taken on the settlement of the West with religious zeal and he wasn't about to give up just because the available land was running out. Reserve land was put on the market in record amounts, whole reserves disappeared, and the people were placed on nearby reserves.

Pheasant Rump and Ocean Man were forced onto White Bear. Young Chipewyan, where the town of Laird now sits, disappeared. And east of the town of Saint Louis, Chacastipasin was liquidated and the people placed on the James Smith Reserve.

The land sales devastated the First Nations socially, politically, and economically, and the effects are still felt.

Following the First World War, the government forced a number of reserves to give up land for soldier settlement. Most of the reserves in the Qu'Appelle Valley were cut in half, with the best part going to provide land grants to returning soldiers.

One of the government's most loyal supporters was an Indian Agent named Graham. Graham was determined to surrender as much land as possible, and his tactics would have landed him in jail today.

For example, he would call a meeting and hold a vote during the dinner break, when most of the people were away. He reduced rations to the point of starving people into submission. His tactics were shameful and caused untold suffering.

At one time, the reserves of Muskeg Lake and Mistawasis were much larger and actually touched. Both reserves lost land to soldier settlement. The proceeds from the sale of the Muskeg Lake land were loaned to the province for the construction of the Borden Bridge west of Saskatoon. The loan was never repaid and the band lost twice.

On May 24, 2000, the Federation of Saskatchewan Indian Nations, the province, and the federal government signed a memorandum of agreement to allow for the transfer of land and cash compensation to correct this injustice.

The agreement isn't a done deal. Negotiations must take place to validate the claims.

This process is currently underway. So far, ten First Nations have had their surrenders validated. This represents 110,000 acres of land. Another 190,000 acres are currently under negotiation.

Saskatchewan First Nations have a history of moving forward together on issues, and this agreement is another example of this political discipline.

Today's First Nations are coming into their own as an exciting political and economic force in this country. We have long since ceased to be the vanishing race, and agreements such as this one stress this fact.

HOME PLACE

GUY VANDERHAEGHE

It was early morning, so early that Gil MacLean loaded the colt into the truck box under a sky still scattered with faint stars. The old man circled the truck once, checking the tailgate, the tires, and the knot in the halter shank, tottering around on legs stiff as stilts, shoulders hunched to keep the chill off him. He was sixty-nine and mostly cold these days.

A hundred yards behind him one window burned yellow in the dark house. That was his son Ronald, asleep under the bare light bulb and the airplanes. Whenever Ronald fled Darlene, the woman Gil MacLean referred to as the "back-pages wife," he slunk back to his father's house in the dead of night to sleep in a room lit up like a Christmas tree. To her father-in-law, Darlene was the back-pages wife because Ronald found her advertising herself in the classified section of a farm newspaper, right alongside sale notices for second hand grain augers and doubtful chainsaws.

Dawn found the old man in a temper, a mood. It was the mare he had wanted when he rattled oats in the pail and whistled, but it was the gelding which had been lured. The mare, wiser and warier, had hung back. So this morning he had a green, rough-broke colt to ride. There was nothing for it, though. He needed a horse because his mind was made up to repair Ronald's fences. They were a disgrace.

Generally that was the way to catch what you wanted, shake

a little bait. It was what Darlene had done with Ronald, but she hadn't fooled Gil MacLean for a second. He knew how it was.

Four years ago his son and Darlene married after exchanging honeyed letters for six months. Ronald never breathed a word to him about any wedding. When Ronald's mother was alive she used to say Ronald was too much under his father's thumb. But the one time he slipped out from beneath it, look at the result.

One morning Ronald had driven off in the pickup. Twelve hours later he phoned from Regina to announce that he and his bride were bound for Plentywood, Montana, to honeymoon. Ronald was thirty-eight then, had never been married, had never been engaged, had never even had a date that his father could recollect. It was a shock and a mystery. The way Gil figured it, Ronald must have proposed by mail before he ever met face to face with Darlene. Ronald didn't have it in him to offer himself in the flesh to someone with whom he was actually acquainted. He would be too shy, too embarrassed for that.

The old man folded himself into the cab of the truck, joint by joint. "The best work, the worst sleep," he muttered to Ronald's lightened window as he drove under it. In the east there were mares' tails on the horizon, fine as the vapour trails of jets, reddened by the rising sun.

It was Gil MacLean's speculation that his son married only to get his hands on land. Not land of Darlene's, she was a waif and a pauper and had none, but his land, Gil MacLean's land. He never entertained the idea that Ronald might have married out of loneliness, or lust, or any feeling of the remotest kin to either. Just land. That was why he was sometimes troubled, wondering what share of responsibility was his to bear for Ronald's current unhappiness. Maybe he ought to have transferred the title sooner, but he had never trusted the boy's judgment. Events appeared to have confirmed his suspicions. Ronald had his own farm now, a wedding present. A married man needed land, so his father gave him the farm that the MacLeans had always called the "home place." It gave Gil satisfaction to see it pass from father to son and he thought it might bring Ronald luck.

The home place consisted of the original quarter Gil's father had homesteaded, the pre-emption, and another 320 acres picked up cheap from a Finnish immigrant who went to pieces when his wife ran off on him. Over the years the MacLean family acquired other holdings, but the home place was special. Situated in a valley, it was a mix of rich bottom land and steep, wooded hills. In the spring, down by the river, blizzards of gulls floated in the wake of tractor and disker, pursuing easy pickings, while hawks rode the air high above the lean hills and, shrieking, fell to plunder these lazy storms of white birds. To Gil it had all been beautiful. It was all he had ever wanted, to possess that place and those sights. A day spent away from the farm made him restless, cranky. Returning to it, even after the briefest absence, he acted oddly, dodging through the wires of a fence in his city clothes to wade about in his crop, hands running back and forth lightly over the bearded heads the way another man might absent-mindedly stroke a cat. Or he might suddenly strike off for the hills with all the energy and purpose of someone hurrying off to keep an appointment, tie flying over his shoulder.

His wife used to say: "Gil's gone off to satisfy himself that nobody so much as shifted a cup of dirt on this place when he was away."

What Gil never confided to his wife was that he felt more present in the land than he did in his own flesh, his own body. Apart from it he had no real existence. When he looked in a mirror he stood at a great distance from what he regarded, but with the land it was different. All that he had emptied of himself into it, he recognized.

The road to the home place ran due east without deviating a hair, rising and falling regularly as a sleeper's breath as it made its way over a succession of bare hills. The emerging sun drew his eyes into a squint when he topped a rise; the blue shadows in the hollows forced them wide again. In the back of the truck the slither and clatter of iron shoes was unremitting. The colt was either highly strung or lacked balance. If it lost its footing and fell it would be a task to get on its feet again; the box was narrow and there was little room for manoeuvring. He'd have to go back and get Ronald out of bed to help him.

Turning Ronald out of bed was not an easy job. Despite his son's difficulties falling asleep, once he was gone he wasn't likely to stir. Often he didn't wake before noon. Gil, on the other hand, roused to the slightest sound. That first night the gritty scraping of the shoes on the stairs had been enough to jerk him out of a dreamless sleep. He'd never been one to lock doors, he had only himself to thank that a night intruder was climbing up to him. It was like the television and its stories of grinning madmen invading houses and arming themselves with drapery cords and butcher knives to strangle and stab. The old man bunched up his pillow and held it out before him, ready to parry the first knife thrust. The footsteps, however, went on past his door. Only when the toilet flushed did he realize it had to be Ronald.

He simply shook in bed for several minutes, too angry and too relieved to ask himself what his son might be up to. Finally he grew calm and curiosity prodded him out into the hallway to investigate. The light was on in Ronald's old bedroom and the door stood ajar.

Ronald was lying flat on his back on the bed, staring up at his model airplanes. As a teenager, even as a young man, he had exhibited little interest in anything other than building models of airplanes from kits, squeezing tubes of glue, pasting on decals, and painting engine cowlings with brushes whose tips he sucked into needle points. The models had never been removed. Forty or more of them hung suspended from the ceiling on fine wires; his room was almost exactly as he had left it when he chose Darlene. Flying Fortresses, Mustangs, Zeros, Spitfires, Messerschmitts, a whole catalogue of warplanes dangled there. The light in the bedroom was also as harsh, pitiless, and glaring as it had ever been. When Ronald was fourteen he had unscrewed the bulb in the ceiling fixture and replaced it with a more powerful one. He also dispensed with the shade because he wanted the models hanging beneath the light bulb to cast their shadows on his bedspread and linoleum in the way fighter planes and bombers passing between sun and earth print their images on country lanes and city squares. These shadows were repeated everywhere about the room, and in their midst lay Ronald, gazing up into the strong light, gazing up at the under-carriages and silhouettes.

"What's all this, Ronald?" his father said. "This is a hell of a time to pay a visit. It's past two."

Ronald said: "I can't stand it. I can't sleep there no longer." He kept his eyes fixed on the planes as he spoke.

Gil knew there was talk going around town about his son and his daughter-in-law, all of it unfortunate. Darlene had come stamped with the word trouble; he'd seen it from day one. The old man sighed and took a seat on the straight-back chair beside the dresser. Ronald was not exactly the forthcoming type; he was prepared to wait him out.

After a considerable stretch of silence his son said: "I should never have left." Gil knew what he meant. Ronald wasn't saying he ought not to have left Darlene; he was saying he should not have abandoned this room and the comfort and solace of those planes that could not fly.

It was strange that, given all the worrying he had done about Ronald and Darlene, Gil had never seen the real danger. Now he did. The realization of what might lie ahead was like an attack of some kind. Before he could proceed it was necessary to relieve the pressure prodding his breastbone and robbing him of breath. He arched his back and squeezed his eyes tight until it eased and he could speak. And speak he did, urgently, for a solid hour without interruption and with a drying mouth. He said it was the government and the courts. They'd gone and changed the marriage property laws so that the women ended up with half of everything these days. Did Ronald know what that meant? Darlene could lay claim to a half share of the home place. "No divorce, Ronald," he repeated. "No divorce. Don't let that bitch break up the home place. Don't you give her that satisfaction." Only when he had wrung this promise out of Ronald did he cease arguing. For a moment he was overcome by his son's loyalty. He patted the back of his hand and murmured: "Thank you. Thank you."

In a month, however, Ronald came creeping back up the stairs. In baffled rage and fear of the future, Gil shouted through his bedroom door: "Don't expect any sympathy from me if you won't try to adjust!"

Ronald explained that he had a problem going to sleep in the same room, the same house as Darlene. That's the reason he came home every once in a while, to relax and catch up on his sleep. Not that it was easy for him to get to sleep in his old room either, but there he could manage it. What he did was stare up at the glowing bulb and planes until the moment arrived when he could feel the sun hot on his back and suddenly he was winged and soaring, flying into sleep, released, sometimes for twelve hours at a time.

Ronald had been paying his visits to his father's to sleep for a year. About the time they started he commenced on improvements to the home place. This meant pushing bush and clearing land up top, above the valley, in the hills. Gil had pointed out this was nothing but sheer craziness. Marginal land like that was suitable only for pasture, cropping it would never repay the cost of breaking and if the hillsides were stripped of cover they would erode. But Ronald, who was usually willing to be advised, wouldn't listen to his father. A cunning, stubborn look stole over his face when he said, "We'll see. I hired another dozer. Pretty soon the brush piles will be dry and ready to burn."

All spring Ronald fired his huge, gasoline-laced bonfires of scrub oak and poplar. The gusty roar of flames was like constant static in his ears, heat crumpled the air around him and stained it a watery yellow, greasy black clouds mounted indolently into the purity of blue skies. The scars of the dozer blades fresh on the earth made the old man indignant. In places the soil had been cut so deep that streaks of rubbly gravel were exposed.

"You won't grow wheat in that," Gil MacLean shouted. "So what'll it be? Carrots?"

Smiling oddly, Ronald said: "I'm not growing nothing. I'll open a pit and peddle gravel to the Department of Highways by the yard."

"That's not farming," his father returned, disgusted. "That's mining."

It was all Ronald had any interest in at present, pushing bush, clawing up roots, burning. His face appeared hot, scorched. His eyes were forever weepy and red, their lids puffy and swollen, lashes singed away. The ends of his hair had crinkled, crisped, and gone white in the furnace-heat. Everything else Ronald neglected. He hadn't yet done his summer fallow and his cattle were continually straying. This morning Gil was determined to mend Ronald's fences because he was ashamed of what the neighbours would think with his son's cows belly-deep in their crops.

The old man crested the last rise and the valley spread itself out at his feet. There were days when he would pull his truck over to the shoulder of the road and look with deep satisfaction at the slow river and the sombre quilt of green and black fields, look until he had his fill. From such a height the home place looked fatter and richer than with your nose shoved in it. Up close the dirt was dirt. There was no time for stopping and admiring this morning though. He was in a hurry.

Gil entered his son's property by a little-used side gate because he didn't want Darlene spying his truck and reporting his doings to Ronald. He parked, unloaded the horse, and slung a duffel bag of tools and a coil of barbed wire on the saddle. Within minutes he was riding down an old trail they had hauled hay on in summer and wood in winter in his father's time.

Neither of those things would be possible now, encroaching wild rose and chokecherry bushes had narrowed it so a loaded wagon couldn't pass. The occasional sapling had taken root between the old ruts. Sunlight and sparrows strayed amid the poplar leaves overhead. Ronald's dozers hadn't reached this far yet, hadn't peeled all this back. Maybe his money would run out before they could, that was Gil's fervent hope.

It was eight o'clock before Gil located the first break in the fence. The wires were rotten with rust and would have to be replaced. He set to work. The old man ought not to have been taken by surprise. He knew the very nature of a young horse was unpredictability. It happened when he was playing out sixty yards of wire, lazy-man style, one end of the coil dallied round the horn, the horse walking it out. It could have been the sound the wire made hissing and writhing after them through the grass and weeds. It could have been that a barb nicked the gelding's hocks. Suddenly the colt froze in its tracks, laid back its ears, and trembled all over like a leaf.

Gil had been a horseman all his life, nearly all of his seventy years. He knew what was coming and he fought with all his strength to keep the gelding from pulling its head down between its forelegs. If the colt managed to get its head down it would be able to buck. It managed. An old man's strength was not sufficient. The horse squealed, wriggled, snapped out its hind legs. Gil's lower plate popped out of his mouth. The sky tilted. He fell.

It was bad luck to get snarled in the wire. The colt dragged him several hundred yards, the old man skipping and bounding and tumbling along behind like a downed water skier without the presence of mind to relinquish his grip on the tow rope.

When it had winded itself the horse came to a halt, stood rolling its eyes and snorting. The old man began to paw himself feebly, searching his pockets for a pair of fencing pliers with which to cut himself out of the jumble of wire. Using the pliers, he had to move cautiously and deliberately so as not to excite the skittish colt. Nevertheless, when the final strand of wire parted with a twang the colt kicked him twice in a convulsion of fear before trotting off a stone's throw away. There it circled about anxiously, stepping on the ends of the dragging reins and bruising its mouth.

The old man lay still, taking stock. There seemed to be a lot of blood, the wire had cut him in many places. He sat up and the blood gushed out of his nose and mouth and spilled down his jacket front. He peered about him, dazed. The colt had dragged him to a desolate place. Ronald's dozers had been at work. Here there was nothing but bare, black earth engraved by caterpillar treads, piles of stones, and the remains of bonfires, charred tree trunks furred in white powdery ash.

While he sat up the blood continued to pour from his mouth and nose. It was better to lie back down. He was feeling weak but he told himself that was because he had taken nothing that morning but a cup of instant coffee. "I'll rest and my strength will come back," he told himself.

Gil closed his eyes and became aware of the powerful scents of sage, milkweed, grass. How was this possible in a place scoured clean? Then he realized they were coming from his clothes; he had been ground into them by the dragging.

During the next three hours he tried a number of times to sit himself up, but the blood always ran so freely from his mouth he resigned the attempt. "Not yet," he muttered to himself. "In a while." He had little sense of passing time. There was only thirst and the stiff, scratchy ache of the wounds on his face, hands, legs.

When the sun shone directly down into his face he realized it was noon. The bright light in his eyes and the time of day made him think of Ronald. He would be waking now, looking up at his airplanes.

He had asked Ronald: "What is it with you? Why do you stare up at those planes?" And Ronald had said: "I like to pretend I'm up there, high enough to look down on something or somebody for once in my life."

Gil had laughed as if it were a joke, but it was an uneasy laugh.

Suddenly the old man was seized by a strange panic. Making a great effort, he sat himself up. It was as if he hoped the force of gravity would pull everything he just now thought and saw down out of his head, drain it away. What he saw was Ronald's lashless eyes, singed hair, red burning face. What he thought was that such a face belonged to a man who wished to look down from a great height on fire, on ruin, on devastation, on dismay.

When the old man collapsed back into the wire he saw that face hovering above, looking down on him.

"You've got no right to look down on me," he said to the burning sky. "I came to fix your fences. I gave you the home place and showed you how to keep it."

His vehement voice filled the clearing and argued away the afternoon. It became harsher and louder when the sun passed out of Gil's vision and he could not raise himself to follow its course. The horse grew so accustomed to this steady shouting and calling out that only when it suddenly stopped did the gelding prick its ears, swing its head, and stare.

SWAP

LEA LITTLEWOLFE

the word passes. be at Fort Pitt. everybody. the people know what's coming. buffalo numbers are down. whites keep coming. the missionaries influence. priest skirts flap in the wind. distant owners control furs and trade goods. agents move around, their government bosses hidden. trees fall and fences rise. forts cluster people. always there's talk of more change. they gather. bands camp on the river bottom. red-uniformed lookalikes. returned hunters. war parties. traders. men who lead. men who move with authority. family groups. roving adolescents. the people think and talk together. mull over the pieces of information. absorb and disperse each new tidbit. send ideas back.

the formal meetings begin. white pieces of paper with orderly scratches. bearded men give their legal description of reality. the pipe is passed. leaders confer. elders are consulted. coats with large brass buttons are handed out to headman and chief. translators interpret, guessing the two sides don't understand each other. youth becoming men shout and gesture, demand their say, learning how to lead. women cook and soothe.

making treaty is about gathering the people. about changing social order. about winner and victim. someone to crow and someone to punish. it's about non-mutual understandings. it takes a while to know what has been agreed to. shoe polish and

pepper to make watered liquor a he-man's drink. movement by
permit only. forced farming. Indian agent control of sales. other-
culture school to unmake family. first-language loss and shame.

the victors, the definers of wealth, become dulled to stolen
bounty. stereotypes veil poverty and social dislocation. you don't
think about reserve life when tiny land parcels are hidden. you
don't have to see the other side of the swap.

ROUNDUP

BARBARA SAPERGIA

Roundup *gives us a look at the crisis in prairie agriculture along with a lively tale of love and marriage in three generations of an extended family. Full of passion, conflict, and humour,* Roundup *encapsulates the love people feel for a way of life and their connection with the land – a connection that may be breaking.*

PAUL *enters, down right (from corral). He opens the screen door and calls to* VERNA.

PAUL: Verna, come outside a moment.

VERNA: Right now? We're almost ready for supper.

PAUL: I don't care about supper.

VERNA: Paul, for heaven's sake.

PAUL: Just come, all right?

VERNA: All right! (VERNA *comes outside.*) What is it?

PAUL: Are you really saying you don't wanna live here any more? (*She doesn't answer.*) Tell me why, Vern. I mean, you said you don't like my attitude. Well, what about you? You haven't been so easy to live with lately. Giving me the cold shoulder. Trying to run Darcy's life.

VERNA: I'm not.

PAUL: You think you got all the right on your side. Well, you don't. You just close your eyes to the truth.

VERNA: Is that so?

PAUL: Darcy and Greg wanna get married.

VERNA: They're not getting married, Paul. Not this summer.

PAUL: They wanna get married now, not when you think it's right. They got their minds made up.

VERNA: They can just unmake them.

PAUL: We could fix up the old folks' place for them.

VERNA: What? Nobody's lived there for ten years.

PAUL: It'd be nice having somebody living on the home place again. You always say it's lonely here.

VERNA: Don't you twist my words.

PAUL: Anyway, it's not in such bad shape. I had a look not too long ago.

VERNA: Paul, no. They've got nothing to live on, and no prospects of getting it.

PAUL: Didn't stop us.

VERNA: Things have changed since then. We don't even know if we'll be here next year.

PAUL: Where the hell else would we be?

VERNA: Farming doesn't work any more. It doesn't work for us, and it's not going to work for the children.

PAUL: Don't call them children. They can do anything we do.

VERNA: Sure, like all farm kids. They learn the job before they're old enough to think about it. If you took one generation of farm kids and raised them in town – that would be it for farming.

PAUL: Why would we do that? Farming's still a good life.

VERNA: No. We spend our lives raising food for city people, and they don't know we exist. They think we're a bunch of hillbillies.

PAUL: I don't give a damn what city people think. Sure, things are tough. But we built this house ourselves. We've ridden over every acre of this land.

VERNA: So?

PAUL: I know you like it too. You used to make me walk with

you in the spring – to see the crocuses.

VERNA: Yes, I thought they were pretty. Now a field of crocuses just means a dry spring and poor pastures.

PAUL: It means the same as it did when we were young. You're the one that's changed. *(He gently turns her towards the hills.)* Verna, look. That line of hills? That's part of me. And the shape of that sky. I know that sky. I don't want another one. Look at it.

VERNA: I can't live here just for the sky. I'm sick of this life. Always fighting to get ahead...always ending up further behind. Having your hopes smashed too many times. Saying "next year" till the words turn bitter in your mouth.

PAUL: You think I've never felt that?

VERNA: I'm not twenty years old any more. I'm afraid.

PAUL: Well...I'm afraid too. Sometimes I'm scared as a little kid.

VERNA: Why didn't you tell me?

PAUL: I don't know.

VERNA: There has to be something between us...something we know for sure. Or I can't stand the bad things.

PAUL: I want to talk to you.

VERNA: You used to.... Look, it's time for supper.

PAUL: This is more important. Verna, you've been acting like I've done something you can't forgive. How can that be? I've never done anything so bad. (VERNA *hesitates.* DARCY *enters, down right.)*

VERNA: Darcy, you are not getting married.

PAUL: Verna, she's been trying to tell you...she's gonna have a baby. That's why she doesn't want to wait.

VERNA: A baby.

PAUL: Now, Verna....

VERNA: You did it on purpose.

DARCY: Mom, for God's sake.

VERNA: Damn it all. Damn it to hell.

PAUL: Verna, it'll be all right.

VERNA: You knew about this? You knew.

PAUL: No! Darcy just told me.

VERNA: (*to* DARCY) You'll throw it all away. Everything I wanted for you.

DARCY: I can't just do what you want.

VERNA: It's the oldest damn story in the world, isn't it? God, you must think I'm stupid.

DARCY: I don't think you're stupid.

VERNA: You did do it on purpose. Didn't you?

DARCY: Yes.

VERNA: Why, for God's sake? You could get married any time. You could have a baby any time. Darcy, you're so young.

DARCY: I'm not your baby any more, Verna.

VERNA: You don't know what you're doing.

DARCY: I do too.

VERNA: You'll have no life outside the farm – but you'll be treated as if you don't count at all.

DARCY: I'll be treated like a farmer.

VERNA: You won't be the farmer. You'll be the farmer's wife.

DARCY: I'll be the farmer and the farmer's wife.

VERNA: You're dreaming.

DARCY: You can't stop me.

VERNA: No.

PAUL: It'll work out. Maybe not like you planned, but it'll work out.

VERNA: I wanted you to have a chance for some dignity.

DARCY: I will.

PAUL: Damn it, Verna, she'll have that.

VERNA: Like I did, I suppose.

PAUL: I thought you did.

VERNA: Because you don't think. If something works for you, you think it must work for me too.

PAUL: What do you mean?

VERNA: I mean that a woman's contribution is not looked at the same way as a man's. Even if she's doing the same work. Are you telling me you don't know that?

PAUL: I don't think I do.

VERNA: Darcy, are you telling me you don't know? You know, all right. (DARCY *won't answer.*)

VERNA: We're a little bit inferior. A little bit of a joke. Oh, look at Verna, she combined this whole great big wheat field all by herself.

PAUL: Verna, I've never said that.

VERNA: If we say something, it isn't noticed. If we do something, it must be easy. It must be less important. Like having a baby. Any fool could do that.

DARCY: Oh, for heaven's sake.

PAUL: I've never said that.

VERNA: Any fool could clean a house or look after kids. I mean, some city people think you should get paid for stuff like that. Can you imagine?

PAUL: Would you slow down. I can't keep up with this.

VERNA: Damn it, I will say this. I will figure it out. I have to make you see.

PAUL: I heard what you said, but damn it, it's just a way of talking. It doesn't mean anything.

VERNA: It does. It does mean something. It means we don't count for as much. The men don't think so, and after a while, neither do we.

PAUL: How can it matter that much?

VERNA: I don't know, but it does.

PAUL: Maybe it's been like you say, I don't know. But things are changing.

DARCY: That's right. It'll be different for me.

VERNA: No! You'll spend your life working as hard as any man

DARCY: Mom –

VERNA: And never once will you hear it said that a woman is as good as a man.

PAUL: But that goes without saying.

VERNA: Does it? If it goes without saying, I'd like to hear you say it. Just once.

PAUL: All right. Women.... (VERNA *keeps looking at him.*) Women are just as good as men.

VERNA: My God. You said it.

PAUL: Sure I did. I couldn't have worked here all these years on my own. I know that. I...appreciate the work you've done. (VERNA *can't answer right away.*) Darcy, go on up to the house.

DARCY: What? Oh...all right. (DARCY *goes up to the house.*)

PAUL: Well? What are we gonna do?

VERNA: I don't know.

PAUL: I'm trying to understand what you're saying. I could try to be more like what you want. Maybe that's not enough any more, I don't know...I'd like to go on if you would.

VERNA: I'd like to be back where we used to be...a long time ago. Maybe there's no way back.

PAUL: How could we be like we were then? We lost a child. We raised a child. All the work we did...thirty years of it.

VERNA: You mean we're no longer the same people?

PAUL: I guess they're still there inside us. But we know more now. Those two people didn't know much about anything.

VERNA: So it's better to be middle-aged and beat-up like some old pickup truck?

PAUL: I don't know if it's better. It's just how it is.

VERNA: It took us thirty years to get to this. It doesn't seem like we got very far.

PAUL: Guess that depends where we were trying to go.... Verna, there's something else.

VERNA: What?

PAUL: Flint made me an offer.

VERNA: For our ranch? How much?

PAUL: Enough to buy a house in town and get by.

VERNA: My God, I didn't know anyone would want it.

PAUL: He wants it, all right. In fact, he'd hire me to help work the place. Just think – fifty years old, and my first regular job.

VERNA: You mean we could stay on here? It might not be all that different. We could live pretty much the same.

PAUL: We'd have to live in town.

VERNA: Why couldn't we live here?

PAUL: He wouldn't be keeping the yard and buildings. It'd just be a few wheat fields and one big pasture.

VERNA: What about our house?

PAUL: Oh, he'd bulldoze and burn it. He don't need anyone living on the place.

VERNA: Why does he want it?

PAUL: It joins up to one corner of his land, and it's got a good spring, which he doesn't have. And then of course, it's there.

VERNA: What did you tell him?

PAUL: Told him we'd talk about it.

VERNA: You said that?

PAUL: Yeah. What did you think? That I wouldn't even talk to you?

VERNA: No....

PAUL: He wants an answer pretty quick. If he doesn't get this, he's gonna bid on the Jackson's place. I guess Jackson already approached him.

VERNA: So what's holding him back?

PAUL: Guess he'd rather have this.

VERNA: So you could live in town and work out here?

PAUL: Or look for some other kind of work.

VERNA: Like what?

PAUL: I don't know. What do you say, Vern? It's what you want, eh?

VERNA: You want me to answer right now?

PAUL: Flint's ready to deal.

VERNA: He'd take down the house? (PAUL *nods.*) Dan and Trandafira's place too?

PAUL: Pretty well goes without saying.

VERNA: But you wanted the kids to live there.

PAUL: Yeah. But I gotta admit, this is probably the best offer we'd ever get.... Well?

VERNA: We could get clear of all that debt.

VERNA: Is that so?

PAUL: Darcy and Greg wanna get married.

VERNA: They're not getting married, Paul. Not this summer.

PAUL: They wanna get married now, not when you think it's right. They got their minds made up.

VERNA: They can just unmake them.

PAUL: We could fix up the old folks' place for them.

VERNA: What? Nobody's lived there for ten years.

PAUL: It'd be nice having somebody living on the home place again. You always say it's lonely here.

VERNA: Don't you twist my words.

PAUL: Anyway, it's not in such bad shape. I had a look not too long ago.

VERNA: Paul, no. They've got nothing to live on, and no prospects of getting it.

PAUL: Didn't stop us.

VERNA: Things have changed since then. We don't even know if we'll be here next year.

PAUL: Where the hell else would we be?

VERNA: Farming doesn't work any more. It doesn't work for us, and it's not going to work for the children.

PAUL: Don't call them children. They can do anything we do.

VERNA: Sure, like all farm kids. They learn the job before they're old enough to think about it. If you took one generation of farm kids and raised them in town – that would be it for farming.

PAUL: Why would we do that? Farming's still a good life.

VERNA: No. We spend our lives raising food for city people, and they don't know we exist. They think we're a bunch of hillbillies.

PAUL: I don't give a damn what city people think. Sure, things are tough. But we built this house ourselves. We've ridden over every acre of this land.

VERNA: So?

PAUL: I know you like it too. You used to make me walk with

you in the spring – to see the crocuses.

VERNA: Yes, I thought they were pretty. Now a field of crocuses just means a dry spring and poor pastures.

PAUL: It means the same as it did when we were young. You're the one that's changed. (*He gently turns her towards the hills.*) Verna, look. That line of hills? That's part of me. And the shape of that sky. I know that sky. I don't want another one. Look at it.

VERNA: I can't live here just for the sky. I'm sick of this life. Always fighting to get ahead...always ending up further behind. Having your hopes smashed too many times. Saying "next year" till the words turn bitter in your mouth.

PAUL: You think I've never felt that?

VERNA: I'm not twenty years old any more. I'm afraid.

PAUL: Well...I'm afraid too. Sometimes I'm scared as a little kid.

VERNA: Why didn't you tell me?

PAUL: I don't know.

VERNA: There has to be something between us...something we know for sure. Or I can't stand the bad things.

PAUL: I want to talk to you.

VERNA: You used to.... Look, it's time for supper.

PAUL: This is more important. Verna, you've been acting like I've done something you can't forgive. How can that be? I've never done anything so bad. (VERNA *hesitates.* DARCY *enters, down right.*)

VERNA: Darcy, you are not getting married.

PAUL: Verna, she's been trying to tell you...she's gonna have a baby. That's why she doesn't want to wait.

VERNA: A baby.

PAUL: Now, Verna....

VERNA: You did it on purpose.

DARCY: Mom, for God's sake.

VERNA: Damn it all. Damn it to hell.

PAUL: Verna, it'll be all right.

VERNA: You knew about this? You knew.

PAUL: Yeah.

VERNA: I wonder if anyone would notice...if we all just went away. If there was no one left on the land...just Harvey and his big machines.

PAUL: So you wanna take the offer? (VERNA *pauses.*)

VERNA: No. I won't sell that man the farm.

PAUL: Okay, then.

VERNA: What about us?

PAUL: I know we might have to sell some time. I tried not to see it, but I know, all right. I even tried to think of other jobs I could do. I thought maybe I could be a welder or a trucker. If we could just try a couple more years. Then if it's not working, maybe we'd have to sell.... I don't wanna leave this place. But I guess I won't die for it either. Just think, we might end up being city people ourselves some day.... I'm sorry it's been so hard. It's not what I hoped it would be.

VERNA: Nobody could have done more than you did.

PAUL: About Darcy. I wish they'd have waited too.

VERNA: Like they say, eh, "If you could be seventeen again, knowing what you know now."

PAUL: Forty-eight's not so old, you know.

VERNA: No.

PAUL: We're not finished yet, not by a long ways.

VERNA: Not finished with each other?

PAUL: No.

VERNA: We'll give it a try?

PAUL: Yeah.... See how it goes?

VERNA: Yeah.

IN MEMORY OF MY KOOCHUM MADELAINE O'SOUP ACOOSE

(circa 1890-1979)

JANICE ACOOSE

Department of Indian Affairs registered her
O'Soup.
The Oblates baptized her
Madelaine.
We called her
Koochum Paul.

She was adopted
Her Irish ancestry...
erased.
Became ANISHNABE.

Flaming red hair, hung
Down the length of her back.
Warm, sun, kissed your brown eyes
Could melt your soul.

An angry word
She never spoke.
A stranger
She never turned away.

Quite unlike anyone
I'll ever know.
My Koochum
May she rest in peace.

(For Koochum Madelaine...one of my teachers)

rior to the signing of Treaty Four, the Oblates of Mary Immaculate made several attempts to set up a mission school among the Anishnabe and the Nehiowak of Crooked Lake. During this time, our Elders tried to show these first blackrobes our ways. They taught them our language, our customs, our values.

Once the Oblates learned our language, they told us that we had to give up our "pagan" ways and become Christians. The blackrobes tried to persuade the Elders to give up their children, assuring them that they would raise them up to be good Christians.

O'Soup, the Chief of the Anishnabe at O'Soup Reserve, answered them. He told them, "If you want our children, give us yours in exchange. We will raise them up to be good people."

Although exchanging children was a common practice among indigenous peoples in North America, the Oblates were unfamiliar and uncomfortable with Chief O'Soup's proposal. They didn't understand that the exchange of children secured peace, built alliances, and formed sacred trusts between nations. However, anticipating a lengthy and co-operative relationship with Anishnabe and the Nehiowaks, the blackrobes agreed.

It took them some time, however, to offer their own children. A Winnipeg orphanage subsequently produced three children.

The Oblates received these children at Crooked Lake in 1886

and they offered them to Chief O'Soup. Gaddie, O'Soup's distinguished headman, opened his home to the young brother and sister of Metis descent. Chief O'Soup accepted the baby girl the blackrobes called Madelaine.

Like all good Christian Indians she was baptized; she was christened Madelaine O'Soup. Like all Indians she also became a ward of the Canadian government and thus, in accordance with the Indian Act, the Department of Indian Affairs registered her with Chief O'Soup's band. She was registered as Madelaine O'Soup of O'Soup's Reserve.

She spent the first eight years of her life on the reserve learning the ways of her people. In her ninth year, the missionaries came for her. Like many school-aged Indian children, her home became the Qu'Appelle Industrial School. At school Madelaine simply became Number 382.

At Qu'Appelle, 382's basic education, combined with domestic and industrious training, produced the appropriate Indian farmwife. From the strict teachings of the principal, Father Hugonard, she also learned obedience to God, father, and husband.

While she was away at school, old O'Soup had arranged for her to marry young Paul Acoose, a descendant of the powerful and respected Acoose family from the neighbouring Sakimay Reserve. Acoose and O'Soup had great hopes for the union between Madelaine and Paul.

Prior to the birth of their children, Acoose and O'Soup had witnessed starvation, malnutrition, and hundreds of agonizingly painful deaths from tuberculosis when they settled on reserves. Their people, once strong and healthy, were reduced to infected bodies, oozing green pus. The dreaded disease plagued many reserves, and only a few healthy people remembered their ways.

Strangely, the blackrobes were not affected. Seeing their strong power, the Indians abandoned their own medicine people and turned to the missionaries for protection and relief from the wretched sickness. Acoose and O'Soup, witnessing the physical and cultural devastation of their people, proposed an alliance between their two families.

As was the custom, old O'Soup brought horses to Acoose. Acoose, accepting the proposal, nodded his head and took the reins. The alliance was secured.

Chief O'Soup's red-headed beauty, Madelaine, was to be joined to Paul Acoose. He was the son of Samuel Acoose, a very prominent and esteemed buffalo runner from old Sakimay's band. Quewich, old Acoose's father, had travelled for many years with Waywayseecapo and his prowess as a runner was well remembered in the oral stories of the Anishnabe.

Many whispered that young Paul had also been blessed by the Creator with strong medicine to run. Indeed, he carried the power in his name – Acoose – Man Standing Above Ground.

The old people wisely predicted Paul would inspire many of his people. In later years, as a councillor to the chief, a committed member of the grass dance society, and an annual participant in the Raindance, he earned the respect and loyalty of the band members. As a runner he set a world record in 1909, acquiring the title "redskin running champion of the world."

Madelaine, as the two old men had arranged, properly became Mrs. Paul Acoose. She bore him nine children: five dark and healthy sons and four fair and sturdy girls. When their children married, Paul would boast that he possessed one hundred and five grandchildren. We saw Madelaine as only an extension of her husband, so we called her Koochum Paul.

She lived in his shadow for seventy-five years, celebrating his achievements and suffering in his failures. In drunken stupors he lashed out, "You white Irish bitch," punishing her for all the things he suffered under white rule. Never one to give in to self-pity, she silently endured his cruelty and humbly asked God's forgiveness for making him angry. When she suffered, Madelaine believed that she had to try harder to please others. She never allowed anyone to go hungry or tired from her door. She encouraged others with a pleasant smile, tea, and polite con-

In Memory of My Koochum Madelaine O'Soup Acoose

versation. Never tiring, Madelaine tended the house and farm chores, many times until late into the evening.

Sometimes, by a dim light, I secretly watched as she unbraided her beautiful hair. Slowly and methodically she'd brush and brush, starting at the top of her head and stopping just below her waist. Her hair was like nothing I had ever seen before, but I imagined there were many fiery red-headed Irish women where she came from.

Just when I thought she was ready to turn out the light and sleep, she'd turn to me: "Good night, noosisim."

In the dark I'd think about how her eyes held mysterious secrets of a foreign land. As I dozed off, dreamily I'd envision her homeland while I silently vowed to someday locate the remains of her family in Ireland. Many times I desperately wanted to ask her about her "real" family. But just before blurting out the words I'd remember her tearful answers, "Wahwah, mister, I don't even know this Irish," as she defended herself against my Mooshum's angry words.

Even as she lay dying, many years later, I thought she'd magically become Irish. Hanging on to each precious moment at her deathbed, I waited for her to mouth the Irish words or recall colourful and exciting stories from her homeland.

She didn't disappoint me. Her last words came from the language of her people – the Anishnabe. In her last senile moments, Madelaine O'Soup Acoose, Number 382, my Koochum Paul, said, "Amo anint wapos, minihkwen nihti," as she motioned for us to gather around the imaginary fire.

2. PARALLEL LIVES

Coal Miners, Saskatchewan Archives

Circa 1931

The struggles for human dignity and human rights have informed the history of the province. From Louis Riel to Tommy Douglas to John Diefenbaker, political issues have provoked great debate and compelled attention. A central issue, strongly expressed by John Diefenbaker, is the establishment of fundamental rights. He says, "I am a Canadian, a free Canadian, free to speak without fear, free to worship God in my own way, free to stand for what I think right, free to oppose what I believe wrong, free to choose those who shall govern my country. This heritage of freedom I pledge to uphold for all mankind and myself." Others have struggled for their rights. And some of those other voices, from Doukhobor settlers to Ukrainian miners, have also attracted the interest of writers. From the conditions of the past, politics emerged. As Rex Deverell says of the time of his play, 1931, "The Great Depression was just beginning. In the Saskatchewan coalfields surrounding Bienfait and Estevan, pay and working conditions had deteriorated to the point of desperation." Writers make discoveries about themselves and their societies as they write. As Greg Nelson says, "I set out to write a play about Doukhobors. In the process, I found myself writing about my own non-Doukhobor history, about the experience of coming (as most of us have) to this country, and this society, from somewhere else." Though our lives are parallel, we are affected by the lives and experiences of others.

PARALLEL LIVES

ELIZABETH BREWSTER

Reading the words of my almost namesake,
Eva Brewster, survivor of Auschwitz,
born in the same year as I was
but into a life wholly other

I struggle to bridge this space
between my own youth with its lesser worries
about grades or money,
my time of gentle studies,
reading poetry in the library stacks
or loitering under elms and willows
daydreaming of handsome sailors
while parents and teachers hovered
protective

and her forced early maturation
in cattle cars and concentration camps,
starved to a skeleton,
terrified of the wolfish dogs
that she saw tear others to pieces

grieving the death
of husband and young child

Parallel Lives

observing much evil done to others:
the innocents used for target practice,
or tortured in medical experiments,
or abused as prostitutes,
the nineteen-year-old girl who looked to be ninety,
the babies thrown alive into open flames;

seeing death in the wreathed smoke
and guessing what it might feel like
to die in the gas chambers
nightmare images for the rest of her life.

And yet she pulled through, managing,
through clever planning and courage,
luck and desperation,
to escape (jumping from a moving train)
to merge with German refugees
in the late days of the war

to hide
to live again
remarried, with other children
here in Canada
not far from me.

I know I could never have survived
such trials
would have fallen with the weak ones
under foot,

saying their last prayers,
vanishing into crematoria
or unknown graves.

Where was God
to allow such difference?

In a cruel world
does one dare (sometimes) to be happy?

Yes, she tells me, yes.
It's right to be happy,
as much as you can.

Only remember.

Excerpt from That'll Be The Day

MOUSELAND

KEN MITCHELL

Tommy Douglas was Premier of Saskatchewan from 1944 to 1960. He was also a storyteller. In the heat of an election campaign, when he spoke to crowds he often told stories like Mouseland.

TOMMY: Let me tell you about Mouseland. It was a place where all the little mice lived and played, were born and died. And they lived much the same as you and I do. They even had a parliament.

And every four years they had an election. They would walk to the polls and cast their ballots. Some of them even got a ride to the polls. And got a ride for the next four years after that too! Just like you and I. And every time on election day, all the little mice used to go to the ballot box and elect a government. A government made up of big, fat, black – cats.

Now if you find it strange that mice should elect a government of cats, you just look at the history of Canada for the last hundred years, and you'll see that they were no stupider than we are.

And I'm not saying anything against cats. They were nice fellows. They conducted their government with dignity. They passed good laws – that is, laws good for cats. But the laws that suited the cats weren't so good for the mice. One law said mouseholes had to be large enough that a cat could get his paw in. Another law said that mice could only run at certain speeds – so that a cat could get his breakfast without too much effort.

All the laws were good laws. For cats. But oh, they were hard on the mice. And life continued to get harder and harder. The mice were finally driven to despair, and decided something had to be done. So they went en masse to the polls. They voted the black cats out. And they voted in the white cats!

Now the white cats had a terrific campaign. They had billboards put up with the slogan, "Mouseland needs more vision!" They nailed together a new platform, saying, "The only trouble with Mouseland is all the round mouseholes. Vote for us, and we'll establish a system of square mouseholes!"

So the little mice did. And the square mouseholes were twice as big as the round mouseholes, and the cats could get both paws in! And life got tougher than ever.

When they couldn't take that anymore, they voted the white cats out, and put the black ones in again. Then they went back to the white cats. Then to the black cats. They even tried half black cats and half white cats. And they called that a coalition.

You see, my friends, the trouble wasn't the colour of the cats. The trouble was – they were cats. And because they were cats, they naturally took care of the cats, instead of the mice.

But by and by, there came along one little mouse – who had an idea. Folks, watch out for the little guy with an idea. He said to the other mice, "Look fellows, why do we keep on electing governments made up of cats? Why don't we elect a government of mice?"

"Oh!" they cried. "Throw him out, he's a communist! Lock him up!" And they tossed him in jail.

Well. You can lock up a mouse. And you can lock up a man. But you can't lock up an idea!

LOCAL NEWS

GARY HYLAND

Meanwhile in the hills
southwest of Moose Jaw
crocus insurgents
have infiltrated
outlying regions

Early reports mention
purple squadrons
apparently armed
with stamens and pistils
of their own design
bombarding defenders
with frequent bursts
of fragrant air

So far skirmishes
have been inconclusive
but civic officials
expressed confidence
their defences were secure
If the worst comes
we have tanks and jets
standing by the mayor said

Local News

The guerrillas are reported
to be demanding equal time
with fiscal considerations
in public and private fields

The effect on school attendance
licence applications
and income tax returns
is not immediately known

Excerpt from
GONE THE BURNING SUN

(KEN MITCHELL)

What Canadian is known by the most people? Wayne Gretsky? Celine Dion? It is Dr. Norman Bethune, a hero to a billion Chinese. He served as a medical doctor in the Spanish Civil War. From there he went to China where he organized the medical units for Mao's revolution.

SCENE TWO

Lights come up on BETHUNE *sitting on the table. He is swinging his legs, wearing a white hospital coat.*

BETHUNE: Good morning, gentlemen! Welcome to the Montreal Royal Victoria Hospital, jewel in the crown of international Medico-Pulmonary surgery. Now – what does that mean to innocent young interns like yourselves? (*Pause.*) You're absolutely right, son – sweet bugger all! Because in fact it's no better than some waterfront abortion den when you look at the statistics. Riddled with bureaucracy and rotten with incompetence. So don't look for a medical utopia – here or anywhere else. The inefficiency will make you sweat. The hypocrisy will make you puke. More patients die in the Royal Vic from the cautious fumbling of old men than they do from TB in the slums of Verdun. (*Pause.*) Cynical? Not at all. Realistic. To expect better would only create disillusionment. And God knows, there are enough disillusioned doctors already. When I was given a second life – through radical pneumothorax – I left general practice and became a lung surgeon. One of the best, according to some. Oh, not these old fossils, of course. There are people here who accuse Bethune of killing his patients. Well, it's true. I do have a high mortality record. In fact, I operate on cases they're all terrified to admit into their offices – the hopeless dying! (*Rises angrily.*)

So to hell with them! If you want to be lung surgeons, you'll follow my technique – fast diagnosis – out there, in the reeking streets of Montreal – fast operation, fast treatment! Yes, they die on my operating table. But remember – Bethune gives them a sporting chance. (*Pulls a stethoscope from his pocket.*)

First demonstration this morning. Identify this object. (*Points.*) Right! I believe you have a future in medicine, son. Well, take a good look at the "stethoscope." The symbol of life – right? Wrong! This little device has killed more lung patients than all the cigarettes manufactured by Imperial Tobacco! My advice – wear it around your neck like a magic amulet. A bit of voodoo never hurt anyone. Remember – the doctor is the holy priest. But for results – stick to your X-ray machine. Five hundred percent more reliable. And when you're ready to work – these! (*Presents a set of heavy rib shears, gleaming.*)

Rib shears. My proudest invention. Look dangerous, don't they? Well, they're not made for delicacy. They're made to cut through bone in one stroke – to collapse the lung – give it rest. We're dealing with an extreme disease, gentlemen – and it demands extreme remedies. Make no mistake. You will get blood on your hands. And other unpleasant organisms. You'll have to overcome some pet aversions, see them for what they are. Maggots, for example. Last month, I introduced forty-six live fly maggots into the chest cavity of a troublesome patient. Couldn't get the septic fluids to drain. Now, maggots love to eat rotting flesh – and would you believe it? – within ten days my little maggots had made him healthy – by consuming the entire infection. The despised vermin of this world can be valuable, gentlemen, if you allow yourselves to think in extremes.

Well, I don't want to shock you – but you'll hear lots of shocking things about Norman Bethune. Playboy – alcoholic – eccentric. Now – I'm a red! Ha! But if I'm ever remembered for anything – it'll be the development of the artificial pneumothorax machine. *(Shows a poster or diagram of it.)*

A pump to collapse the lung. With this machine, I am able to maintain my patients' lives – as well as my own. Yes? *(Chuckles.)* No laddie – medical inventions will not make you rich. Unless you're a psychiatrist. Or a plastic surgeon. *(A bell rings.* BETHUNE *rushes off.)*

Consider these thoughts as you memorize your Latin. Tomorrow's lecture: Bedside Manners and Bigger Fees!

SCENE SEVEN

BETHUNE: Salud, Canada! This is Radio Station EAQ, Voice of Spanish Democracy. Norman Bethune reporting from Madrid. Thanks – Canadian cameradas y companeros – for the shipment of medicine and bandages. Our medical unit, Instituto Hispano-Canadiense de Transfusion de Sangre, has become famous in this bitter war. The first blood transfusion service in military history! A hundred transfusions a day, along a thousand-kilometre front.

The carnage is incredible. In February, the Fascists started bombing Malaga. The entire population forced to flee a hundred miles to Almeria. Hazen and I drove to help them. Thousands and thousands – so dense the van can't push them through. They flash past our windshields like millions of snowflakes in a blizzard. The old ones give up, lie down in the ditch to wait for death. Children younger than ten. Barefoot. Slung on mother's shoulders. Clinging to her hands. A man staggers along with two children on his back, hidden among the pots and pans. Suddenly the van besieged by a mob of frantic parents. "Receiberne este! Take the children to Almeria!" Holding out their lifeless arms. Eyes swollen from the dust and sun. "Este esta herido!" Blood-stained rags around their limbs. Crying from pain and hunger. Planes machine gun the road by day. They tramp all night in a stream of men, goats, children – crying the names of the lost: "Gustavo! Gustavo!" Three days and nights, we ferry the multitude, more precious than our bottles of blood, to Almeria.

But the final barbarism awaits. On the evening of February 12th, 1937, forty thousand refugees have reached sanctuary in the little seaport. Huddled in the main square of Almeria. Sirens wail. Mussolini's planes darken the sky. Ten huge bombs drop in the very centre of town. A strategic military target! Bodies and limbs fall through the air like a torrent of bloody rain. Three children dead on the pavement in front of the relief office. Killed waiting for a cup of milk. The street a shambles of dead and dying, lit by the bright orange glare of burning buildings. In the darkness, children's screams. The curses of men rise in a massive cry – higher and higher. They cry for pity. They cry for revenge. My body heavier than all the dead. Hollow, empty. In my brain, a bright flame of hate. *(Sings.)*

> Spanish heavens spread their brilliant starlight
> High above our trenches in the plain.
> From the distance, morning comes to greet us,
> Calling us to battle once again.
> Far off is our land
> Yet ready we stand.
> We're fighting and winning for you –
> FREEDOM! *(Makes the Republican salute – a raised clenched fist.)*

This is Norman Bethune signing off in Madrid.

SCENE TEN

BETHUNE *lights a candle in the darkness.*

BETHUNE: Yes? Who's there? Ah, Tong – what is it? Chairman
Mao wants to see me? It's after midnight! No, no – wait. Just
a minute. Can we take Jean along too? It would be a great
honour for her – and she's come so far. *(Calls.)* Jean! Come
on, wake up and grab your boots! We're meeting the great
man himself! Tong is here to take us to headquarters. Come
on! Forget about a skirt – those pants look great. This isn't a
king you're meeting, it's a guerrilla leader. The man who led
the Red Army through the Long March – how far, Tong?
Eight thousand miles! Fighting Nationalist soldiers all the
way – through swamps, over mountains, across every river in
the country! They lost over a hundred thousand men! And
you know how many made it here to Yan-an? Just ten thousand! But oh, god, what men! And women! Now, in these
hill-caves in the desert, they've built a revolutionary capital.
In just two years! A university, a hospital, factories. Oh – he's
incredible – a genius – a leader – *(Halts, surprised.)*

In here? A – cave? *(Pause.)* Well of course, it's a cave!
Dammit, they all live in caves! The bloody hospital's in caves.
(Lighting change. He enters MAO's *presence.)*Ni hao, ni hao.
We're very well, thank you. *(Turns to* TONG.*)* And please tell
Chairman Mao that we – Comrade Ewen and I – are very
impressed by everything we've seen. We're eager to begin
work. I've made a tour of the hospital and I'm afraid I must
report that it's badly in need of – yes of course – please
translate. *(Pause.)* Spain? Well, I'm afraid there are many
problems. Disorganization. Factionalism. The German
weapons of the fascists. *(Pause.)* Who? No, I never met
Lorca. They'd killed him before I got there. But I did run

into Hemingway in a taberna in Barcelona. (*A trifle impatiently.*) Mr. Chairman, I was at the front. I am a soldier, my job was to save soldiers' lives. That's why I request that you order your generals to assign me to the battle front. To set up mobile units, as I did in Spain. If you are not mobilizing medicine, you have troops dying without purpose. In Spain, we operated at the front. Seventy-five percent recovery. Seventy-five percent! So if I could just get permission to go to the front – (*Pause. He sags with disappointment.*) I see. Yes, the base hospital needs attention. But Mr. Chairman, Comrade Ewen can do that as well as I. In fact, if your medical officers took my advice, they'd blow the place up and start all over! Oh yes – the caves are a good defence against aerial bombing, but – the dirt! Everywhere. I haven't seen a patient covered with a warm blanket, never mind clean sheets. They sleep on mud kangs in their old uniforms! You might as well put bullets through their – Never mind, don't translate. Tell Mr. Chairman Mao that I – we – will start work in the morning. Of course, we'll need a few basics. First, elementary classes in hygiene for all personnel – nurses, doctors, even the janitors. Two – a power generator for the hospital – for lighting and blood refrigeration. Pardon? Then who should I speak to? No, wait – just say I've tried to have this done, but the hospital bureaucrats say it must be approved by "higher authority." And I believe we're speaking to the highest authority in the Eighth Route Army. Right? (*Smiles.*) Good, that's settled. We're making progress, Tong! Third! My nurses will need at least two heavy trucks to carry the blood unit to the front. In Spain, I had – What? No nurses? Or doctors? (*Pause.*) No trucks? (*Explodes with frustration.*) NO ROADS? Impossible! I'm not a miracle worker! I refuse to take assignment! What the hell does this man expect – everything? (*Pause.*) He does? Everything? (*He stares at* MAO, *astonished. He sags for a moment, overwhelmed, then blows the candle out.*)

DOUKHOBOR

JOHN NEWLOVE

When you die and your weathery corpse
lies on the chipped kitchen table,

the wind blowing the wood of your house
painted in shades of blue, farmer

out from Russia as the century turned,
died, and lay at the feet of the wars,

who will ever be able to say for you
what you thought at the sight of the Czar's horsemen

riding with whips among you, the sight
of the rifles burning on bonfires,

the long sea-voyage, strange customs endured,
officials changing your name

into the strange script that covered the stores,
the polite brown men who spoke no language

you understood and helped you
free your team from Saskatchewan winter mud,

Doukhobor

who will be able to say for you
just what you thought as the villages marched

naked to Eden and the English
went to war and came back again

with their funny ways, proud
to speak of killing each other, you, whose mind

refused the slaughter, refused the blood,
you who will lie in your house, stiff as winter,

dumb as an ox, unable to love,
while your women sob and offer the visitors tea?

Excerpt from

SPIRIT WRESTLER

(GREG NELSON)

In 1897 the Doukhobors left Russia to escape from religious persecution. They settled in Saskatchewan where they wished to live collectively and to refrain from fighting in wars. However, ten years later, the Canadian Government decided to enforce a particular aspect of its immigration policy, requiring each male to sign for a homestead. The Doukhobors were not to be allowed to live in villages with all land registered in the name of their leader, Peter Verigin. The majority refused the order. They abandoned their prosperous farms and resettled in the interior of British Columbia.

SCENE THREE

A meeting hall. A table. On the table: bread, salt, water. Several Doukhobors, including NIKOLAI *and* ZIBAROFF *are behind the table.* NIKOLAI *has a newspaper. They address a large group of Doukhobors.*

NIKOLAI: *(To* ZIBAROFF.) Are you crazy? Do you realize what you have done? *(To the meeting.)* We are now a laughingstock in this country. A punchline. Those crazy Doukhobors.

ZIBAROFF: We are –

NIKOLAI: *(Interrupting, holding up newspaper.)* The Manitoba Free Press: "...hundreds of men, with the light of insanity in their eyes, roaming whither and for what they know not, driven by a belief that brings the dark ages into the twentieth century!"

ZIBAROFF: That is –

NIKOLAI: *(Not stopping.)* Why do you think the government wants a meeting? They think they've made a mistake! And frankly, I don't blame them!

ZIBAROFF: I wish to speak.

NIKOLAI: If I were them –

ZIBAROFF: *(Overriding him.)* I wish to speak. You have spoken. *(NIKOLAI looks at him for a moment. Then he sits. ZIBAROFF turns to the meeting. He has a telegram.)* Friends. Brothers. This is the telegram. Here it is. From the Government of Canada, written in English. It says: come to Ottawa, come to our meeting...or else.

NIKOLAI: *(Standing.)* That's not what it says.

ZIBAROFF: I am speaking.

NIKOLAI: But it doesn't say that. It's very polite. *(ZIBAROFF looks at him.)* All right. *(He sits.)*

ZIBAROFF: They ask us for a response. Well, my friends, I have a response. This is my response. *(He tears the telegram in half. NIKOLAI almost gets up again, but restrains himself.)* We must not forget! Yes we are in a new country. It isn't Russia, there isn't a Tsar, but there is a government, my friends, and we do not trust governments!

NIKOLAI: *(Back on his feet.)* Wait a second –

ZIBAROFF: *(Overriding him.)* How does it begin? With a telegram. A meeting. "Come to Ottawa." And so we go, and this, and that, and then it's "Oh, and by the way, we want you to swear this oath."

NIKOLAI: *(Shaking head.)* No.

ZIBAROFF: "Oh, and by the way, we want to conscript you."

NIKOLAI: That's –

ZIBAROFF: We cannot serve two masters! What would Peter Verigin say, if he saw this telegram? He would say: "Ignore it. Do not go." He would tell us: "We are subjects of God. We must serve God. We must cast away our riches, and our worldly goods. We must free our animals from servitude, and we must leave this place, this barren place, and search, however we can, for Paradise. The land of God. Where the sun is ever warm." That's what he would say! And I tell you, friends, I promise you, that Verigin will join us there! The Lordly! He will live with us, in Paradise! We must prepare the way! (ZIBAROFF *sits, abruptly. Scattered clapping.* NIKOLAI, *who has watched* ZIBAROFF's *performance in silence, now stands. He waits for silence.*)

NIKOLAI: (*Pause.*) Well. I don't agree. I don't think Verigin would say that. Any of that. And you know, I don't think he'd be very...proud. Of us. Of how we're getting on. (*He pauses.*)

I wonder what he would say. If he were here, in this room. If it were he that stood in front of you today, instead of me. Perhaps he would turn to Zibaroff here. "Tell me, Ivan," he'd say, "how would you define this paradise? A place where there is land? A place where we can cultivate? And build, and grow? A place where we can live in honest toil? Is it a place where we no longer have to suffer?" (*Slight pause.*)

And then perhaps he'd turn. And point outside. And say to Ivan: "Look. Look out there. Stretching out in all directions. Under the snow. Beneath the wind. Surrounding us. You don't have to search any further, my friend. You've found it. You've discovered Paradise. It's name...is Canada." (*He looks out at the meeting.*)

I believe it's a gift. All this. Not from Ottawa. From God. Because we suffered. Perhaps we should act a little more grateful. (*He looks at* ZIBAROFF. *He picks up the torn bits of telegram.*)

I propose that we accept this invitation. That we go to Ottawa, and tell them we are happy.

We must stop this madness. We must work together. So that when, at last, he arrives, Peter Verigin will be proud. Of us. His people. (ZIBAROFF *rises, to speak. But someone has started singing a psalm. Voices join in.*)

ZIBAROFF: My friends – (*The singing gets louder.* ZIBAROFF *looks at* NIKOLAI, *who starts singing along. Finally,* ZIBAROFF *is forced to sing too. The meeting ends: the people parade out, singing.* NIKOLAI *remains behind, looking after them.* ANNA *approaches.* TANYA *is in the background.)*

ANNA: You're a good speaker.

NIKOLAI: *(Sees her.)* Mother.

ANNA: You make a good impression.

NIKOLAI: Really?

ANNA: Everyone is impressed. They talk about you. They agree with what you say.

NIKOLAI: *(Looking after* ZIBAROFF.*)* I hope so.

ANNA: Nikolai. *(He looks at her.)* I'm proud of you. *(He smiles.)* Come here. *(*NIKOLAI *goes to her.)* You don't believe me?

NIKOLAI: Sure.

ANNA: I'm your mother.

NIKOLAI: I know.

ANNA: You're becoming an important man. It's true. Don't argue. Why don't you go?

NIKOLAI: What?

ANNA: To Ottawa. This meeting. You should go.

NIKOLAI: I should?

ANNA: Yes. Because you're linked. You and Peter Verigin, you always have been. Why? Because you have his faith. And then you can go to Siberia.

NIKOLAI: Mother –

ANNA: Why not? Stop in Ottawa, have your meeting, and then... keep going. All the way to Siberia. Sure you could. They have to send someone.

TANYA: *(Approaching.)* What's this?

ANNA: *(To* NIKOLAI.*)* Because you're linked.

NIKOLAI: *(To* TANYA.*)* It's nothing.

ANNA: *(To* TANYA, *defiant.)* I was saying Nikolai should go to Siberia. *(Slight pause.* TANYA *with a hint of a smile.)*

TANYA: Siberia.

ANNA: That's right. To bring us back the Living Christ. What's funny?

TANYA: Nothing.

ANNA: *(Getting angry.)* Someone has to go!

TANYA: I know –

ANNA: He can't just leave.

TANYA: You're right –

ANNA: He can't just walk across the ocean. Someone has to get him!

TANYA: Yes –

ANNA: It might as well be Nikolai.

TANYA: That's right. It might as well. You're absolutely right. *(ANNA is unsure if TANYA is making fun of her.)*

ANNA: I have work to do. *(To NIKOLAI, as she goes.)* Think about it. *(ANNA leaves.)*

TANYA: *(Smiling.)* I'm sorry. I can't help it!

NIKOLAI: Neither can she.

TANYA: I know. I'm sorry.

NIKOLAI: So?

TANYA: So what.

NIKOLAI: So what did you think?

TANYA: About what? *(Slight pause.)* You know what I think.

NIKOLAI: Tanya –

TANYA: You know how to talk, you've always known how to talk. *(Slight pause.)* It makes me nervous.

NIKOLAI: What does.

TANYA: All of it. Zibaroff. Verigin. I mean, what is he going to do? When he gets here? Wave his hand, and everything will be perfect?

NIKOLAI: No –

TANYA: You're placing all your bets on him, that makes me nervous.

NIKOLAI: Tanya, we're like children. Look at us. We don't know how to act, we, we've been dropped here, in this country, where we can do anything, anything! Of course we're going to disagree! That's the point! What we need is leadership! That's all we – *(He realizes, stops.)* Am I talking again?

TANYA: Nikolai. You're not a child. You're a man. *(Slight pause.)* Come here. *(He goes to her.)* I love you.

NIKOLAI: I love you.

TANYA: I don't want you to go to Siberia.

NIKOLAI: Okay.

TANYA: I don't want you going anywhere.

NIKOLAI: Okay.

TANYA: I want you staying here. Right...here.

SCENE FOUR

SIFTON's *office, in Ottawa.* SIFTON, MAVOR, *and* NIKOLAI.

MAVOR: Minister, may I introduce Mr. Kalmakoff. Nikolai Savelyevitch. Nikolai, The Right Honourable Sir Clifford Sifton, Minister of the Interior. (SIFTON *speaks as if to a child.* NIKOLAI *speaks slowly, haltingly, with a thick Russian accent.*)

SIFTON: Hello! Welcome to Ottawa.

NIKOLAI: *(Bows low.)* God be praised.

SIFTON: *(Not sure whether to bow in return.)* Yes. Thank you. Same to you.

MAVOR: Nikolai's English is surprisingly good.

NIKOLAI: I don't have many chance to speak with English.

SIFTON: Well you're doing brilliantly.

NIKOLAI: Thank you.

SIFTON: Smashing.

MAVOR: *(Slight pause.)* Well.

SIFTON: *(Gazing at* NIKOLAI.) I'm most interested in your people. I'm a great fan of East Europeans. Frankly, I don't know where this country would be without them, they've almost single-handedly opened up the west.

MAVOR: That's right.

SIFTON: Unfortunately they – you – also have your critics. People who believe that you aren't willing to integrate, to become...Canadian. They say, quite rightly, that we are building a new country, which, as such, requires unity.

MAVOR: Yes, but surely –

SIFTON: (*Not stopping.*) However. Their comments are all too often tinged with a racist overtone. Which I cannot abide. (*Slight pause.*) I'm not sure where I stand on integration. Somewhere in the middle, I suppose. As usual. (*He smiles charmingly. There is a slight pause.*)

MAVOR: Mr. Kalmakoff has come with a request.

SIFTON: Has he.

MAVOR: It's regarding Peter Verigin.

SIFTON: Ah.

MAVOR: I spoke of the matter before, you may remember.

SIFTON: I do indeed.

MAVOR: Mr. Kalmakoff would like us to negotiate for his release. Personally, I think it's an excellent idea.

SIFTON: (*Suddenly.*) What can I give you?

MAVOR: I'm sorry?

SIFTON: Tea? (*To* NIKOLAI.) Yes? Tea?

NIKOLAI: Yes.

SIFTON: Professor?

MAVOR: Yes. Thank you.

NIKOLAI: Thank you.

SIFTON: (*Gestures for them to sit.*) Please. (*They sit.* SIFTON *serves the tea.*)

MAVOR: As I was saying, Minister, bringing Peter Verigin to Canada, the reuniting of the leader with the people, would have an unquestionably stabilizing effect.

SIFTON: (*Handing tea to* MAVOR.) Professor.

MAVOR: Thank you. Now, I've been in touch with Russia. I've made some enquiries. And I think it's possible.

SIFTON: (*To* NIKOLAI.) One lump or two?

NIKOLAI: Thank you.

MAVOR: All it seems to require is clout. Political clout.

SIFTON: (*Handing tea to* NIKOLAI.) There you are.

NIKOLAI: Thank you.

MAVOR: Such as you possess, Minister.

SIFTON: You flatter me, Professor.

MAVOR: Not at all. I'm simply stating the facts. (SIFTON *sips his tea.*)

SIFTON: You know, it's rather embarrassing, but...I don't think there's anything that gives me greater satisfaction...than a good cup of tea. (*Pause. He has their full attention. To* NIKOLAI.) You've been in this country now for...five years?

NIKOLAI: Yes.

SIFTON: And you're doing rather well.

MAVOR: Extremely well.

SIFTON: You've built your villages, you've broken some land.

MAVOR: They built the railway.

SIFTON: I understand you're pacifists.

NIKOLAI: Yes.

SIFTON: Admirable. Very Christian. And...communists, too?

NIKOLAI: Yes.

MAVOR: Minister....

SIFTON: (*Ignoring him.*) Fascinating. Tell me, what does that mean, exactly?

MAVOR: I've explained it to you –

SIFTON: (*Interrupting, to* NIKOLAI.) Mr. Kalmakoff. Why don't you tell me what it means. (*They both turn to him. Slight pause.*)

NIKOLAI: I wish to say. Doukhobors are happy in Canada. Happy. For Doukhobors, Canada is Paradise. Thank you. (*Pause.*)

SIFTON: Yes. (*Pause.*) Look, Mr. Kalmakoff. I'd best be entirely frank. The west is filling up. Good, fertile land, such as yours, is becoming valuable. And a lot of people want it. (*To* MAVOR.) How much does he know about the Hamlet Clause?

MAVOR: Well, he –

SIFTON: (*Interrupting, to* NIKOLAI.) There is something called The Homestead Act. This is how it works. A man, a settler, registers for a piece of land. He is given three years to "improve" it. This means he must break it, till it, and live upon it. He must homestead. If he does so, he is allowed to own it. All right?

MAVOR: Minister –

SIFTON: Now. Your people were given special privileges. You are allowed to live and work, as you say, "together," communally, in villages, or "hamlets." As well, you are exempt from the responsibilities that come with owning land. Such as military service. That was the deal.

NIKOLAI: Yes.

SIFTON: However. Your land must still be registered. And it must be tilled. Up to this point, neither has occurred.

MAVOR: That's not true.

SIFTON: Some of it has been tilled, but some is not enough. Large tracts remain unbroken. And now there are people, voters, who are looking at this land, and seeing that it isn't tilled. And then they are looking at the book and seeing that it isn't registered. And when they are told about special privileges, they are getting upset. And complaining rather loudly.

MAVOR: They're not "privileges," Minister, they're terms. Of an agreement.

SIFTON: Which is in peril. Do you understand? Of being revoked. (*Pause.*) I support you, Mr. Kalmakoff. I can hold the wolves at bay. But you must do something for me. You must behave yourselves. All right? No more of these marches.

MAVOR: Minister –

SIFTON: And more importantly, you must sign. For your land. We must have your names in our book. Professor Mavor has agreed to travel out to get these names. You must help him. You must tell them to sign the book, and till the soil. Do you understand?

NIKOLAI: Yes.

SIFTON Can you do this?

NIKOLAI: Yes.

SIFTON: Good. Because otherwise –

NIKOLAI: I can do this.

SIFTON: Excellent. Because otherwise –

NIKOLAI: But I am only one.

SIFTON: I'm sorry?

NIKOLAI: I am only one. The people will not listen. Not to me.

SIFTON: They won't.

NIKOLAI: They will listen to Verigin. To Peter Verigin.

SIFTON: (*Pause.*) Ah.

NIKOLAI: Verigin will solve every problem.

SIFTON: Will he tell your people to sign?

NIKOLAI: He will solve every problem. (*Pause.*)

MAVOR: By all reports, he's an excellent man.

SIFTON: Is he.

MAVOR: Tolstoy speaks most highly of him.

SIFTON: Does he.

MAVOR: Yes. Most highly. (*Pause.*)

SIFTON: All right. Why not. One more can't hurt. Where is he, Siberia?

NIKOLAI: Yes.

SIFTON: Right! Siberia. No problem. We'll send for him.

NIKOLAI: Minister. I promise. Peter Verigin will take Doukhobors...and make them into Canadians.

Excerpt from

BLACK POWDER

REX DEVERELL

In 1931 a strike took place at the Estevan coal mines. The RCMP stopped the strikers' parade on the main street of Estevan, where three miners lost their lives. What follows here is a segment of the coal strike story.

SCENE 9: ANNIE BULLER

Annie Buller is addressing a meeting of miners and their families. She is tall, imposing, a little on the heavy side. Her comrades have described her as beautiful, auburn, with an infectious smile. She is obviously and unapologetically an agitator.

ANNIE: My name is Annie Buller. I've been sent down here by the Workers Unity League in Winnipeg to tell you that this Sunday afternoon the workers of Winnipeg stand solidly behind you and the action you have taken.

Your fight is the worker's fight all over Canada. You will receive ammunition for your fight – ammunition in the form of food and clothing from workers all over Canada. All the unions are in sympathy from coast to coast and they have promised assistance.

I have spent the morning touring the mines in this district. I have examined some of the houses where miners are forced to live and I have found them not fit to live in! Men and women and children are living in houses that look like pigpens. The men are working in mines that look like pigpens and they are working in mines where they are treated no better than pigs!

Who is going to stand by you? Not the mine owners. Not the Government – not Bennett – not Premier Anderson. Not Bennett's hirelings, the Royal Canadian Mounted Police. They have not been sent down here to help the miners. They are here as Bennett's stool pigeons and they are here to assist capitalism and the mine operators.

No – believe me, your friends are your fellow workers. They stand beside you.

A few years ago I made a trip to England, Sweden, Holland, Germany, and Russia. I have to tell you that the conditions we are struggling against in this country are duplicated many times over in other parts of the world. In Germany, for instance, conditions for the working class are so bad that thousands of young women are forced to turn to prostitution. I learned that in the city of Berlin alone there are forty thousand prostitutes.

Comrades, the world is ripe for revolution. Only in Russia did I find that miners like yourselves are well paid. They have good houses with hot and cold running water and they get three weeks holiday with pay every year. They have libraries and cultural institutions and their lives are so much better than here or anywhere else.

But your lives can be better too – if you are prepared to fight and keep fighting. I have admired the solidarity you have shown. I hope you will continue to stay together and go over the top and prevent those men from operating the machines at the Truax mine. You will have no difficulty with the police. They are a mere handful and you can go through them like that.

In Toronto the Women Garment Workers were striking for better conditions and better pay. When the scabs and the others came to interfere with the striking girls in their fight they fought like lions. They grabbed them by the hair and choked them by the throat. That's how the girls in Toronto won out – and you can fight too – or are you yellow?

CROWD: We can fight!

ANNIE: *(Smiling upon them)* Yes – and I know you will. I know you are not yellow. I know that you are going to defend your wives and children. I know you are not going to let them go hungry or barefooted. *(Great shouts.)*

ANNIE: I am going back to Winnipeg next Sunday. I have to be back there. But before I leave I promise we will have another meeting combined with a demonstration. I know some of the boys can make signs and banners and I know they'll do it for us – won't you boys? So, I ask you – will you stay together?

CROWD: Yes, we'll stay together!

ANNIE: Will you fight?

CROWD: We'll fight!

ANNIE: Yes, I know you will! *(She steps down to great cheering.)*

OWNER: *(In spotlight.)* The owners and operators of the mines in this district want the public to know the real truth. We have prepared a statement. *(He has a paper in his hand.)* The eight deep seam mines in the Bienfait and Estevan districts with an aggregate capital investment of three million dollars and paying an aggregate amount yearly in social taxes of over twenty thousand and four of these mines paying royalty to the government on coal mined are now lying idle due to a strike fostered 100 percent by Communists. These Communists and agitators openly boast they are financed by Soviet Russia.

For nearly twenty years our deep seam mines have employed a maximum of over 500 men from October to March inclusive and in very large measure, by their payrolls aggregating hundreds of thousands of dollars yearly, have contributed to the growth and prosperity of Estevan,

Bienfait, and the surrounding districts.

Notwithstanding an attempt to resume, our deep seam mines (financed entirely by British and Canadian capital) continue to stand idle because of the fact that we have not been provided with proper police protection. Mob law has ruled – while hundreds of men in the district are desirous and anxious to go to work.

The newest and largest operation in the field, a machine operation financed 95 percent by American capital, employing approximately fifty men, notwithstanding our mines are idle, is running to capacity. Together with the influx of coal mined outside the province, our deep seam mines will very rapidly lose their market!

Information spread over the country by the Communist movement of deplorable working conditions in this field is entirely false, and the operators welcome a Royal Commission to investigate. It is our right to operate the plants and it is our right to demand the necessary police force. The police are not doing their job! (*Spotlight on an Inspector from the* RCMP.)

INSPECTOR: We have the situation well in hand.

OWNER: We could have gotten those new men in there and the mines would be operating today!

INSPECTOR: We were prepared to act.

OWNER: Over at the Western Dominion Collieries while the mob was still assembled the police were completely withdrawn from the vicinity.

INSPECTOR: That's not true. The force was there. We were prepared to act upon any information laid by the mine operators or anyone who had a grievance. We have the situation well in hand.

ESTEVAN, SASKATCHEWAN TRANSPORTATION COMPANY BUS STOP

ANDREW SUKNASKI

three of us walking the empty street   where the bus is parked
we enjoy the silence   and fresh evening air
while the driver   has another coffee
before carnduff   the end of his route

finally the old woman   in a babushka
protecting her   from the flowering cold
stands beside   the coke machine   by the depot
while I edge over   closer
to ask her   how far she's going

    'I going bienfait   spen tenksgeeving dare
    veet ole veedo fren'

I tell her
'I'm going there myself'

    'you knoh peeple dare?'

Estevan,
Saskatchewan
Transportation
Company Bus Stop

'no   I'm just going there
to find someone who can tell me
about the three miners
who were shot during the estevan riot   of '31'

        'oh....'

she says quietly
turning slightly   away from me
in the cooling silence
to gaze into the southern sky
where dark clouds
knowing no country   drift south
through her evening dream

Excerpt from

THE TESTIMONY OF LOUIS RIEL

(LOUIS RIEL)

1885

Your Honours, gentlemen of the jury: It would be easy for me today to play insanity, because the circumstances are such as to excite any man, and under the natural excitement of what is taking place today (I cannot speak English very well, but am trying to do so, because most of those here speak English), under the excitement which my trial causes me would justify me not to appear as usual, but with my mind out of its ordinary condition. I hope with the help of God I will maintain calmness and decorum as suits this honourable court, this honourable jury.

You have seen by the papers in the hands of the Crown that I am naturally inclined to think of God at the beginning of my actions. I wish if you – I do it you won't take it as a mark of insanity, that you won't take it as part of a play of insanity. Oh, my God, help me through Thy grace and the divine influence of Jesus Christ. Oh, my God, bless me, bless this honourable court, bless this honourable jury, bless my good lawyers who have come 700 leagues to try to save my life, bless also the lawyers for the Crown, because they have done, I am sure, what they thought their duty. They have shown me fairness which at first I did not expect from them. Oh, my God, bless all those who are around me through the grace and influence of Jesus Christ our Saviour, change the curiosity of those who are paying attention to me, change that curiosity into sympathy with me. The day of my birth I was helpless and my mother took care of me although she was not able to do it alone, there was someone to help her to take care of me and I lived. Today, although a man, I am as helpless before this court, in the Dominion of Canada and in this world, as I was helpless on the knees of my mother the day of my birth.

The North-West is also my mother, it is my mother country and although my mother country is sick and confined in a certain way, there are some from Lower Canada who came to help her to take care of me during her sickness and I am sure that my mother country will not kill me more than my mother did forty years ago when I came into the world, because a mother is always a mother, and even if I have my faults if she can see I am true she will be full of love for me.

When I came into the North-West in July, the first of July 1884, I found the Indians suffering. I found the half-breeds eating the rotten pork of the Hudson Bay Company and getting sick and weak every day. Although a half-breed, and having no pretension to help the whites, I also paid attention to them. I saw they were deprived of responsible government, I saw that they were deprived of their public liberties. I remembered that half-breed meant white and Indian, and while I paid attention to the suffering Indians and the half-breeds I remembered that the greatest part of my heart and blood was white and I have directed my attention to help the Indians, to help the half-breeds and to help the whites to the best of my ability. We have made petitions, I have made petitions with others to the Canadian Government asking to relieve the condition of this country. We have taken time; we have tried to unite all classes, even, if I may speak, all parties. Those who have been in close communication with me know I have suffered, that I have waited for months to bring some of the people of the Saskatchewan to an understanding of certain important points in our petition to the Canadian Government and I have done my duty. I believe I have done my duty. It has been said in this box that I have been egotistic. Perhaps I am egotistic. A man cannot be individuality without paying attention to himself. He cannot generalize himself, though he may be general. I have done all I could to make good petitions with others, and we have sent them to the Canadian Government, and when the Canadian Government did answer, through the Under-Secretary of State, to the secretary of the joint committee of the Saskatchewan, then I began to speak of myself, not before; so my particular interests passed after the public interests. A good deal has been said about the settlement and division of lands, a good deal has been said about that. I do not think my dignity today here would allow me to mention the foreign policy, but if I was to explain to you or if I had been allowed to make the questions to witnesses, those questions would have appeared in an altogether different light before the court and jury. I do not say that my lawyers did not put the right questions. The observations I had the honour to make to the court the day before yesterday were good, they were absent of the situation, they did not know all the small circumstances as I did. I could mention a point, but that point was leading to so many that I could not have been all the time suggesting. By it I don't wish it understood that I do not appreciate the good works of my lawyers, but if I were to go into all the details of what has taken place, I think I could safely show you that what Captain Young said that I am aiming all the time at practical results was true, and I could have proved it. During my life I have aimed at practical results. I have writings, and after my

The Testimony of Louis Riel

death I hope that my spirit will bring practical results....

No one can say that the North-West was not suffering last year, particularly the Saskatchewan, for the other parts of the North-West I cannot say so much; but what I have done, and risked, and to which I have exposed myself, rested certainly on the conviction, I had to do, was called upon to do something for my country.

It is true, gentlemen, I believed for years I had a mission, and when I speak of a mission you will understand me not as trying to play the role of insane before the grand jury so as to have a verdict of acquittal upon that ground. I believe that I have a mission, I believe I had a mission at this very time. What encourages me to speak to you with more confidence in all the imperfections of my English way of speaking, it is that I have yet and still that mission, and with the help of God, who is in this box with me, and He is on the side of my lawyers, even with the honourable court, the Crown and the Jury, to help me, and to prove by the extraordinary help that there is a Providence today in my trial, as there was Providence in the battles of the Saskatchewan.

I have not assumed to myself that I had a mission. I was working in Manitoba first, and I did all I could to get free institutions for Manitoba; they have those institutions today in Manitoba, and they try to improve them, while myself, who obtained them, I am forgotten as if I was dead. But after I had obtained, with the help of others, a constitution for Manitoba, when the Government at Ottawa was not willing to inaugurate it at the proper time, I have worked till the inauguration should take place, and that is why I have been banished for five years. I had to rest five years, I was willing to do it. I protested, I said: "Oh, my God, I offer you all my existence for that cause, and please to make of my weakness an instrument to help men in my country." And seeing my intentions, the late Archbishop Bourget said: "Riel has no narrow views, he is a man to accomplish great things," and he wrote that letter of which I hope that the Crown has at least a copy. And in another letter, when I became what doctors believed to be insane, Bishop Bourget wrote again and said: "Be ye blessed by God and man and take patience in your evils." Am I not taking patience? Will I be blessed by man as I have been by God?"

I say that I have been blessed by God, and I hope that you will not take that as a presumptuous assertion. It has been a great success for me to come through all the dangers I have in that fifteen years. If I have not succeeded in wearing a fine coat myself I have at the same time the great consolation of seeing that God has maintained my view; that He has maintained my health sufficiently to go through the world, and that he has kept me from bullets, when bullets marked my hat. I am blessed by God. It is this trial that is going to show that I am going to be blessed by man during my existence, the benedictions are a guarantee that I was not wrong when by circumstances I was taken away from adopted land to my native land. When I see British people sitting in the court to try me, remembering that the English people are proud of that word "fair-play," I am confident that I will be blessed by God and by man also.

Not only Bishop Bourget spoke to me in that way, but Father Jean Baptiste Bruno, the priest of Worcester, who was my director of conscience, said to me: "Riel, God has put an object into your hands, the cause of the triumph of religion in the world, take care, you will succeed when most believe you have lost." I have got those words in my heart, those words of J.B. Bruno and the late Archbishop Bourget. But last year, while I was yet in Montana, and while I was passing before the Catholic church, the priest, the Reverend Father Frederick Ebeville, curate of the church of the Immaculate Conception, at Benton, said to me: "I am glad to see you; is your family here?" I said: "Yes." He said: "Go and bring them to the altar, I want to bless you before you go away." And with Gabriel Dumont and my family we all went on our knees at the altar, the priest put on his surplice and he took holy water and was going to bless us, I said: "Will you allow me to pronounce a prayer while you bless me?"

He said: "Yes, I want to know what it is." I told him the prayer. It is speaking to God: "My Father, bless me according to the views of Thy Providence which are bountiful and without measure." He said to me: "You can say that prayer while I bless you." Well, he blessed me and I pronounced that prayer for myself, for my wife, for my children, and for Gabriel Dumont.

When the glorious General Middleton fired on us during three days, and on our families, and when shells went and bullets went as thick as mosquitoes in the hot days of summer, when I saw my children, my wife, myself and Gabriel Dumont were escaping, I said that nothing but the blessing without measure of Father Frederick Ebeville could save me, and that can save me today from these charges. The benediction promised to me surrounded me all the time in the Saskatchewan, and since it seems to me that I have seen it. Captain Deane, Corporal Prickert, and the corporal of the guard who have been appointed over me have been so gentle while the papers were raging against me shows that nothing but the benediction of God could give me the favour I have had in remaining so respected among these men. Today when I saw the glorious General Middleton bearing testimony that he thought I was not insane, and when Captain Young proved that I am not insane, I felt that God was blessing me, and blotting away from my name the blot resting upon my reputation on account of having been in the lunatic asylum of my good friend Dr. Roy. I have been in an asylum, but I thank the lawyers for the Crown who destroyed the testimony of my good friend Dr. Roy, because I have always believed that I was put in the asylum without reason. Today my pretension is guaranteed, and that is a blessing too in that way. I have also been in the lunatic asylum at Longue Pointe, and I wonder that my friend Dr. Lachapelle, who took care of me charitably, and Dr. Howard are not here. I was there perhaps under my own name.

Even if I was going to be sentenced by you, gentlemen of the jury, I have this satisfaction if I die – that if I die I will not be reputed by all men as insane, as a lunatic....

The agitation in the North-West Territories would have been constitutional, and would certainly be constitutional today if, in my opinion, we had not been attacked. Perhaps the Crown has not been able to find out the particulars, that we were attacked, but as we were on the scene, it was easy to understand. When we sent petitions to the Government, they used to answer us by sending police, and when the rumours were increasing every day that Riel had been shot here or there, or that Riel was going to be shot by such and such a man, the police would not pay any attention to it. I am glad that I have mentioned the police, because of the testimony that has been given in the box during the examination of many of the witnesses. If I had been allowed to put questions to the witnesses, I would have asked them when it was I said a single word against a single policeman or a single officer. I have respected the policemen, and I do today, and I have respected the officers of the police; the paper that I sent to Major Crozier is a proof of it: "We respect you, Major." There are papers which the Crown has in its hands, and which show that demoralization exists among the police, if you will allow me to say it in the court, as I have said it in writing.

Your Honours, gentlemen of the jury: If I was a man of today perhaps it would be presumptuous to speak in that way, but the truth is good to say, and it is said in a proper manner, and it is without any presumption, it is not because I have been libelled for fifteen years that I do not believe myself something. I know that through the grace of God, I am the founder of Manitoba. I know that though I have no open road for my influence, I have big influence, concentrated as a big amount of vapour in an engine. I believe by what I suffered for fifteen years, by what I have done for Manitoba, and the people of the North-West, that my words are worth something. If I give offence, I do not speak to insult. Yes, you are the pioneers of civilization, the whites are the pioneers of civilization, but they bring among the Indians demoralization. Do not be offended, ladies, do not be offended, here are the men who can cure that evil; and if at times

I have been strong against my true friends and fathers, the reverend priests of the Saskatchewan, it is because my convictions are strong. There have been witnesses to show that immediately after great passion I could come back to the great respect I have for them.

One of the witnesses here, George Ness, I think, said that I spoke of Archbishop Taché, and told him that he was a thief. If I had had the opportunity I proposed I would have questioned him as to what I said, so that you would understand me. I have known Archbishop Taché as a great benefactor, I have seen him surrounded by his great property, the property of a widow whose road was passing near. He bought the land around, and took that way to try and get her property at a cheap price. I read in the Gospel: "Ye Pharisees with your long prayers devour the widows." And as Archbishop Taché is my great benefactor, as he is my father, I would say because he has done me an immense deal of good, and because there was no one who had the courage to tell him, I did, because I love him, because I acknowledge all he has done for me; as to Bishop Grandin, it was on the same grounds. I have other instance of Bishop Taché, and the witnesses could have said that the Reverend Father Moulin, "When you speak of such persons as Archbishop Taché, you ought to say that he made a mistake, not that he committed robbery." I say that we have been patient a long time, and when we see that mild words only serve as covers for great ones to do wrong, it is time when we are justified in saying that robbery is robbery everywhere, and the guilty ones are bound by the force of public opinion to take notice of it. The one who has the courage to speak out in that way, instead of being an outrageous man, becomes in fact a benefactor to those men themselves and to society.

When we got to the church of St. Anthony on the 18th, there was a witness who said, I think George Ness, that I said to Father Moulin: "You are a Protestant." According to my theory I was not going to speak in that way, but I said that we were protesting against the Canadian Government, and that he was protesting against us, and that we were two protestants in our different ways.

As to religion, what is my belief? What is my insanity about that? My insanity, your Honours, gentlemen of the jury, is that I wish to leave Rome aside, inasmuch as it is the cause of division between Catholics and Protestants. I did not wish to force my views, because in Batoche to the half-breeds that followed me I use the word, carte blanche. If I have any influence in the new world it is to help in that way and even if it takes 200 years to become practical, then after my death that will bring out practical results, and then my children's children will shake hand with the Protestants of the new world in a friendly manner. I do not wish these evils which exist in Europe to be continued, as much as I can influence it, among the half-breeds. I do not wish that to be repeated in America. That work is not the work of some days or some years, it his the work of hundreds of years.

My condition is helpless, so helpless that my good lawyers, and they have done it by conviction (Mr. Fitzpatrick in his beautiful speech has proved he believed I was insane) my condition seems to be so helpless that they have recourse to try and prove insanity to try and save me in that way. If I am insane, of course, I don't know it, it is a property of insanity to be unable to know it. But what is the kind of mission that I have? Practical results. It is said that I had myself acknowledged as a prophet by the half-breeds. The half-breeds have some intelligence. Captain Young who has been so polite and gentle during the time I was under his care, said that what was done at Batoche, from a military point of view was nice, that the line of defence was nice, that showed some intelligence.

It is not to be supposed that the half-breeds acknowledged me as a prophet if they had not seen that I could see something into the future. If I am blessed without measure I can see something into the future, we all see into the future more or less. As what kind of prophet would I come, would it be a prophet would all the time have a stick in his hand, and threatening, a prophet of evil? If the half-breeds had acknowledged me as a prophet, if on the other side priests come and say that I am polite, if there are general officers, good men, come into this box and prove that I am polite, prove that I am decent in my manner, in combining all together you have a decent prophet. An insane man cannot withhold his insanity, if I am insane my heart will tell what is in me.

Last night while I was taking exercise the spirit who guides and assists me and consoles me, told me that tomorrow somebody will come t'aider, five English and one French word t'aider, that is to help you. I am consoled by that. While I was recurring to my God, to our God, I said, but woe to me if you do not help me, and these words came to me, in the morning someone will come t'aider, that is today. I said that to my two guards and you can go for the two guards. I told them that if the spirit that directs me is the spirit of truth it is today that I expect help. This morning the good doctor who has care of me came to me and said, you will speak today before the court. I thought I would not be allowed to speak; those words were given to me to tell me that I would have liberty to speak. There was one French word in it, it meant I believe that there was to be some French influence in it, but the most part English. It is true that my good lawyers from the Province of Quebec have given me good advice....

I am glad that the Crown has proved that I am the leader of the half-breeds in the North-West. I will perhaps be one day acknowledged as more than a leader of the half-breeds, and if I am I will have an opportunity of being acknowledged as a leader of good in this great country....

The only things I would like to call your attention to before you retire to deliberate are: First, that the House of Commons, Senate and Ministers of the Dominion and who make laws for this land and govern it, are no representation whatever of the people of the North-West. Second, that the North-West Council generated by the Federal Government has the great defect of its parent. Third, the number of members elected for the Council by the people make it only a sham representative legislature and no representative government at all.

British civilization which rules today the world, and the British constitution has defined such government as this is which rules the North-West Territories as irresponsible government, which plainly means that there is no responsibility, and by all the science which has been shown here yesterday you are compelled to admit if there is no responsibility, it is insane.

Good sense combined with scientific theories lead to the same conclusion. By the testimony laid before you during my trial witnesses on both sides made it certain that petition after petition had been sent to the Federal Government, and so irresponsible is that Government to the North-West that in the course of several years besides doing nothing to satisfy the people of this great land, it has even hardly been able to answer once or to give a single response. That fact would indicate an absolute lack of responsibility, and therefore insanity complicated with paralysis.

The Ministers of an insane and irresponsible Government and its little one – the North-West Council – made up their minds to answer my petitions by surrounding me slyly and by attempting to jump on me suddenly and upon my people in the Saskatchewan. Happily when they appeared and showed their teeth to devour, I was ready: that is what is called my crime of high treason, and to which they hold me today. Oh, my good jurors, in the name of Jesus Christ, the only one who can save and help me, they have tried to tear me to pieces.

If you take the plea of the defence that I am not responsible for my acts, acquit me completely since I have been quarrelling with an insane and irresponsible Government. If you pronounce in favour of the Crown, which contends that I am responsible, acquit me all the same. You are perfectly justified in declaring that having my reason and sound mind, I have acted reasonably and in self-defence, while the Government, my accuser, being irresponsible, and consequently insane, cannot but have acted wrong, and if high treason there is it must be on its side and not on my part....

For fifteen years, I have been neglecting myself. Even one of the most hard witnesses on me said that with all my vanity, I never was particular to my clothing; yes, because I never had much to buy any clothing. The Rev. Father André has often had the kindness to feed my family with a sack of flour, and Father Fourmand. My wife and children are without means, while I am working more than any representative in the North-West. Although I am simply a guest of this country – a guest of the half-breeds of Saskatchewan – although as a simple guest, I worked to better the condition of the people of the Saskatchewan at the risk of my life, to better the condition of the people of the North-West, I have never had any pay. It has always been my hope to have a fair living one day. It will be for you to pronounce – if you say I was right, you can conscientiously acquit me, as I hope through the help of God you will. You will console those who have been fifteen years around me only partaking in my sufferings. What you will do in justice to me, in justice to my family, in justice to my friends, in justice to the North-West, will be rendered a hundred times to you in this world, and to use a sacred expression, life everlasting in the other.

I thank your Honour for the favour you have granted me in speaking; I thank you for the attention you have given me, gentlemen of the jury, and I thank those who have had the kindness to encourage my imperfect way of speaking the English language by your good attention. I put my speech under the protection of my God, my Saviour, He is the only one who can make it effective. It is possible it should become effective, as it is proposed to good men, to good people, and to good ladies also.

HUMAN RIGHTS

RT. HONOURABLE JOHN GEORGE DIEFENBAKER

Excerpts from a speech to the House of Commons, July 1, 1960

Right Hon. J.G. Diefenbaker (Prime Minister) moved the second reading of Bill No. C-79, to provide for the recognition and protection of human rights and fundamental freedoms.

M r. Speaker, on this Dominion Day once more we think of the genius of the fathers of confederation and the contribution they made in their day and generation to the setting up of a national political organization which, despite the many vicissitudes of national and international events, has proven one of the most for-ward-looking constitutional accomplishments among the nations of the democratic world. Today we have reason for celebration when we look back over the years and recall that the purpose of the legislation which brought about confederation, in the words of its major architect, Sir John A. Macdonald, along with Sir George Etienne Cartier, was "to make a great people and a great nationality."

We have been able during the intervening years to add steps which more and more have expanded the democratic rights of Canadians as a whole. At the present session, we have passed legislation which provides for the first citizens of Canada, the Indians, the full right of the exercise of the franchise, thus removing any suggestion that they or any other Canadians are in the position of being second-class citizens.

It is in this context that I rise for the purpose of speaking on a subject on which I have spoken through the years, which has to do with the maintenance and preservation of freedom against governments, however powerful they may be, for in the words of an organization which was set up some years ago by our great neighbour, the United States, "freedom is everybody's job." On this day there should be a realization of the responsibilities of citizenship, with pride in the achievements of the past, and the added assurance that individuals will know that henceforth under law they will at all times have preserved to them the rights and benefits of that institution.

These ten amendments cover the fundamental freedoms of religion, speech, and security of the individual. In general, they are those which, with the necessary additions that have to be made in the light of present day conditions, are in the bill of rights which I now bring to parliament.

The bill in question can be summed up in a few words. In clause 2, the following fundamental freedoms are provided:

a) the right of the individual to life, liberty, security of the person and enjoyment of property – and the right not to be deprived thereof except by due process of law;
b) the right of the individual to protection of the law without discrimination by reason of race, national origin, colour, religion or sex –

Pausing there, Mr. Speaker, may I say that above everything else in the world today, there is no element more dangerous to the legions of freedom everywhere and to the nations which espouse freedom, than the practice of discrimination.

Clause 2 continues:
c) freedom of religion
d) freedom of speech
e) freedom of assembly and association; and
f) freedom of the press

I am going to set out some of the abuses which have taken place. I am not going to be partisan. I am going to quote from the submission of the committee for a bill of rights.

Why, then, is it now necessary to state explicitly in the constitutional document what is already implicit? The answer is that experience has shown that what is only implicit is in fact endangered by lack of recognition and acceptance, and that an explicit statement of rights is not only advisable to create public recognition of the fundamental basis of our society but also to prevent definite infringements of those rights. The exigencies of total war and the inevitable growth in the functions of government have naturally and inevitably resulted in a tendency to the abrogation of these civil rights.

Then it goes on to point out a few examples, and I know all of us regret those examples today. It says:

Under the sweeping powers conferred by the War Measures Act, the executive (or cabinet) in December 1945, some months after the cessation of hostilities and without reference to parliament, passed three orders in council, which if they had been enforced...would have exiled...to Japan some 11,000 or more persons of Japanese origin, a large proportion of whom were Canadian born citizens.

When we talk about discrimination and its dangers we recall that the only offence committed by these people in 99 percent of the cases, as it turned out subsequently, was their colour.

I wish to say that the bill of rights, as I see it, will deny the right of any government to interfere with my right to speak within the law, my right to be free from the threats of the activities of a police state, whether consciously or unconsciously administered. It will deny anyone the right to prevent me living my own life within the limits of the law without regard to race or colour or creed. It will remove from any government the right to deny me the right to belong to an unpopular minority anywhere in the country. It will deny any government, however powerful in the future, the right to deny recourse to the courts.

Those are some of the benefits that will come from the passage of this legislation.

I hope the house will support this measure. It is introduced on Dominion Day. It is one of those steps which represent the achievement and the assurance of that degree of liberty and freedom under law that was envisaged by the fathers of confederation. I think it embodies a pledge for all Canadians, a pledge which I place before you not as something original but changed to meet the fact that I am speaking in the Canadian parliament.

I am a Canadian, a free Canadian, free to speak without fear, free to worship God in my own way, free to stand for what I think right, free to oppose what I believe wrong, free to choose those who shall govern my country. This heritage of freedom I pledge to uphold for all mankind and myself.

3. RELUCTANT BLACK HAWK

The Hockey Game, Allen Sapp

Acrylic on canvas, 71.3 x 86.5 cm, 1968

Allen Sapp's painting stirs memories of the burn of chill air on cheeks, of taking skates off and rubbing freezing toes. What could remind us more of Saskatchewan than hockey and winter? Or blizzards and the smell of an aspen forest in an early thaw? "Sometimes we would play hockey on a slough behind my old home," Allen Sapp says. "There would always be a few boys who would like playing out in the open. Many times we didn't have skates, but that didn't stop us from playing." But hockey isn't all good memories. As Stephen Scriver says, "Over the years I have met, played with, observed, taught, and coached kids who have had great hopes riding on them, hopes that are usually not fulfilled for a multitude of reasons. Consider that only one in 100,000 kids who starts playing hockey ever makes a living at it, and most of them for just a short time." Winter isn't always pleasant; sometimes it's difficult just to survive. As David Carpenter says about his story, "Above all, read this story in winter, but read it in a warm and cosy place." And sometimes the experience of winter can teach us about other things. Sheila Stevenson hopes that the winter trip in her story "raises awareness of how fear prevents us from transcending borders of race and culture, and how the anger and humiliation common to our experiences can be channelled into a specific triumph, a unique form of expression leading towards healing."

STANISLOWSKI VS. GRENFELL

(STEPHEN SCRIVER)

It is noted
without metrics or mourning
that the world's foremost violinist
played in Grenfell
to the assembled chairs of the Legion Hall

while two-thirds of the populace
was attending a four-pointer
between the Spitfires and Whitewood
at the Community Recreation Centre

No surprise in a town where
there's more agriculture
than Culture, and Art
is the guy who runs the Paterson elevator

THE RELUCTANT BLACK HAWK

(BRENDA ZEMAN)

So you want to find the Indian guy who walked out thirty years ago on the Chicago Black Hawks? Good luck. Freddie Sasakamoose has no phone. Nor does he return a phone message passed on to him by his friend, Ray Ahenakew. Maybe, you think, he's had his fill of strangers asking him why he gave up a Canadian boy's dream to play in the National Hockey League. Yet, because you want to understand how it happened, you decide to jump in your car, go look for this Freddie Sasakamoose, track him down.

You head north from Saskatoon into Doukhobor country beyond the North Saskatchewan River. In the Lucky Dollar store at Blaine Lake, a fair-haired woman looks at you, then says "Nyet" to a baby fussing in a grocery cart.

North of town, past the Muskeg Lake Reserve sign, you veer northwest. The road is paved and bales of hay and swaths of wheat lie on golden hills set into the blue sky. To your relief you see people ahead, a road crew. You ask directions but even the road crew doesn't seem to know the road. About thirty miles, says one fellow. Sixty, for sure, says another. A third says, Better ask at the garage this side of Shell Lake.

Simonar's Repair Service and Café. The old garage man eyes you curiously when you say you want to go to Sandy Lake.

I'm looking for Freddie Sasakamoose, you add.

So am I, he says.

Why?

He owes me, he drawls, his face crinkling into a slow smile, no sign of malice in his tired blue eyes.

Three teenage girls stand hitchhiking on a reserve road. You stop and they pile in. They don't know much about Freddie Sasakamoose. One girl says, He used to be Chief of Sandy Lake and he used to play for the Sandy Lake Chiefs.

That's all you know? you ask. What about the slapshot? What about his ambidexterity? The rink-long rushes? His magic on the ice?

The girls are puzzled and they giggle, not knowing what to say. No, they've never heard about Freddie going to Chicago when the NHL only had six teams. Or about the time in 1974 when Freddie was in Edmonton making final preparations to take a young Saskatchewan Indian hockey team to Finland. Howie Meeker heard about it and invited Freddie to a Team Canada (World Hockey Association) practice. Later, in the dressing room, Bobby Hull greeted Freddie with, I know who you are! You're the Indian who played with Chicago. You're the beggar with the slapshot I had to live up to!

You drive on in the silence wondering what is beyond the next hill. From the top you see the centre of the reserve, a cluster of buildings just down the road. You breathe a sigh of relief.

The name "Atahkakoop" is everywhere. On the rink, on the school, finally at the entrance to the band office. After the hereditary chief, one girl says. You ask why the name "Sasakamoose" isn't on the rink, but the girls get out saying they don't know.

You go in the band office and ask for Freddie Sasakamoose, former elected chief of the Atahkakoop Indian Reserve. He's in there, a man points to a door three steps away. At an all-day meeting, he says, only happens once a month. He goes inside to get him. You notice a sign in the office, NO LONG DISTANCE TELE-PHONE CALLS.

Councillor Freddie Sasakamoose emerges from the meeting room. Your eyes meet at the same level; he can't be more than five feet seven inches tall in his Texaco cap and he's stocky. He doesn't know you from Eve. You tell him you've come to find him, to ask him if he'll tell his story. His black eyes are amused. Oh yeah, he grins, I was gonna phone you sometime.

You find yourself grinning with Frederick George Sasaka-moose.

FREDDIE

I was born December 25, 1933, over at Whitefish Reserve, now they call it Big River Reserve, just neighbourly out from here, about fifteen miles from this reserve, Sandy Lake. My mother's father, old Gaspar Morin, lived at Victoire. It used to be a Metis settlement near Whitefish. My grandmother Morin was an Indian from Sandy Lake who married out to a Metis. That made my mother Metis too, until she married in to a Sandy Lake Indian. My mother's name is Sugil.

Them days in the thirties it was tough. My father, Roderick Sasakamoose, was into loggin'. Very hardly did I see my old man trap. His father was Alexander Sasakamoose and he married a Favel, Julia was my grandmother. Old Alexander musta been into some farming. I remember the time he chased me for jumpin' on some haystacks. He was mute, he couldn't talk or hear, but he could run, that old man. Caught me too, and gave me a good lickin'.

I had a good childhood, real good. It musta been 1937 or '38. I had these bobskates. Old Gaspar used to clean up ice for me ta skate. It wasn't long till I started makin' hockey sticks from red willows. I'd find a branch, one that was crooked at the end, and chop it off. I'd use any damn thing I could find for a puck. Stones or rocks or cans. Maybe even a frozen apple or two, eh?

Trouble was we didn't have too many horses in them days. Or any good transportation. That was one of the reasons I missed quite a bit of school. I went to school in this area for about a year. What made it tough, I had to walk two-and-a-half miles in the morning and then home again. Five miles in the winter, that was too much for a little guy.

When I was about eight years old my parents sent me to school at St. Michael's over at Duck Lake. Maybe they seen something ahead for me, I don't know. It wasn't too far, only about sixty miles, but it seemed like the other end of the world away.

SUGIL

I really missed my kids when I had to send them so far away from home. I had eleven kids but only five lived. I've lost two sets of twins and another boy and another girl, they all died from illness. I knew Freddie and the others would be well taken care of at the residential school. It was better I send them because we didn't have no bus and I didn't want them to get sick. I've sent all my children away to school, including Clara[1] who was five when she left.

I never went to school and my late husband only a little bit. I never learned to read or write at all until my husband showed me how to play bingo. One night I won $2800. I spent it in the best possible way, on household things, and I put the rest in the bank.

My mother, her name was Veronica Bear, she raised us really good. My Dad, he was Joe Morin, he died when I was about eight. Later, my mother married another Morin, this time Gaspar. Anyway, she raised us alone. She taught us not to steal, not to do anything wrong. In fact, she used to always tell me, Sugil, that's my nickname, my real name is Judith, she'd say, Sugil, if you don't do this right, the cops are gonna come and get you!

My mother taught us to do a lot of things, to bake bread, to make bannock, to sew and how to make moccasins. A lot of

---

1 Clara Sasakamoose Ahenakew translated her mother's Cree to English for this story.

times when I used to do beadwork, she would rip it out, tell me it wasn't good enough. She would make me do it properly. I guess my mother was right in bringing me up the way she did.

I always tried to do the right thing. But sometimes, even if you try to do the right thing, things go wrong. One day three of us ladies decided to go pickin' berries up north. My friend Alice picked us up in her van. Alice didn't know she had guns in the back, they belonged to her son. After awhile we decided we were gonna stay overnight. We didn't know whose place it was but there was bedding and everything we needed right in the cabin.

Next morning we decided to start pickin' berries. But the game warden came.

He saw the guns in the van and he charged us a hundred dollars for illegal possession. We decided to pay up on the spot because we didn't want to go to court. We didn't want to be in the newspapers.

The game warden took our hundred dollars and the guns to the RCMP barracks at Big River. It wasn't until Alice's son wondered where his guns had gone to, we had to tell. Pretty soon everybody knew about it. Now they called us "The Outlaws."

None of my children were outlaws like me! I tried to pass down all the good qualities from my mother. I think Freddie tried to do his best in hockey. I remember my husband and I used to listen to the radio. My husband was a great sportsman in his day, a really good soccer player for this reserve. He used to travel all around and he scored lots of goals, just like Freddie did in hockey. Anyway, my husband and I used to listen to the radio. I didn't understand many words but I used to hear "Chicago" and "Sasakamoose, Sasakamoose," so I knew Freddie was good. I don't know why he quit. He never talked about it. My husband and I were kind-hearted, we never spoke in anger to each other, we never asked him about it.

But I know one thing. The reason he played hockey so well is because his Indian name is *Ayahkokopawiwiyin*. My Indian name is Red Thunder Woman. When I hear thunder I am not afraid, I enjoy it. My youngest son Leo was given the name Morning Star. He is calm and quiet, that makes Leo a good golfer. Freddie got his name from Bertha Starblanket, she's an old woman on this reserve, more than a hundred now. I know Freddie had strong legs for hockey because the old lady named him according to the spirit of a young bull. His Indian name means "to stand firm."

FREDDIE

Maybe three times I tried to run away from St. Michael's School. Once there were three of us boys. We started out in the morning and we hid out until three or four o'clock. It was spring and there used to be a ferry just south of Duck Lake called Carlton Ferry. This ferryman wouldn't cross us. He knew we were from that school. He'd delay us, give us something to eat and he'd grab hold of the phone and call up those priests. Sure enough, in about an hour, the priests would show up and take us back to school. In them days priests were tough. They shaved our heads and made us sit in the middle of the floor on the cement to embarrass us. All the kids would watch us sittin' there eatin', even the girls.

We were also punished for speakin' Cree at school. Whipped sometimes. We did not speak very good English at that time and I still don't. We had a hell of a time tryin' to communicate in English with our fellow little students. We'd usually talk Cree when we were away from the scene, eh? Today I speak Cree real good, it's what I was born with and I enjoy it.

We didn't have no excuse for runnin' away. We were bein' fed good and were bein' treated right. In about seven or eight years after the priests and the sisters had offered me everything into my life, I didn't feel so bad about school. But I wouldn't go back to that kind of system. I guess when you're young like that you like to come back home. I was lonesome.

Come August I never wanted to go back to school but my

parents were determined. They wanted me to be somebody edu-cation-wise. And then there was hockey, hockey was the main issue for me. And for the priests too. They were French and a lot of them were from down east, eh, from Montreal, and they were crazy about hockey.

I remember Father Roussel. He believed in a system of obe-dience. He was just like a Russian trainer. What would happen is that old Father Roussel had maybe fifty pucks in the middle of the bloody ice and if a guy was coastin', not movin' on the whis-tle, Father Roussel would fire a puck right at him. Of course, when it gets 20 or 30 below, these pucks freeze and in them days we didn't have no padding, everything was homemade, maybe just a few sticks here and there in your pants to stop you from gettin' hit on your charleyhorse.

Father Roussel, he taught me to shoot both ways. I started out shootin' right but one year he was kinda short on left wing. So he says, Who can shoot left? I says, I'll try. Wouldn't you know it, ends up I'm better shootin' left than right.

You know, Father Roussel used to say, you gonna hate my guts through the year round. You gonna hate it cause I'm gonna train you hard, call the extra effort outta you. But at the end of the season you're gonna thank me. And that's what happened.

FATHER GEORGES ROUSSEL OMI

I first met Frederick Sasakamoose in September, 1944, when he was a student at St. Michael's in Duck Lake. I came there to teach and was in charge at the mission at Batoche across the river. I was also sports director and in charge of the brass band too.

I was born in Saskatchewan twelve miles south of St. Walburg. My first language is French, eh? I started teaching in a country school and then I went down to St. John's College which is now part of the University of Alberta. After that I went one year apprenticeship, novitiate, at St. Laurent in Manitoba. From there, I went six years to Lebret and then to Duck Lake.

As you would know, the Oblates were the first ones to help the Indians to receive some education; it was not the government! We have been criticized for taking them out of their cultural milieu. But we had so little money and they were so scattered. At the Indian school at Duck Lake, for example, we had students from Muskeg Lake, Mistawasis, Sandy Lake, Montreal Lake, Sturgeon Lake, Fort à La Corne plus the odd one from some other place.

From the very beginning you noticed Frederick Sasakamoose. He played in the brass band, trombone or bass, something big to make a lot of noise! He was puffing all right, sometimes his notes were not correct but he seemed to enjoy it.

He showed more promise on the ice. Let's put it this way, let's acknowledge the gifts that God has given to us. I was quite observant. I could quickly see the strong points and the weak points of my players. As well, I know my own strong points and weak points. Frederick was kind of short and stout, he was taller than he was wide, of course, but I would say he was the short strong type. He had strong legs, he was steady on his skates and had some nice motions feigning to the right or left. I realized that right away. Lots of times when he was a boy, he came to me and said, When I get older I will be playing in the NHL. And in his case I believed it and I would answer, If you work hard, you will succeed. Do your best and play cleanly.

There was only once I had to discipline Frederick and he learned his lesson. He was playing dirty. He got beat by the other guy who managed to bypass him. So he tripped him and that was against my regulations. Our reputation as clean hockey players was good, excellent I would say. No dirty stuff. Oh, there was some checking, but no bulldozing or ramming into the boards.

Afterwards, the boys were all sitting in the dressing room and I was maybe eight, ten feet away from Frederick. I said, This isn't the way to play, and I threw a glove in his direction. I could throw straight enough. Of course, it peeved him, naturally. He said, If that's the case, I won't play any more and you'll lose the game. I answered, I prefer to lose honourably than to win in a shameful way.

The next day was a nice day. Usually, at noon, I'd give the senior team a hockey practice. When it was warm, everybody outside! Take exercise, run around, shoot some snowballs, whatever, but get some oxygen to the brain! Frederick stayed in on the first day. On the second day he was standing by the window so he could see us on the rink. The third day he came out and stood along the boards. He was shouting to the boys, Come on, hurry up, get going! Hockey was getting the best of him.

When I came in, Frederick was standing firmly in the doorway, blocking my entrance. He said, If you want me to, I'll play. I said, If you want to do what I tell you, okay. If not, no deal. He said, I will, and from that time, no trouble.

He followed my orders from that time on. I believe in conditioning. I used to give the boys gymnastics, bench work, and some mat work. They did a lot of running when the ice was bad, and I had them roller skating in the off-season. When the ice was good, I'd get them out skating. I could skate enough to move ahead. To make them move, I'd use my hockey stick, a little tap on the seat, not a big one, for the ones who were lagging behind. The boys used to enjoy that. They'd say, Look at him, slowpoke, go after him. Shoot the puck at them? No, well, maybe shoot towards them, on the side. I could shoot straight enough.

As for Frederick's shot, I believe in the wrist shot, quick and accurate. Frederick developed a good, excellent, I would say, wrist shot when he played at St. Michael's. He practised all the time, even taking practice with the younger boys when I was too busy. I would say Frederick lived for hockey. And so did the other boys on the team.

You know, those who say the Russians showed us how to play hockey don't know what they are talking about. In 1948 Joe Primeau, he was a scout for the Toronto Maple Leafs, he saw my boys play in a provincial championship game in Weyburn. My boys were like scrubs, so short compared to the Weyburn boys.

But we had all but two returning the next year. Joe Primeau said to me, Father, your boys do not play as fast as the professionals but they play positional hockey.

And that was true. Frederick knew what he was doing on the ice by the time he left St. Michael's. He had confidence. The exciting thing about watching Frederick was this: you knew he was going to score. You just didn't know his plan of attack. And that provided the suspense. Maybe, when he got to Chicago, he didn't work hard enough or maybe he married too young. I don't think Frederick would mind me saying this, I've been to his house and he received me well several times, but maybe his heart took him out of the play.

FREDDIE

In the spring of 1949 we beat Regina and won the midget championship of Saskatchewan, eh? That's when I thanked Father Roussel. That time was something I'll never forget. Of course, the team rode back to the school in one of those big damn grain trucks we used to use, squeezin' together to keep warm.

After that I came back home and I had no intention of goin' into junior hockey. None at all. Never had no dream. You just go back home, that's all. Maybe we figured we weren't good enough to go to junior hockey training camp. Our dream was never NHL, never.

I was back here in the fall, about this time of year. We were stookin' over at Blue Heron, my Mum and Dad and me, it was thrashin' time. All of a sudden a car pulled into the field and I thought I seen Father Roussel comin'. I thought he was comin' to take me back to school and I said to my Dad, Oh, no, I'm not goin' back. I'm fifteen and I'll be sixteen in December and I don't have to go back.

Ends up it was Father Chevrier, he was gonna be boss at Duck Lake, and two other guys. He said, D'ya wanna go to trainin' camp in Moose Jaw? And I said, Where's that?

When he told me where, I said, No, I'm not goin'. No damn way was I gonna go any place now that I'm back home. Then Father Chevrier says, I'll tell you what, I'll give you fifty dollars a month for spendin' money and I'll dress you up real good. I still wasn't gonna go. I thought he was talkin' about those old combination overalls the sisters used to make us at Duck Lake.

Finally, Mum came over and Dad came over. He says, You have a good offer. After about an hour of coaxin', my mother demanded that I go and I gave up. I musta done good in Moose Jaw. I showed up real good, I musta. That's when George Vogan of the Canucks told me to come live with him and his wife Flora and his daughter Phyllis. Treated me real good, those people.

PHYLLIS VOGAN HENDRY

My Dad was general manager of the Moose Jaw Canucks. I was sixteen at the time. I came home late one night and I heard something in the living room. I went upstairs and asked my brother's girlfriend – she was visiting from Michigan where my brother was playing minor pro – I asked her who was in the living room. Phyllis, she said, your father brought home another hockey player and this time he's an Indian!

Just a few days before, this same girl and I had gone to the train station because my father was out of town and he asked us to go meet Ray Leacock, a defenceman from Montreal. Ray was surprised I spotted him so quickly on the platform. Ray, I said, you're probably the only black guy in Moose Jaw. For sure you're the only one in a hockey jacket. This was too much for my brother's girlfriend, first Ray, then an Indian fellow. She was American, eh?

You better get used to it, I told her, that's the way we do things in this house.

I got up the next morning and there was Freddie. He had on a pair of real heavy plaid pants and a thick plaid shirt and a cap pulled down over his ears, and he was very, very dark-skinned. Before the year was out he was as light as I am. Anyway, there he sat, looking just terrified. About like Metro Prystai looked when he'd come to live with us about seven years before.

Freddie had never seen plumbing so that night I told Dad, You better take him up and show him how to use the bathtub. We'd done that with Metro. So Dad took him up. Freddie's Mum had made him black silk shorts and that's how Dad left him in the bathroom. Freddie was in there for about an hour and a half. Finally I said, Dad, you better go see what he's doing in there. Dad went and there was Freddie sitting in an empty tub in his black silk shorts.

But Freddie learned very quickly, he was very bright. He was such a beautiful handwriter. He used to write "Frederick Sasakamoose" over everything, sheets, tablecloths, you name it, until one day I said, Freddie, I don't care if you're practising your autograph, this has got to stop. The other thing I was really impressed with was Freddie's reflexes. He used to catch our budgie out of the air as it flew past him. And he could throw five pennies in the air and catch them before they hit the floor.

Freddie wasn't the first Indian person to live with us. One day in about 1943, Dad showed up at the house with an American Indian. Dad ran into Chief Iktomi in Fir Mountain. The Chief had about six university degrees and he was going around doing a book on North American Indians until his tires went flat at Fir Mountain. Tires were hard to come by during the war so Dad offered to help get him some tires. Ended up the Chief moved in with us and Metro and the other eight hockey players and stayed with us for six months.

Freddie lived with us for four years, three years with Mum and Dad, and when my husband and I got married he moved in with us next door for a year. Freddie couldn't have lived with just anybody in those days. He needed to be looked after in lots of ways. He was so honest he'd always pay up what he owed at Doraty's pool hall. Once he came home and said, Phyl, I lost a hundred dollars and I paid up but there's two guys owe me more than that and they won't pay me. They were orderlies from the hospital and I had to call up the Mother Superior. She forced them to pay up.

Money literally flew by Freddie. I remember after he went up to Chicago for a few games in the spring of '53. He came home with a big cheque and he wasn't supposed to cash it till he got to Saskatchewan. When he got here almost the first thing he shows me is a big photo of a beautiful Indian model. I think he said she was Cherokee, he'd met her in Chicago. She was modelling something pretty scanty in the photo and I thought, Oh boy, Freddie, you may be in the big leagues but this girl is outta your league!

When Freddie lived with us hockey was his life. He socialized with the rest of the team, but always as a part of the group, you know, everybody going out and having a good time together. I remember he used to correspond with an Indian girl named Rose, a nursing student I think, and an Isbister girl named Loretta from up north. But he rarely saw them and it was more a friendship thing. Still this girl from Chicago was supposed to have had him running around missing practices.

Anyway, next day after Freddie got to Moose Jaw, he went out and bought a big car with the cash he had on him. He still had his cheque when he headed off to Humboldt to see Rose.

He didn't make it. I got a frantic call, well about as frantic as Freddie ever got. Phyl, he said, my tire went flat and when I was changing the tire the wind came along and blew my cheque away. What am I gonna do, Phyl? he says.

Dad phoned Chicago right away to put a stop payment on the cheque and I phoned "The Mailbag" on CHAB Moose Jaw to tell people to be on the lookout for a Chicago Black Hawk cheque made out to Frederick Sasakamoose. Wouldn't you know it? A farmer found it in his field and called up the radio station.

I called Freddie and he said, But Phyl, I gotta go see Rose. I said, Freddie, you go get that cheque and thank the man for his trouble. He went, but that was Freddie. He lived for the moment.

Haven't seen Freddie since he was on his way to see Rose. But I remember getting a Christmas card and him telling me he'd named his oldest daughter, Phyllis, after me and his oldest son, Elgin, after a friend of his in Moose Jaw. Freddie was happy here, he was part of our family. When he left for Chicago I said to Tiny Thompson, the scout, I said, Tiny, they won't care about Freddie in Chicago the way we care about him here.

FREDDIE

The year I went to Chicago we'd lost out in junior hockey to Regina or somebody. I was in the Canuck dressing room takin' my stuff off. Nobody was talkin'. We were sad about bein' taken out. I was thinkin' about goin' home.

First person I seen was George Vogan. That man and his family offered me everythin'. He was just like my Dad and my Dad was a good man. George walked towards me, he had a suitcase. I said, What's this, George? He said, Didn't you hear the good news? I said, Nobody ever told me anything yet. Well, he didn't tell me, he just kinda looked around a little bit at the coach and the manager.

All of a sudden the manager came up to me and said, Here's a telex. Here's your plane ticket. You're goin' to Chicago Black Hawks the remainder of the season.

So I didn't know what to do. I just stood there and I looked at the players. They were astonished, me bein' an Indian to be called and go play in the big leagues. Then people walked in there with a watch and my name engraved and a ring and two suitcases filled with clothes so I'd look respectable on my way in. It was a real joy.

METRO PRYSTAI

I was the first guy to go from the Vogans to the NHL. I was a lot like Freddie, Moose Jaw flabbergasted me, such a big place. And radios and indoor toilets. I thought I was in heaven. In Yorkton we had a crystal set and when nature called we just ran a hundred feet from the house to the biffy. My mother and father didn't speak much English, so my mother said in Ukrainian, My Metro can go to Moose Jaw if he goes to school, he goes to church, and he doesn't get paid much to play hockey. She didn't need to worry about me bein' a good boy. Instead of going to the pool hall, I'd go skating every night. It was indoors and it was free.

I was gone from Moose Jaw by the time Freddie moved in with the Vogans. I was nineteen when I went up to Chicago in 1947. A couple of years later George Vogan started telling me about this great kid Sasakamoose, what a helluva hockey player he was and I started seeing him in the spring when I'd drive from Chicago to Saskatchewan with Doug Bentley.

FREDDIE

I took the plane the next day. I'd never been on a plane before. I met the team in Toronto. Some of the people from Moose Jaw followed me too. They wanted to see me play. I got in the dressing room and they gave me #16 and I didn't know what the heck to do.

Anyway, I got on the ice and I was skatin' around warmin' up. At that time I was just like a...I'm not braggin', but I could skate and skate and shoot, real good. I had my slapshot by then. I don't know where it come from. I don't know where I seen it. Nobody was usin' it much then. It just came natural to me. So I took a shot or two and a referee come up to me and says, Somebody wants to talk to you on the phone. I went over to the penalty box and some guy said over the phone, How the hell do you pronounce your damn name? Saskatchewan Moose? Sack-a-Moose? Sask-a-moose? I said, Who am I talkin' to? And the voice said, Foster Hewitt. My gosh, I said, Foster! You know, I heard so much about Foster. Back home and at the school we used to listen to Saturday-night hockey all the time. So I was talkin' to Foster and I gave him my name properly, Sa-sa-ka-

moose, and I guess that's how he done it, bein' the professional
he was. I was in the big time now.

METRO PRYSTAI

I'd been traded to Detroit by the time Freddie went up to
Chicago. Chicago wasn't doin' that well at the time and Freddie
was supposed to be the saviour. Since he'd done so well in amateur hockey he was supposed to pick up the franchise. And, of
course, management made a big ballyhoo about him bein' the
first treaty Indian to make the NHL. They wanted Freddie to fill
Chicago Stadium.

I know Freddie musta been afraid when he first went up. I
know I was. He had to contend with jumpin' right from junior
to the NHL and he had to contend with Chicago. And that was
scary. Ya gotta remember, Al Capone died in prison from
syphilis the year before I went up to Chicago. And then Freddie
had to contend with livin' at the Midwest Athletic Club. We all
did. I had to live there too when I played with Chicago.

They called it a hotel but really it was a dive. They had a
place downstairs where gamblers used to hang out. It was a box-
ing club. I remember one guy fought under the name of Rudy
Valentino. And all these hoodlums used to sit at ringside in their
white and black fedoras. The gangsters used to feel sorry for us
poor hockey players. They used to tell us they could get us jobs
payin' a lot more. But I wasn't gonna carry a gat like those guys.

The biggest gangster I ever ran into at the Midwest was
Matty Capone, Al's younger brother. Once, when I was playing
for Detroit, Matty was in the crowd. I tried to avoid skating by
his corner of the rink but he kept calling me over. I was afraid to
go and I was afraid not to. Finally, I went and he says real tough-
like, Hey, Metro, get me an autographed stick. I got him an autographed stick.

I remember Detroit playin' a home-and-home series with
Chicago shortly after Freddie cracked the lineup. There'd been a

lot of publicity and when Freddie came out there was a big cheer. I was glad I wasn't playing defence or goal against him. He had a very hard, accurate slapshot and his wrist shot, well, he could get away with nothin'. A lot of guys have to wind up, but not Freddie. He had tremendous wrists. He could be fallin' down and still get a good shot away. And he could skate. He could stop and start on a dime and he could hit top speed in two, maybe three strides. He had the best reflexes I've ever seen, better'n Gordie Howe.

It's hard to know why I lasted and he didn't. But I know one thing. If he'd been with a better organization, maybe like Toronto or Montreal or Detroit, they could have afforded to bring him along more slowly, they could've groomed him better. Chicago's general manager, Bill Tobin, wasn't the hockey man that Conn Smythe, Frank Selke or Jack Adams were. Freddie was most likely with the wrong organization.

I remember, though, when I was with Chicago we used to joke in the dressing room about Doug Bently, he sorta had a big nose, eh? Nothing against it at all, but we used to tease him about being the only Black Hawk with a picture of himself on the front of his sweater. Then we'd say, When Freddie Sasakamoose comes up, he'll be the real thing. Doug used to laugh, he kinda enjoyed it.

FREDDIE

I don't know how in hell I ever come to have a crest like that one, me bein' a treaty Indian and playin' for Chicago Black Hawks.

Chicago was really somethin'. It kinda helped me along with city life, havin' lived in Moose Jaw. In Chicago you were just like another Joe walkin' down the street. In Moose Jaw you knew who you were. Freddie Sasakamoose. But in Chicago nobody knew you.

I guess some of the hockey people knew me. When I played my first game in Chicago I ended up on TV and they gave me a transistor radio and a box of cigars. That night about 19,000 people come and see the Indian play. And when I first walked in, the organist started playin' the *Indian Love Call*. He was kind of a comical fella.

In Chicago I stayed in a hotel and I used to have a friend who roomed with me called Gerry Topazzini. He used to take me all over. Once he took me to shake hands with Louis Armstrong. Another time I remember standin' in the doorway talkin' with Jack Dempsey in his restaurant in New York. I just don't know about it, I met some of the great ones.

When I come back after playin' for those first two months I had a little bit of money, about seven, eight thousand dollars. When I turned pro they gave me three thousand and I had to sign the 'C' form to be affiliated with Chicago. Maybe it was ten thousand, I don't know, it was so damn long ago. Then they gave me the day wages of that time, about a hundred and fifty a day plus room and board.

I come back home that spring after I turned pro. I bought a car. I never owned no car, I used to take cabs. I bought a big DeSoto, a fluid drive, and everybody knew I was back. You shoulda seen me when I walked in to this reserve when I come from Chicago when I was nineteen. It was just like I was outta this world. People looked at you, amazed. It was a wonderful feeling. It's something I have to thank the Creator for, my younger life. Jesus, I was called from all over to play exhibition games, a hundred dollars a game. There was still ice in Saskatchewan and every place I went was filled. I was young and I was single and everyone wanted to see me play.

LORETTA SASAKAMOOSE

I thought it was pretty good of Freddie to come and see me, little Loretta Isbister from Bodmin, when he could have had almost anybody, eh? We kinda got together through my brothers. They had this thing about Freddie. Wherever he played hockey they wanted to go see him because he was such a good player.

We lived out in the sticks and my Dad farmed, mixed farming. My mother was from Sandy Lake reserve till she married my Dad, Miles Isbister, he's Metis. Then automatically, she was classified as non-Indian. In her heart she was always Indian and to us, we classified ourselves as Indian too because there's not much difference with Metis and Indian.

My mother died when I was fourteen which was tragic for all of us. From then on I raised my youngest six brothers and sisters. There was no one else to do it. I was young but you grow up pretty fast when you have to.

I was sixteen when I met Freddie and he was eighteen. I think there was quite a bit of difference there. I was kinda tied up at home whereas he was from one city to another seeing all those places. But we hit it off real good as friends and he'd write letters to me and send me a Christmas present, a valentine card, this and that.

My brothers were really happy when I married Freddie four years later. But I don't know about my Dad. Well, you know, most dads have this thing about trying to hang on to their girl for as long as they can. I had raised the family and probably they hated to see me go. Leaving them behind I sorta felt like I was neglecting them and, finally, my Dad said, You did your share for this long and it's fine. But I still had that feeling.

The thought of going to Chicago was a bit much. I don't know much about cities and at that time I didn't know nothing about big cities! There's a lot of good things about people here. They tend to be a little backward, a little shy. You can't just say, I'll make a friend here, I'll make a friend there. It just wasn't in me.

You know, I even had a hard time moving from the south end of Sandy Lake to the north end when we built this new log house. The old house, that was where we raised our nine children, where Freddie started farming and we had the three buses. He started getting machinery little by little and now don't ask me how many acres he's farming! After we moved here, I'd find

myself back at the old house two or three times a day and it's
only seven or eight miles away! I even spent a couple of nights
there last year and I had a *very* good sleep. But now, we've
been here better than a year and I like it now. This is the place
we'll raise our second family as long as our son-in-law wants
us to. Our oldest daughter passed away three years ago. Oh,
it was so hard on all of us, especially on Freddie. Now we have
her three children to remember her by.

The only time I've ever been away was when I lived for
three years with Freddie in Kamloops. I read and I read and
I read when I was alone during the day. At night there were
times we'd sit together and Freddie would say, It's so lonely
Lorett, I'll be glad when hockey season's over.

FREDDIE

I was in the '55 Chicago training camp in Welland and I was
expectin' some letters from Lorett, we'd just been married
July 22, that summer. Every day I looked and there was
nothin'. I kept on wondering about my old lady and what was
gonna become of her. I'd phone her, of course we had no tele-
phone, so I'd have to phone the store. Somehow or other I
couldn't get her on the phone. After about twenty days I got
worried. What the hell am I gonna do? And I was just doin'
so good in training camp.

About ten days before the thirty-day camp was over I got
hold of my wife. I said, I'm gonna make the team, Loretta, now
you come over here. I got a house all ready, I'm makin' good
money. She held back, she didn't want to come. She told me
no. Well, then it was a problem. I had to talk to the management, Tommy Ivan. I said, Tommy, I'm havin' a heck of a time
with my old lady, she don't want to come to Chicago. Is there
by any chance you could send me to western Canada? Some
place I could be close to my wife, some place she'd enjoy.

That's when I went to New Westminster to play for the

Royals. Kenny MacKenzie was the manager. I said, Kenny, I gotta go for my wife. I want a couple of plane tickets, give me a coupla days and I'll be back in three or four. Away I went.

Got over to Saskatoon airport, phoned a taxi nearby here in Debden and said, Rainey, come and pick me up. So he come and a coupla, three hours later we got back here, about six, seven in the morning, it was a little daylight. Got to Lorett's Dad's house, everybody's sleepin' and I was yellin' from the outside. Knocked on the door, nobody answered, so I went upstairs. Loretta opened the door a little, she knew it was me, ha ha, she said, What do you want? I said, Open the door. I want to talk to you.

She didn't tell anybody about that, ha ha. Maybe I guess she never will but I'm glad I could be able to tell a little bit about it. Anyway, old Miles, my father-in-law, was happy to see me, the old fella. Sat down and had a little breakfast and coffee. Meanwhile, Rainey's waitin' for me in the taxi outside.

After a little while I said, Loretta, I got a couple tickets here. Want to take you back, got a good house, makin' a good living, about another year or so we'll go back to Chicago and continue playing NHL. And she said no. I don't know what she thought at that time. Still don't.

So I went back and see Mum and Dad and I told them the problems and they said, Well, it's best that you go back. You got a good life, a good future ahead of you, you're young, you done what you wanted to do for the best of her. She didn't want to come so I went back.

I moved to New Westminster, to Calgary, to Chicoutimi – Quebec league – bouncing all over the damn place. I guess maybe it was a little bit of control, that was the problem, not using alcohol, not using anything, just that I kinda fell apart because she wouldn't come with me. My wife was a beautiful girl and I loved her very much.

Two years after, I went back to Calgary and I was playin' in Saskatoon in that old western pro league and my Mum and Dad were there and a few people from the reserve and some Indians in Saskatoon come to watch me play. My mother brought me a beaded jacket, a real beautiful jacket she made for me. My parents were real proud of me, eh, real proud.

Durin' the hockey game I was kinda lookin' around where all the Indians were sittin', tryin' to see my wife. Didn't see her no place. After the game I asked my Mum where Lorett was. My Mum didn't know why she didn't come.

After, I went back to the hotel. Decided I was gonna go. I was gonna quit right then, pack my gear and go home. I was still affiliated with the Black Hawks. Anything they say I had to do. So I knew this was the end of my playin' NHL, the end of my younger life.

I played this bush league in Debden for a couple of years and I lived with Lorett. Then I got a call from Kenny MacKenzie in Kamloops, double A Senior. I got to know the people at the Kamloops Indian Reserve, Lorett was with me and I could still play a little bit of good hockey.

MURIEL GOTTFRIEDSON SASAKAMOOSE

I first met Freddie in 1957 when he came to Kamloops to play for the Kamloops Chiefs. Before the hockey season was over I married his brother Peter.

My reserve, Kamloops Reserve, is situated right across the river from the city of Kamloops. "Kamloops" comes from the interior Salish word meaning "meeting of the rivers" and we had a population of about 300 at that time.

People were very impressed by Freddie when he came out there. At first we saw him as a star. We had some real different ideas about him. We didn't think of him as quite human. People were a little bit distant and hesitant to come up to him and be friendly and talk to him. They held him in awe. To Indian people he was the equivalent of Elvis Presley as a celebrity. He was an idol, yet he was a role model for young people. Indian people from all around bought season tickets and filled up a whole sec-

äüçéñ

tion of the Kamloops arena.

To this day he's the only person from the plains who's ever been made Honorary Chief of Kamloops Indian Reserve. My band hosted a traditional ceremony. They had dancers come from the Shuswap Nations next to our reserve and from the Thompsons, the Okanagans, and the fringes of the Chilocotin tribes. They went up on top of Mt. Paul and sent signals to all of the tribal groups and they gathered and honoured him. My people named him Chief Thunderstick because Freddie was very famous for his slapshot.

FREDDIE

I'd say I was famous, in Indian eyes I was famous. It was a great disappointment that I had given them, I imagine I did. Even the white people in Canwood and Debden were disappointed I was not playing in the NHL, even them, they knew me. But it was more so for my parents because they saw great things in life for me.

The people on this reserve, they treated me real good when I came back. I knew their life, how their world was and how they made their livin'. Of course, I had to learn how to live on the outside. But I didn't want to force that way of life on Indian people. I think you have to leave the Indian people, how they enjoy life, how they enjoy themselves, leave that alone. I adjust myself real good. Not once did I leave this reserve since I come back. Although there's a brighter future on the outside, there's freedom here.

You see, when you were playin' hockey you were never free. You were more or less looked at, told what to do. That's part of life as a professional and you're paid well for it. When I turned pro, I knew damned well I was dressed good, I'd be able to get the things I want. Every two weeks I was gettin' paid and I was gettin' wiser. I was twenty-one, twenty-two at the time and I thought, God damn, I'm gonna make it and I'm gonna go through the life of bein' in the NHL. God, it was good. A lot of times I sat down and asked myself what went wrong with my hockey life. I do not blame it to my wife, I do not blame nobody. Maybe there were just some things I could not adjust to. The only thing, it makes a guy kinda wonder what he coulda done with some of these big contracts today.

MURIEL SASASKAMOOSE

After Peter and I lived for a time at Sandy Lake I got to know Freddie as a person. He has a lot of self-confidence. He's a survivor. He's also a bit of a trend-setter, you should see his new log house. He's outgoing, he's musical, he plays guitar and sings and he can really dance. Freddie's a good person to have at a party. People crowd around him because he's energetic and he's a good storyteller. Freddie can talk to down-and-outers, drunks, and he can also talk to the Prime Minister of Canada.

Now that I'm Band Administrator for Sandy Lake, I get the opportunity to see Freddie in a different light. I'm the first woman to ever hold this office and most people here really felt, you know, me coming from a matrilineal society such as the Interior Salish and this being a very male-oriented society at Sandy Lake, well they had a hard time adjusting to me. I always thought in terms of women, children, and men, the total community, whereas the men tended to think more of what the men wanted to do. The women here are quite silent compared to me. The men often said, That Muriel, she's a women's libber, and a lot of the flak came from my brother-in-law Freddie!

Freddie and I realized our differences right away. Freddie tends to be a bleeding heart and he believes every sob story that comes his way. Freddie's a dreamer. I am most often a realist and I sort of say, Give them a swift kick in the ass, and that's the direction they should go. But Freddie and I both believe in the community and the betterment of Indian people and see that change has to take place.

I admire Freddie very much. You've got to remember when he first got into hockey, Sandy Lake didn't have roads, telephones, or electricity, and there were only two vehicles on this reserve. The only things he really knew were trapping, hunting, farming, and hockey. To go from here to Chicago, that's a big jump. And he did it. I really think if he wasn't so tied to his family and his community, he would probably have stayed longer. But it doesn't matter. Freddie gave us all something to be very proud of. But he rarely talks about it. Freddie doesn't live in the past.

FREDDIE

If I was to die today, I wouldn't cry for my life. I've met a lot of good people, a lot of good Indians and a lot of good white people. The enemies I created through my hockey life, the fans that called me names, you know, every one of them came back, I know every one of them. I hear them when I'm on the ice, you know. You're an Indian and this and that, but, you know, I never looked. It never hurted me because I always had pride in me. Enemies from that time come up now and shake hands with me and say, Remember when I used to call you names? I don't know, I say, did you? Well, I say, that's gone.

Now I meet people who say, Any of your children as good as you were? I don't think so, I say. People look at me and think I should be able to produce all good hockey players. But I never did go out there with my kids and support them by trainin' them.

I lost my oldest daughter three years ago when I was chief. I knew that my daughter was killed in a car accident due to alcohol. At that time I too was drinkin', but not heavy; I was chief. I knew it hurt my life and hurt my family so I very, very seldom used alcohol. I was blessed with a good wife. She never drank, she's a beautiful woman, she took care of my children when I was not always there. I'm blessed. Funny thing, I didn't know till I was almost fifty. When I lost my daughter it changed me.

Now I'm fifty-two, almost fifty-three. I'm a community man. I was chief for four years, served my people well. I believe in the system of competition with the outside white society. When I was a kid I learned to compete with the outside and I had to be able to do things twice as good to continue to play hockey with them.

But the thing I remember is comin' home from school every summer, eh? It was wonderful when we come on top of that hill over there. We used to drive up in that big three-ton grain truck, you know, fifty or sixty of us piled in there. About six, seven miles south of here I could see the hill and at the top, oh boy, what a feeling, to see this reserve.

MARTY COULDA MADE'R

STEPHEN SCRIVER

Marty coulda made'r   they always say
he was the best there ever was in this rink
that's sent three other guys to the bigs

but Marty liked the good times too much
after he'd made'r to the Pacific Coast League
he'd come back here every spring
an really cut a swath

there was no end to his appetite
for food an beer an the girls
so by fall he'd be thirty, forty pounds overweight
lookin at trainin camp three weeks down the road

so he'd go around town
tellin us if we saw him on the road
beggin for a ride he'd kill us
if we ever picked him up

many's the Sunday me and the old lady'd
have the kids out for a tour
an we'd come across Marty miles outa town
with about ten sweaters an five pairs of pants on
crawlin along the road

he'd see us an start wavin us down
but we'd just drive on by
so the next time Marty'd see me
he'd say thanks

that went on for three years
till his knees finally gave out
but you ask anyone around here
if it isn't a damn shame

only pucks he touches now
are the ones he gathers up after practice
just before he scrapes the ice

DAVID GOES TO THE RESERVE

SHEILA STEVENSON

I invited one of my white friends at university from my Native Studies class back to the reserve. He offered to pay half the gas. It was one of the coldest days in January. The heater even on full defrost couldn't keep up, and I drove looking through a small clear area on the windshield, snow drifting from the sides of the road. The semis we met threw snow at us and at times you couldn't see a thing. That night we followed the tail lights of the car in front. David was tired, didn't have much to say as we drove. He kept biting the inside of his mouth. We were both anxious to get in the house when we finally saw the turnoff. David really wanted to meet my Kohkum.

Kohkum had been waiting the evening through, and there was a light in the window and she had some food on the table before too long. Both stoves, in the basement and upstairs, were going. The TV turned up loud made it too hard to talk. Kohkum probably couldn't hear half what David said anyway. He was doing that weird thing of not looking at my Kohkum when he was speaking, that thing they teach you in university about talking to Indians. Cultural differences.

I hadn't been home for a long time. It's so far. No wonder my guest slept so late the next morning. At first I wanted David to get up and then I wanted him to sleep as late as he could. He managed to sleep through my Kohkum feeding the wood stove with scoops of coal, and I remembered how tired he'd been when we finally pulled in last night. I was still seeing highway, while he was just starting to butter up my Kohkum, making me jealous.

"If she brings a boy out there, he'll sleep in the basement." I was visiting my Mom when she lectured Kohkum on the phone, her eyes on me. I could also "Stack some of that wood, do some good," even though Kohkom could ask just about anyone. My Mom has this myth that back home no one helps anybody.

I could tell that Kohkom was not too thrilled with David, his carrying on the night before with endless questions as he talked to the table, or the salt and pepper shakers. Kohkum was probably worrying – meeting David – that I must not be doing too good in school, but really it was for friends like him that I wanted to do the best I could, given my lack of serious ambitions.

Times like this when I come home, Kohkum eyes my clothes, my backpack, and she always makes it a wash day. She'd "dry the clothes for a bit in the dryer," she told me that night, hustling up some bannock and jam. "No – it's no trouble. Do you have any clothes needs washed? I have room in the washing machine," she asked David too, because that's the way she is.

That morning waiting for David, I went out to get some wood with the cardboard box. The coal smell in the air is oily and maybe an old person would feel it in their chest, taste it in the food, but Kohkum's gone to old ways even more since Mooshum died, and coal is cheaper and lasts longer. The coal is a part of Kohkum's old person smell. I can't get used to it on my Kohkum. I can't get used to her watching Oprah Winfrey either. Kohkum had just asked me if maybe David had been using drugs. I told her that David hadn't been using drugs, not since he'd been with me. Kohkum is always able to look anyone in the eye and know the truth.

The yard was ice with a pitted complexion, frozen and spotted with the soot. The wind was rattling the clothesline and the taste from the coal fire was on the lump at the back of my throat, on that somehow unexpected bit of homecoming feeling. To the right the Chevy truck stood marooned under a load of dried wood like some disintegrating buffalo in an ancient wallow. A magpie leaping was arching to the wind and doing jumping jacks, and there, my old car looking like it never left the reserve.

From inside my grandmother rapped on the window. She motioned – a skinny dog was just out of range, in case I threw a chunk of wood, or had scraps to feed him. I didn't know if he was a stray or not. He was kind of watching me and he would follow. I hoped Kohkum would think to put the coffee pot to the back of the stove to keep it warm for David, but then I knew she would.

I filled the box with wood, thinking we might as well use wood for the time being, while we're on "the reservation," that American word David used. Just that word makes me think of the reserve as somewhere exotic, like maybe Wounded Knee. Maybe it makes a place where my Kohkum is a wise elder, maybe where I walk in the valley deciphering meanings in the wormwood, churning up fresh paths on snowmobiles with my new university friends.

In Saskatoon, David was pretty excited when I had asked him if he'd come back home with me for the weekend. That felt good. The ice in the yard broke like glass in each frozen footprint. I stomped some and saved some for David to do. Suddenly again, I was fiercely glad he was here instead of gone skiing, or maybe at another skidoo party at his parents' cottage that I'd not been invited to. And he wanted to meet my Kohkum, that too made me feel good.

David finally woke up to the sounds he's not used to. I'd shut the door behind me loud and firm to keep the warm in. Kohkum lifted the lid from the stove, added wood, and the sparks flew upward. The door on the stove was squeaky. The wind was still whipping up a little snow. David must have heard the sound of the wind in the chimney change to country music when Kohkum turned on the radio, making him quit his "stinking in bed." Sometimes Kohkum's phrases make us sound like hillbillies. Kohkum asked me how school was going, and I made it sound okay, then again, not too okay, then she started the washing machine, the old tubs ready to catch the water to use again.

David finally came up in his baggy jeans and his poor boy sweater. He got the eggs fried hard and toast greasy warm under a bowl, and he was complimenting everything. He must have thought that he was really roughing it. I remember thinking that. Normally David is a vegetarian, vegan. He has that luminous transparent skin like those dolls with those baby shoes and tiny bottles.

After David finished, he wanted to go for a hike. If we were going out hiking, Kohkum had it that David could borrow the coat used for bringing in the wood and save his ski jacket.

"I hope we see some game," he said. I'd already told him that the reserve didn't have any game, no deer really, no moose – because if anything moved out here, there would be ten hunters go and shoot it up. David still had it in his head that Indians live on big game reserves or something.

The TV was on – Kohkum always watches talk shows from Los Angeles in the morning and does her work around and between that time she turns on the TV. Those old cook stoves heat up the house pretty fast, and so I was ready to go out again. There's always an extra coat, and a snowmobile suit from when my cousin was staying here before. I put on the snowmobile suit, having a silent fit of conscience about David wearing Mooshum's green coat, something my Kohkum keeps using and using, keeps hanging behind the door. Reserve style.

I stayed by the door as David got dressed in Mooshum's coat. It was like putting a mattress cover on a fence post. David is cute, he's got grunge style. He covered his throat with a flourish, and stretched a toque widely to cover his ears. I was half wanting and half afraid he'd ask for that coat as he put on work mitts and then the old corduroy cap; that feeling I get.

I had half forgotten the beebee rifle behind the door. It was one of the last of the toys not given away or hauled off by some kid. I slung it over one shoulder. I slipped the little orange tin of beebees into my pocket and I mimicked what I thought was David's exaggerated surprise. I said, "It's for targets, silly." He did-n't know it was just a toy. He kept looking away, just watching his footing on the wooden step, I guess I hoped.

The wind had gone down as David and I emerged into the cold white-and-blue world. The sky was bright. The snow under the eaves was dented with the tiny avalanches of the day before, melted with holes and marked where a bird's flight disturbed it. It was preserved like a plaster mask and as delicate and hard as china. Dirt, curls of bark, and edges of crushed puddles marked the driveway.

"It's good you're up," I said as we walked. "This morning I already walked past the railroad tracks. That's far." Again, I could see the pile of exposed grain, a flight of winter birds, the chick-adees, my cousin's horses huddled together in the coulee, and that dog with ice clinging to its muzzle. David, in the patched coat, kind of fit in like a happy tramp.

"Poor creatures," he said. I remembered he'd used that word first referring to us, that day I met him the first time away from campus. He had been rummaging for vintage clothes at the sec-ondhand store, and he remembered me from class. I didn't know him, except I'd seen him before; an artist maybe, I thought to myself. Afterwards we ran downtown in the snow, catching flakes on our tongues, laughing at ourselves on the mirror window of an office building – my hair wild and tangled and his face to me the face of a Dickens' boy in his Sally-Ann clothes. How should I act, what should I say, I often thought. I still can't explain "the grunge look" to Kohkum.

David walked on top of the snowbanks, jumping from peak to peak singing "Along the mountain track, Val-der-ree, Val-der-rah," his breath making frost on his eyelashes and on the edge of his scarf. When he turned his head, it was as if his voice came from far away.

There was a New Year's party hat on the road and I kicked

at it, but its tassel was stuck fast in the frozen snow, reminding me of something. I remembered that other time, that New Year's night I was babysitting, running at two in the morning in minus twenty degrees, and I surprised some deer. I remembered I was telling Kohkum about surprising these deer that night, and how they rose round the edge of the clearing. All she could see was how dangerous it had been. I know that. It would have been irrational, except I know when to stop. I try and tell her that.

At night in winter the cold and dark makes the distance between landmarks shrink and expand, the scorching cold dilates and explodes inside your lungs. When that happens, it's like a warning. Burns you like a first kiss. But you forget sometimes.

It was the magic of how the first deer rose up and the rest exploded out in front of me, ice fog between their legs that swirled around me as I ran after them. I told David that, so he wouldn't know I might have preferred to go to a party in the city. I don't know what he thinks we do on New Year's out here.

Kohkum had said, You shouldn't be out running in the cold. Even with a scarf, people freeze their face, their lungs that way, and you get tired and you freeze to death. Her voice rose and fell in the old time way. I should have stayed over at my cousins, and why did they let me walk home anyways. I should be more careful. Kohkum had kept her arms folded. You should listen. It's no joke, and you don't feel it coming on when you're freezing. Or you could get run over. You never know.

I was thinking about these "you never knows." It's like when you are driving and you see a car pulled over on the shoulder and you see a car coming towards you. Kohkum says you always pass both other cars at the same part of the road, and you've got to hope to hell that no one makes a mistake. You never know. After a while, I started to notice this phenomenon of passing parked cars when Kohkum wasn't with me, and so then that's when I tried to notice the times when it didn't happen. "You never know," my Mom and Kohkum say. But it's funny – it's like you get programmed, and for the rest of your life you're resisting someone else's notion of Fate. That's what makes you act illogically.

My Mom and Kohkum, they're the same, no matter how differently they see the world, or talk about us kids. Kohkum will always think my Mom was wrong to start up with my Dad, maybe wrong to leave me there with her. Mom will be stubborn and they won't talk about it together, but I see it when Mom and her disagree about me, or about something my aunties or my cousins are up to.

But my Kohkum believes in a power and presence of what must be a God, and that God is in each of us, full of light. She made me believe that people have souls and we're only contained in our bodies and sometimes very lightly, like babies are sometimes, or the very old or dying are. Kohkum said that when she looked up in the sky, she was afraid of what was up there, and I always think of that. I think of her telling me not to whistle at the Northern Lights. I'd do that when I was a kid. Just because. Just because that was superstition. They teach you about superstition in grade three.

I leapt from footstep to footstep, breaking through where David had been a second before. He didn't wait up. He looked like an old man from the back – Relic, from the Beachcombers.

But it was the old pattern, the way when I was a kid, Kohkum's talk as we left. "Kohkum, we're going walking, hiking! And we won't run, and I won't get lost." I had to laugh, Kohkum is always worrying. Just because that's the way she is, worrying about everyone. I remember wondering, the twin sundogs overhead, if she could ever see the Zenlike purity in a day like this one. A black crow's rush of wings startled me, and the sound moved thickly in the frozen air. When I opened my eyes, David was below me, had jumped down to the road, just the two of us, our colours bold and vivid. Kohkum was too old to appreciate the crystal beauty, to be young, that must have been what I'd decided. I vowed, then, to remember and keep that day forever. I saw that scruffy reserve dog following us.

The snowbanks were piled up about five feet high to be a windbreak. The shock goes up your legs when you land. David was ahead again, disappearing behind the other side of the snowbank. It's funny how playful he is, and it's one of the things that attracted me to him. I told him that, and he sort of dodged an imaginary punch, looking at me sideways. He was a clown that day, wearing Mooshum's coat and hat. Elmer Fudd. I've admitted to myself since then that I had a crush on David.

This car I recognized comes around the corner, I see it's the priest's car, him, so I have to say something to David. "It's the priest, now be good...." As the priest passed by looking at us curiously, I said, "I think his head turns all the way around."

I had gone to church almost every week with my Kohkum when my Mom left me on the reserve after Dad and she broke up. And I didn't like the priest. At the funerals, telling the people they sin, recycling sermons in the dilapidated church every Sunday. The sermon I remember was in the fall, after Mooshum died. How can we judge the servants by what each did with the money given him while the Master was away? In this Bible story, the Master is gone for years, and he returns to see how the money he has divided unequally among his servants had been invested. I know that I'm on the side of the one He called no good, lazy, the one with the least amount of money to invest in the first place, the one who was afraid to lose the Master's money and so went and buried it. The one the Master beats around the head when the poor bastard digs it up for him and tries to explain and loses everything anyway. That useless bastard of a priest left my old grandpa to die in hospital and he didn't bother to visit. We felt no need to explain that we only asked him to come for Kohkum's sake. Kohkum wanted him to visit. Often now I keep my opinion to myself, but I can't help the way I feel when I remember Mooshum's funeral. Kohkum still goes to Mass on Sundays, just like how she keeps that old coat. David must have looked like Mooshum too, to that old priest. It's funny the way now my memories spark around Mooshum that day.

We came up to the big coulee. The bush was like a venetian blind against the sun, stirring an illusion of depth and of distance, the filigree of a confessional. Single file we walked, like dropping to the bottom of a cool well. We followed the track of a snowmobile into wider white coulees, invisible from the view above. Everything was quiet, the berries of rosehips red like blood in the snow, the waxwings small grey flurries disappearing into the sun. The path itself was set above the snow and we sank up to our knees unexpectedly. And David, single-mindedly, obsessively followed the linked design in the snow in front, off in his own world.

I had never really known my grandfather. But he wanted me to go to school and get the education the whites get, get me off the reserve. He made me stay in town with my Auntie's kids, although I was back almost every weekend on the reserve, always just a few miles away. But then I felt he was just running my life, that he really didn't love me, I guess. It is a lifetime ago now, I convinced myself of that. I was having a good time I thought then. Came the day I didn't want to go back to my Mom's either. After I managed to finish high school, Mooshum hurt his back real bad. And after that he just faded away. He became an old man in the kitchen. He was there getting sicker, and after a while Kohkum and I did everything, and maybe just Kohkum after that. He didn't talk much except when he had an opinion. Except about the old days and about people I didn't know, and then never saying much to me anyway.

In those days with David, the schoolbooks just lay in the corner, and I would feel guilty. I was doing okay, but I could have been doing better. Now I think of Mooshum always there before, giving me money that he could have used for himself, helping me buy my first car and fix it up. And I think about that night of my high school grad. He was still wearing that label they sew on the sleeves of new suits. I think of that. I could have taken it off with my little pearl-handled nail file. I remember that.

David and I climbed the side of the coulee towards the snow that was less deep. When we reached the top we stopped to get our breath. Our clothes stopped rustling. It was quiet. By two hours after midday, the temperature was the highest it would be. I looked at David and his cheeks were like apples, his blue eyes clear like the sky shining behind them.

"This is great!" he repeated, and I suddenly felt the same way. The blessing of that day. I wanted to say something.

He was yelling and whooping and then, far below I saw two humans appear at the edge of the clearing. They were hunting. They both had rifles. I nudged David, motioning him to be quiet. He shut up right away. He was holding the pellet rifle. The air seemed frozen and the trees below like smoke.

"Hey – who are you?" one yelled after a minute of sizing us up. We were sizing them up ourselves so I didn't answer.

"Who are you?" the bigger one yelled again, his voice cracking a little. Then I recognised them. I saw them lots before at the arena in town. They go to the hockey games, the Spencer boys, Rodney and Tom. They're just kids. I decided to see what they were going to do next.

I yelled back, "Who are you?"

I turned to David to share the joke, surprised to see the way he was holding the gun, his hand under the barrel. He looked ready to swing that gun up. He looked scared in his body, and us outlined against the sky. Maybe like a man to those boys. I must have gone grey. David said "Shsh." The boys below consulted each other.

"Jesus, David, it's okay," I hissed at him, and he looked at me without certainty. I pushed David to get him going, back from the edge, to break the spell and his robot expression.

"No – who are *you*?" Rodney yelled. That really gets my goat. It's like my Kohkum says, you never know.

"I *live* here!" I threw back at the boys. I was annoyed at David. I didn't want to talk to him. I just walked, fuming, thinking. David was saying, "Wait, this thing isn't loaded. Hey, this is a beebee gun."

When my Mooshum passed away, this old man, the elder

who gave his tribute at the wake, said Mooshum wanted me to go on and get my education. The undertaker had Mooshum wearing that grey suit in the casket for the funeral and that label that was on the sleeve was – gone. I found myself looking at that place on his sleeve where it had been and I burned with shame. I remember I was still skipping a lot of my classes then too. There was lots of food at the wake, and the band hall was packed with everyone from the community, Mooshum's friends and our relatives. I listened to the stories and the tributes, but all I could think of was how I never really knew him. I was just a dumb, ignorant, and ungrateful kid, and I couldn't stay around. I went home with my mom. I remember that I knew what I was.

After that winter break with David, I began to find something in university for my own reasons. I adopted the persona of Little Oka Annie looking for Daddy War Buck. After a while I was able to start feeling right about Mooshum. And the reserve. I was the only one who knew what happened.

I have not been much for staying with Kohkum, spending my time in the city, "with friends, maybe." Monel, my mom, is always thinking she is covering for me, but it's tough going out to the reserve to hear Kohkum or my aunties. Sometimes it's us miserable kids, or then band office politics, or complaining about my mom or one of us kids who never grew up. Sometimes I can't stand it. I hate knowing I'm being used as an example – what to be, what not to be.

I am a year closer to getting a degree in the program they have for us and finally I am starting to learn how to pick electives. I find the professors and the white students will still look to me to give "the" Native perspective in discussions in class. Me.

David was the first of my university friends, White, Indian, or Non-Indian, that I thought I could just be myself with. "Just be yourself," is the advice you hear from people who enjoy beating their gums. They tell that to people maybe they think are shy, that don't know how to act.

I don't know if David noticed I was mad at him.

Kohkum had a hot soup and bannock waiting for our lunch that day. I'm thinking now of that day when Kohkum asked me about David. David went and called his brother-in-law to pick him up in town after lunch. I drove. We waited at the Service Centre until this car pulled up. A guy waved, and David was gone like a shot.

Kohkum never made any judgement that I know of when I told her what I thought had happened. She got ahold of my jeans and mended the fashionable rips before I went back to school and I guess she let me think about it, to make up my own mind. Now when I see the mending it makes me feel Love.

I guess David is okay. He's not to blame. We're still friends, or still just friends, or whatever you call it. He sure liked meeting my Kohkum, he said the last time I saw him. I think he must have been embarrassed to have been so afraid, that must be it.

TURKLE

DAVID CARPENTER

A long time ago there was a great storm, a blizzard that pummelled the prairie for one night and one day and another long night. Old-timers from the district use it as a benchmark for other memories. One of the hardest hit was a farmer who owned more than a section of land along the North Saskatchewan River. On the morning of the great storm, this man awakened before dark, walked out into the yard, and noticed that even on the path he took to the barn the snow was up to his knees. In the midst of doing his chores, he discovered that during the night his cow had wandered away through an open gate. He was fairly sure that, unless something had driven it off, the cow was not going to wander far. The cow's name was Turkle, but the farmer never used that name. This was just the family cow as far as he was concerned, and it didn't pay to get sentimental about animals.

On the morning of the storm, his wife and children got up as though nothing were different. The immense snowfall was exciting, perhaps almost a novelty for them. And so the children dressed for school.

It was a three mile walk. The farmer announced that he would take his almost new 1924 Model T out of the shed, put on the chains, and drive them all to school. This would give him a chance on the way back to check for the missing cow because *Someone had left the gate open.* He knew every pebble on the road, he was proud of what his new car could do with chains on the wheels, and he was too stubborn to let a snowstorm divert anyone in his family from their daily routine.

Apparently his wife protested. She felt that the children should be allowed to miss school, stay home, and do their lessons in the kitchen next to the wood stove. It was twenty-five degrees below zero that morning, and dropping. But the farmer must have brushed aside her protests with his usual admonition, that *Only babies are meant to stay home in bad weather, and the children aren't babies any more, so why baby them?*

He went outside and cranked up his new Model T, and in a minute they were gone. They were gone long before it was light.

For some reason, perhaps a small act of rebellion, the youngest daughter, the one who they say left the gate open, smuggled her cat from the barn into the car beneath the folds of her winter coat. The cat was a tabby named Albert. The names of the children were Clarence, who was ten; Eleanor, who was nine; and Berta, the girl with the cat, who was six.

The farm was less than one hour's drive north of Saskatoon, a section of grainland with a large coulee that flows into the river southwest of Hepburn. The road the farmer drove runs through this coulee, and so in a tough blizzard, it would be sheltered from a north or a west wind. Away down in the coulee, you could underestimate even the severest storm, which explains why the farmer thought he could negotiate the road in his car. But when you climb up out of the coulee and onto the flat land, these prevailing winds can catch you very suddenly with a wall of driving snow.

And that's what must have happened to the farmer, whose name was Elmer Foster, as he wheeled the Model T out of his coulee so many decades ago. Still more than a mile southeast of the schoolhouse, he drove into a massive whiteout, and before he could stop or turn back into the coulee, he was off the trail and spinning his tires in snow up beyond the running board. The farmer tried to extract his car from the snowbank, but when he spun his wheels, something seemed to blow its top (my grand-mother's words), and the car's engine went dead. He tried to crank it up again, but to no avail.

The farmer waded all around the car. He was almost blinded by the driving snow which by now was propelled by a barn-crushing wind that greeted the first rays of daylight with one long demented howl. As the story is told, the farmer was a fear-less man, and less unnerved by the storm than angered by this turn of events.

As well, Elmer Foster was a tall man. Ducking his head back into the car, he must have had to hunch over to deliver his speech to his three children. He was by reputation a man of few words, so this speech must have seemed something of an occasion to the children. "Better stay put," he is reported to have said. "I don't care how much yiz want to go out there or how long yiz have to sit in the car, do not – I repeat do not – leave for so much as a minute in this storm. If it gets cold, huddle up, light this here candle, sing songs, nibble away at your lunches, and keep the blanket over top, but don't try to make it to that school or yiz won't last three gulldam minutes."

One of the children asked him where he was going.

"I'm going to get the horses."

With his coat flapping like the wings of a great stricken bird, he staggered back towards the coulee and disappeared into the driving wind.

The three children and the cat arranged themselves together in the back seat, and their voices were almost silenced by the ter-rible wind. They sat so that little Berta was in the middle between the bodies of the two older children. In return for this favour, Berta allowed them to hold her cat inside their coats, and all day long they passed Albert back and forth beneath the blanket.

As I write this down (in a warm house in the city), I'm sit-ting merely one room away from the same blanket. It is a faded and worn but still red Hudson's Bay blanket with black stripes. In one corner are four parallel black bars woven into the wool.

These indicate the heaviest gauge, a fourstar, as they used to say. The four bars are there for native trappers who could count but not read. This family heirloom is probably about seventy-five years old.

But as I was saying, the children lit the small candle offered to them by their father and nibbled away at their lunches until the last crumb was gone.

The farmhouse was sheltered from the storm at the lower end of the coulee. The children's mother could hear the wind rising, she could see the snowfall increase, and for half an hour or so, she went about her chores half distraught and half denying the peril that had enveloped her children and husband. When at last she went outside to the henhouse, she had to catch her breath in the cold. Instead of feeding the chickens, she plunged a short way up the road to see if she could see her husband's car coming back. But there was no sign of the car, and the tracks the car had left had already filled in with snow and disappeared. Elsie Foster retreated to the house, filled the stove with firewood, and waited by the kitchen window. Even down in the protected coulee, she could now tell that this was one of the worst storms she had ever seen.

The window she waited by looks out onto the trail her husband took to drive the children. On all but the foulest days, the view from this window conjures a remarkable illusion. The viewer is closer to the riverbank and to the cottonwoods and willows that line the river than to the vast prairie up above, and so from the Foster house, the tableland that constitutes this prairie looks more like the top of a ridge of hills or a plateau – anything but a prairie. If you *had* to live away out there, my grandmother used to say, that was the place to be.

There was no telephone, so Elsie Foster waited. The wind got worse and worse, and the temperature sank below thirty. Several times during the day, in moments when the wind seemed to taper off, she left the warm house and tried to break trail up the road through the ravine that led to the schoolhouse. Each time, the driving snow forced her back inside. Sometimes she imagined her husband and her little ones safe inside the schoolhouse and merely unable to return home in the storm. But these short respites of desperate hope soon gave way to agonized mourning for each one of them. She never slept that night.

When she got up in the morning long before daybreak, the storm had passed, the wind had fallen, and the temperature had risen dramatically. When she left the house the temperature was still rising. In Alberta, this sudden warming after a cold spell is called a chinook, but in Saskatchewan, this phenomenon is so rare that back then it didn't even have a name.

The farmer's wife harnessed two horses to the cutter and grabbed a scoop shovel. She sat in the driver's seat beside a supply of blankets and a large round stone heated on the stove that she had wrapped in cloth. She urged the horses all the way up the coulee to the place where the car had gone into the deeper snow. It looked like a huge humped animal asleep in the ditch. She could not scrape the snow off the new Model T; she had to shovel it off in great scoops. It was some time before she managed to yank open the door on the driver's side.

The first thing she discovered was that her husband was gone. The second thing she saw, as a waft of candlewax and urine passed through her nostrils, was her three little ones still as death beneath the blanket, and then, nosing its way out from where they lay, the tabby named Albert. She cried out the names of her children, *Clarence! Eleanor! Berta!*

Slowly, one by one, they opened their eyes as though called back from the dead. Their candle had burned to a stub.

She carried the children from the Model T to the cutter and bundled them in with the cat and the hot bound stone. Then she led the horses back on foot and carried the children into her own bed. She massaged their limbs and fed them tea and soups and anything else they would take down, and though the two eldest turned feverish, she could see that her children had a good chance of making it back from their long sleep. One of them told her that their father had gone for the horses, so she realized he must have fallen somewhere between the Model T and the barn.

Berta, the small one, seemed strangely unaffected by the ordeal in the model T. Her mother spent more time tending to the needs of the two older children while little Berta slept between them in her parents' large bed. When Berta woke up, she said that she would come with her mother to find their father. But her mother made Berta stay home to care for Clarence and Eleanor if they should wake.

Elsie Foster knew she had to hurry. Once more she climbed into the cutter, though this time without the heated stone and the blankets, and urged the horses up out of the coulee and toward the schoolhouse. The snow was whipped and banked in bluewhite folds beneath a clearing sky, yielding not a sign of her husband. Perhaps he had gone in the other direction and found his way to the schoolhouse. If not...and she prayed all the way to the sound of the wheezing horses and the hissing runners.

There was a jubilant crowd of survivors at the schoolhouse. Some of her neighbours had kept their children home; others had accompanied them to school and spent the entire day and night in the teacherage. When Elsie Foster broke into the schoolhouse, the happy mood gave way to one of great urgency. Elsie's neighbours set out at once to find her lost husband. All day long they kept arriving with food and fresh horses for the search. A team of horses managed to tow the Model T back to the Fosters' yard. The men waded back and forth over the trail poking and kicking at anything that might have fallen in the deep snow. But no one found a trace of Elmer Foster, the children's tall, strong, fearless father. Their indestructible father.

Elmer Foster, people said, would sooner have taken a horse or a car than walk a hundred feet. When he left the Model T, he half sailed, half stumbled down the trail back through the coulee, but even there, the wind was almost unbearable. It drove him along like a tumbleweed, sliced through his winter coat, and every time he drew breath, the air sank like a cold thin blade into his lungs. He managed to walk for half a mile, and then the trail turned west so that he had to face almost directly into the wind for a painful stretch. At this point on the trail, he must have seen very quickly that he wasn't going to make it. As the story goes, he ran into something huge and motionless somewhere near the trail. It was Turkle, the missing cow. She was still alive, in fact still standing and covered with a deep layer of snow, but the storm had been so intense the poor animal was played out, her breath coming in short feverish whistles. When he kicked the unfortunate creature, she scarcely even moved.

Foster always carried a big jackknife in his pants pocket. Perhaps the knife was in his hand before any clear messages had reached his half-frozen cranium. He had no sledge, of course, with which to stun the animal before he stuck it, so with the cow standing there in a state of frozen immobility, he probed the dewlap for the hole that cows have at the front of their brisket, and drove the long blade into the lower part of the cow's throat. As he had always done at the smokehouse, he twisted the blade, severing Turkle's jugular. The blood fountained out, the cow shuddered in the man's arms, and her old legs buckled.

Away from his ropes and pulleys outside the smokehouse door, Elmer Foster had never slaughtered a cow, so the work was clumsy and rushed. At first he could scarcely feel the knife in his hands, but when the warm blood covered them, the hands seemed to revive on their own. He opened up the cow, pulled out her intestines, and with them a sizeable calf fetus, and slowly wedged himself inside. Caught in a lesser storm, he might have chosen to fight his way down the coulee, but something must have told him that this was absolutely his only chance. He went into the foul steaming carcass feet first so that his head and nostrils would remain closest to the opening, and like the womb's former inhabitant, Elmer Foster closed his eyes to the awful storm. It howled over his head all that day and all the following night.

I have always wondered what Elmer Foster thought about in his moments of consciousness. Did he fret about his children in the car or his wife alone in the house? Did he hear his own words to his wife that same morning? *Only babies are meant to stay home in bad weather, and the children aren't babies, so why baby them?*

During the warmest part of the day, the search continued up and down the trail from the point where the car had foundered to the Fosters' yard. Clarence and Eleanor, the two oldest children, slept and woke throughout the day in a state of feverish recovery. Their mother left them in the care of their sister and joined in the search. As the afternoon wore on, a neighbour boy brought little Berta out on the trail so that she too could search for her father. She had been told that either they would find him and take him home, or that God would find him and take him to Heaven. This seemed a reasonable explanation, so the little girl, bundled up and drawn by her older companion on a toboggan, remained calm all through the waning afternoon. The boy left her and went to help the men search through some snowdrifts a short way off the trail.

Sitting on her sled, Berta thought she heard a noise. She made her way over to the sound and discovered after some vigorous digging that she was standing on a massive object beneath the snow. She began to dig down, singing and talking to herself. From time to time, the men would walk by, and perhaps note with some surprise that the girl was helping in her own way. As the light began to fade, she had uncovered the head of her beloved Turkle.

The name, I'm told, had come from Berta herself, a mispronunciation of turtle, and was applied to the big cow for her painstakingly slow movements around the farm. Apparently the name had stuck for everyone in the family except Elmer.

"Moo," Berta said to Turkle, and the cow seemed to moo back.

"What are you doing in the snow?" said the little girl.

Turkle grunted a faint reply.

"Are you deaded?" said the girl. This time there was no reply. "Turkle, you are a bad cow. You should go home and get warm."

The cow seemed to agree. It even growled her name, or seemed to. Turkle had spoken many times to Berta, but never in a voice so strange and anguished. The girl stood up and began to back off.

When her mother came to take her home, she found Berta hitting the massive head of the cow with her mittened hand. She explained to her mother that Turkle was a bad cow, but that was because she was sick and cranky, and maybe they should take her home too.

"It's too late for Turkle," her mother said. "Turkle is dead, Berta."

"No, she's not," said the little girl. "Are you, Turkle?"

Without so much as the flicker of an eyelash, Turkle stared like a mother, sadly, and perhaps a little bit offended, up at the rising moon. *I know what I know,* she seemed to say.

"Come over here," said Elsie Foster. "Mummy wants to have a word with...." She never finished her sentence.

Much of this story, perhaps too much, was told to me by my grandmother. She signs her name Mrs. Judson Gerald Steward, but back then she was a girl named Eleanor Foster. She has a small flare for the dramatic, and I find I have pared her story back some. For example, she swears that the coyotes had already gotten to Turkle and her precious cargo, which is highly unlikely. She has little Berta standing triumphant upon the head of Turkle, signalling to the searchers in a gesture made all the more dramatic by the setting sun and the rising moon. If this were such a big moment for little Berta, why does she still avoid talking about the day they found her father? My grandmother simply shrugs. This is an older sister's gesture. In her rendition, brother Clarence is holding Albert the cat and openly weeps to a reporter as he tells the story his mother cannot bring herself to tell. This description doesn't quite square with my old taciturn Uncle Clarence, a solitary alcoholic whose memory of his father seems pretty shaky.

But the story survives in an even more pared-down version in the *Saskatoon StarPhoenix,* and from there it was carried all across the nation. It is typical of my family that the only national fame they ever attained was entirely unsought.

But one dramatic detail of Eleanor's that I cannot bring myself to leave out is the moment in the smokehouse when all six feet of Elmer Foster's body were finally pried free of the great carapace of Turkle's body like a thawing T-bone, and, O, she moans, O, the sight of his clotted head when he first smelled the air of the barn and he opened his mouth to wawl and cry in Mother's arms.

4. PUT ON MY MASK

Things to Come, Dennis Bruce

Acrylic on matboard, 81.0 x 101.6 cm, 1992

Here we look with new vision into the places of all our ancestors. There is a common ground here, where an exploration of the spirit of the place can lead to mutual understanding. To do this, one must truly see the points of view of others. There are those who can guide us, like Louise Bernice Halfe's Nohkom, or Rita Bouvier's Medicine Man. For Marie Annharte Baker, "Instead of the proverbial 'walk a moccasin mile,' the poet asks the readers to take off their false fronts or masked selves and cleanse or apply a healing mask of appreciation for the beauty and self-worth of another person." And as Joanne Gerber says about her story, "It's...about looking at the world through different eyes, listening through attentive ears." When we do that, we make amazing discoveries about what seems perfectly ordinary. As Lorna Crozier says, "When people's thoughts turn to the sacred, many think of what lies above us. They look at the sky. Instead I want to honour what's under our noses, under our feet, the common but holy inhabitants of our world."

THE ELECT

ANNE SZUMIGALSKI

Here in the saintly dark, all is so cleanly dank, all is ordered and cradled. Nothing is sinful. Even the suck of the worm's mouth upon us is preordained, therefore right.

Suddenly, it's dawn up there. It comes with the silver squeal of birds, a sound like thin trumpets. "Crack the box," it says. "Arise, this is the day."

Obedient as buds, our heads appear in the open grass, and a rain of golden yods falls down upon us. So this is light. We had forgotten it.

We, who lay long in holy depths of earth, have all at once become small and new, can't even remember our names, and the passers-by won't tell us. They stop. They smile. They stare and then move on.

At last a child in blue cotton leans down to us. "Daffs," she says, and, taking each of us by the neck, yanks for the love of God.

NŌHKOM, MEDICINE BEAR

LOUISE BERNICE HALFE

A shuffling brown bear
snorting and puffing
ambles up the stairs.

In her den
covered wall to wall
herbs hang...carrot roots, yarrow,
camomile, rat-root,
and *cācāmosikan*

To the centre of the room she waddles
sits with one leg out, the other hugged close.
She bends over her roots and leaves
sniffs, snorts and tastes them
as she sorts them into piles.

She grinds the chosen few
on a small tire grater,
dustdevils settling into molehills.
Her large brown paws take a patch
of soft deer skin
and wrap her poultice
until hundreds of tiny bundle-chains
swing from the rafters.

The brown labouring bear
Nôhkom, the medicine woman
alone in her attic den
smoking slim cigarettes
wears the perfume of sage, sweetgrass
and earth medicine ties.

PUT ON MY MASK FOR A CHANGE

ANNHARTE (MARIE ANNHARTE BAKER)

See the stripe that divides my face in two.
A vermilion dot marks the tip of my nose.
Take this ancient advice and face up to me.
This is not some recent ritual I picked up.
My beloved cave sister let us dab mud together.
Let us meet at the creek to apply the clay.
Make our healing salves original cosmetics.
Anoint bites, scratches, bumps and lumps.
We then wouldn't mistake each other for ugly.
Let us take back ceremonies to paint our skins.
You be my Zingu mother designing my face.
I the Zingu daughter lift my face from water.
Then you, then me, take turns smiling Jaguar.
The corners above your lips curl in laughter.
Under healing masques we are twinning spirits.
We are masks within each other holding out.
Whatever we must face is in the winking eye.

LISTENING TO THE ANGELS

JOANNE GERBER

When he comes back at last – his body simply unstrung and shivering with weakness – his eyes are the clue. Oh, they've always been blue, against all odds and theories of heredity, bluer than Lake Huron on the kindest of days, and brighter, so it isn't the extraordinary colour or even the light in them that tells me. No. It's the misleading absence of light. Stephen's been listening again.

He's listening now, the rattan settee creaking and groaning as he rocks himself. One hand grips his hair as though presenting it to someone for inspection, pale curls snagged like a fleece on his fingers. His other arm wraps his head, stopping both ears. His knees meet his brow. He's a curve, a bow, quivering with oblivious concentration. Within the circle of his bent form, within the silence of his muffled ears, whisper angels exclusive to Stephen. At least, that's what I think.

It's his knees that bother me most, drawn up like that. They hide his face. I want to see even his shuttered eyes, his intent chin, to read something there. Some tiny thing.

Our parents don't believe there's anything to be read. As always, Mother has fled the room, espadrilles flapping. Her exit was followed almost at once by the squeal and clatter of the drawer under the oven, where the pans are kept. She needs to bake. I can picture her out there, in her gingham apron, puzzling, running through the list of what's already on hand, what we could do with. She's stingy with goodies, preferring to serve up a pair of ginger cookies which have lost their snap, than to recklessly give us three fresh at one sitting.

Wait, she's calling me.

"Ireeene, honey! What was that pie your father was asking about last night? Peach? Coconut cream?" A panicky edge to her voice. He does that to her.

"Lemon chiffon." She'll fuss and fret over the meringue, trying to get it perfect, even on an afternoon like this. First week of September, wilting weather; until the breeze quickens off the lake, I've abandoned my packing.

Packing – I fret over Stephen. Who will sit here with him when I'm back at Carleton? Who will make conversation – *milk* it out of thin air – at the dinner table? Mother and Father don't speak much to each other. To Stephen, either. Mother saves her comments for her wheezy Electrolux, for the cantankerous washing machine, for Alex Trebek on the television, and for me, when I'm here, because she thinks I need to master domestic dialect, being female. (She's wrong. I will never, never. Never. I will elope with a boyfriend and plant aspen on the Kamchatka Peninsula first. I will pitch a nylon dome tent on the blistering slopes of K2. I will barter for goat's cheese and black bread with elaborate pantomimes in a Turkish bazaar. Anything.) But what about Stephen? He may suffocate, wither, become a mute, alone with the two of them in this house.

Technically, the angels are only conjecture. My own. I invented them in sixth grade, when one of my classmates came across Stephen in action. A cover story, created on the spot, without a moment's thought, launched into the shocked silence like a comet. But in its wake, seeing my little brother through my friend's awestruck eyes, I started to think that maybe I'd had a brush with Mystery. Ten years later, I'm a true believer. Though Mother is forever warning me that my overactive imagination will be my downfall. That, and my saying whatever comes into my head.

Stephen has never said a word about what's in his head when

he leaves us like this. Everyone else assumes he's in limbo: unconscious, lights out, lost. But no. Definitely, no. It's to presence, not absence, that he relinquishes himself, his interest in the outer world suspended absolutely. You only have to watch him.

His body moves, there's a current in his limbs, you can feel it lift the hair on your arms, if you sit tight beside him. His head stirs ever so slightly as in answer to a delicate cadence. If he isn't trying to hear something, why that arm thrown up around his head, fiercely guarding his ears? He's listening for a voice in his inner ear.

And the squeezed eyelids? A screen that from the inside becomes a window for him. A well-lit window. Does he step through it? I can't say. But he *sees*.

My brother's eyes afterwards are opaque and sad in the way of clear water inadvertently muddied. He's reluctant to look through them. After whatever he's been seeing, we must present a bleak vista. I want to whisper, sorry. Sorry, Stephen. Because I'm part of the everyday world he has to deal with, a world diminished and diminishing. Diminishing in part because, at eleven years old, my brother doesn't write. He won't write. He could get all of them – a pretty substantial them – off his back with one paragraph. He's never written a paragraph, though. Has yet to produce a sentence. And he's not dyslexic.

Reading is nothing to Stephen, he's prodigious. Since I've been back here this summer, he's borrowed Chekhov, Dostoyevsky and Turgenev, Bulgakov and Zamyatin, and the twenty-odd novels (*Monsignor Quixote, Henderson The Rain King*) I picked up used along Bank Street. When he was just five, he worked his way through one of those children's series which torque reality to teach kids their place in the world. Mother couldn't help quizzing him afterwards about what he'd learned. Stephen told her, "Books are like yogourt. You have to get through all this stuff that doesn't taste good before you get to the fruit at the bottom."

Intrigued, I asked, "What fruit?"

Stephen blinked at me and whispered, "Cantaloupe." Melon of any kind nauseates him. "*You* know, Renie – the message."

"Message?" He was a preschooler.

"Kid stuff." He left the room.

School has been a crucible for him; he's hardly die-cast, reading like a whiz but not writing. They can't help speculating, wielding verdicts. "Hand-eye coordination," one theory went. (Had they ever seen him draw?) "Compromised linguistic connections." "Highly functioning autism." (Heard him talk?) "Repressed psychological trauma." That last one got my attention. But in a house where everything is suppressed, there'd be no trauma to *repress*. Would there?

The truth is, he confounds them. By grade five they had him inscribing spirals and loops and uncrossed *t*'s for a Hungarian tutor of penmanship who finally threw up his hands in melodramatic despair and consigned the child to a life of mock illiteracy. Officially, Stephen's an unclassified *Special Ed.* (On the school bus, a *Sped.*)

He must hate the label, for its vagueness as much as the stigma. He's dismayed by imprecision. That may be what prompted his conscientious objection to inscription in the first place. Grade one, those blunt ball-and-bat consonants and vowels. The pencils thicker than his thumb. The words themselves – the *at bat fat cat that sat on a mat in a hat* – between lines a *pat* inch apart. No wonder he resisted. And once he'd taken a stand.... He's stubborn. Implacably stubborn. Always has been.

Still, I say hats off to him. How dextrous does a kid have to be to spend years in directed doodling, in creative ciphering, without one lapse into a recognizable character? Pretty dextrous. He will write when he feels the need. I can just see him nonchalantly penning uncials, upper case and lower case, each letter round and satisfying and perfect. He did serve that time as a calligrapher's (albeit uncooperative) apprentice.

His standoff is awfully hard on Mother and Father, who hunger for public proof that their boy's not stupid. Stephen recognizes their predicament with small kindnesses. A portion of breaded liver eaten without ketchup. Dandelions, bluebells, and cornflowers with Queen Anne's lace for the breakfast table, after one of his sunrise rambles. (He wanders off regularly. At sunset too. Like Father when the fancy strikes, there's no keeping him.)

Then, his pictures.

He makes pictures with pastels. Not tawdry sidewalk portraits, enlarged eyes brightened by two starpoint dots of white. And not a child's ball-on-a-stick tree, apple-studded, immobile under a tentacled smiling sun. No. No approximations. What Stephen draws is awesomely observed. He gets it right.

His landscapes are recognizable at once. As Lake Huron in certain weather from a particular gap in the screen of trees across the Bayfield bluff. As the hedgerow with blackberries on the way to the Rasmussens' rundown A-frame. As the spot on the breakwater where we're convinced one of the boulders, metallic and mysteriously scorched, is a meteorite.

Recognizable, that is, as minutely observed strips of Lake Huron, or the laneway, or breakwater. Tantalizing slices, fourteen-by-three-inch vertical strips, always. Why Stephen sets himself these boundaries, works within these parameters, I can't say. No one can. He lets me watch him, though. Like yesterday.

"Renie," he said quietly, standing just outside my bedroom door, "I need to work. Coming?"

Work. He's eleven. I was glad to go, though. My room a sweltering warehouse of heaped clothes and so-called essentials for off-campus housing.

"Where's –"

"She's out back," he said gravely. "Getting a zucchini and tomatoes for supper."

"Okay, give me five minutes." I had my hair on top of my head in a plastic banana clip. I'd stripped down to camisole and cut-offs against Mother's indignation. (Is it my freckles or exposed flesh she so objects to?)

Stephen nodded and retreated to wait as I dug for a T-shirt I wouldn't be taking back to school.

Quickly, I packed along something to read. I put almonds and raisins in a Zip-loc and towel-wrapped two cans of (Father's) Pepsi. Threw sunscreen into my sisal tote in case Mother caught us. Hurried to join Stephen.

He was crouched out here, on the veranda, watching a pair of ants hoist a crouton. I tossed his Blue Jays cap at him like a Frisbee. "Ready?"

He grinned and ducked. "All set."

With his oversized sketchbook under one arm, and a fluorescent fanny pack full of pastels, he whistled a bit while we hiked to wherever it was he planned to draw. Good, towards the lake. Turning off the gummy road, through the bit of meadow, the woods and scrub bush before the beach. Our beach, more rugged and breathtaking than the summer people's.

We had it to ourselves. How did he always seem to manage this?

The lake was spectacularly blue. I dropped to unbuckle my sandals. Winced and counted to ten. The sand was a kiln.

"Over here, Renie." Stephen had skipped ahead in his runners. Was halfway to the breakwater that girdled the curve to the point. "You know where we watched the meteor shower that night? Those rocks."

Bone numbing, they'd been. Ankle wrenching (or jean drenching) to get to. But the waves at two a.m. like glimmers of mother-of-pearl. The sky like glimpses into a vast Pandora's box, intermittent jewels, gemstones thrown across the velvet haphazardly, trailing stardust. It had been worth creeping away from the house like cat-burglars. Worth limping home afterwards in damp, wind-stiffened denim. Because Stephen was incandescent. Ecstatic.

"Sure, wherever," I told him. "But give me a second to get wet." I waded out thigh-deep to splash my face and arms, blessed cool, then followed.

Even in full daylight, with bare feet, the rocks were a challenge to negotiate. No point arguing, though. Stephen never headed out randomly to sketch, never took my suggestions. He scouted, I guess, on his dawn and dusk rambles.

I stepped carefully into a tepid pool between boulders. Felt for a bit of roughness to give me purchase.

"I'll wait for you to catch up, Renie." His feet swinging over a four-foot granite drop.

We scrambled on together. Next week, I couldn't help thinking, he'd be doing this alone.

When we reached his spot, Stephen climbed up to the inner edge of the rocks, where they met the low bluff well back from the water. Then he sat for the longest time, just looking. Not a fixed gaze, but this horizon-to-horizon, earth-to-zenith sweep, dreamily intent. Next he felt the wiry dune grass. Poked at the nubbled dirt, ran his thumbnail over the ridges of a clamshell. Baptized his hands and lips with sand, both white-hot and damp. He sniffed things, and got me sniffing too, in spite of myself. A bit of purple crown vetch, the wind full-face from offshore, a licked stone with green indications of the lake bed in its cracked marble surface. (He always does this. What is it he's after?)

Then, propping his sketchbook on his knees, he unzipped his pastel pouch, sighed – and settled down to study the sky and landscape all over again. As though he were about to sketch a Grand Canyon of a scene. But, inevitably, a three-inch slice of what's out there.

I squinted, panned for an invisible seam, a strategic shimmer, even, in the atmosphere. Nothing. I scanned what he'd drawn in grids, casual about glancing from paper to panorama, so as not to alert him. Then I sat asking myself: Do his eyes have a frame I'm not seeing; is this the most he can take in? Or is he trying to enlighten us about something with these fastidious cross-sections? Offering us an angel's-eye view?

I thought suddenly of the print I'd bought for my dorm room

last fall. "Wounded Angel," Scandinavian, turn-of-the-century. It reminded me somehow of Stephen. Two boys carrying an angel. Young boys, one dressed like a sombre Lutheran pallbearer, black-hatted, plodding eyes-ahead-stoically, old before his time. The other taller, more graceful, a close-cropped blond farmer's or fisherman's son, but troubled, frowning inscrutably out from the tableau. Seated suspended between them on a wooden-poled litter, the wounded angel. Girlish, a few pale field flowers in one hand, her head and body bowed a little despite her radiance. And across her eyes, tied around her corn silk hair, a strip of dazzling cloth, a homemade bandage. One wing seems bent slightly, torn as though she'd snagged it. Beyond the little procession, tundra-coloured flats and water, a listless lake or river.

That enigmatic blindfold, about three inches wide. Stephen's luminous three-inch landscapes. Did he see the painting somewhere when he was small, before he took up pastels? Or was there another, more tangible, connection?

My brother was a boy full of secrets. I knew better than to trespass by asking. Leaving my book in my tote bag, I watched Lake Huron swell to vibrant life under his hands. Wondering when I would have the privilege again.

Nothing but nothing will tempt him to expand his vision. Teachers have tried laying in reams of good-sized manilla paper, bristol board, even quality watercolour stock with the offer of a matte thrown in. Stephen says no thanks and negotiates access to the paper cutter.

At home, Mother has ventured roundabout remarks with Father or me in attendance. "Oh my, from the back, honey," she'll say to Stephen, "your pictures could almost be taken for flypaper! Who would guess they're so lovely?" (Flypaper – even Father snorted at that.)

"Just look at this little *bit* of the lake, Irene! Imagine if your brother drew the *whole scene!*" At least she dutifully hangs them from the kitchen ceiling with thread. Like flypaper. (Or like tubular wind chimes, like parchment Haiku). They rotate, slowly, shivering with the seismic pressure of our footfalls. Poor spick-and-span Mother. Her primrose kitchen's festooned with her son's anomalous impressions of the world, each proportioned like the satin Miss Huron County banner of her glory days, but infinitely more provocative. Earth and sky and water between them, stunningly rendered.

Adjusting his perspective is a dead issue with Stephen. Like the fixative.

That was one of my blunders.

It isn't oil pastels he uses, but the other kind. The chalky, crumbling ones, which have a tendency to smudge. We drink a fair bit of tea in our house, and the warning whistle on the kettle isn't what it used to be: those meticulous, multi-coloured fronds suspended from the ceiling. The surreptitious steam. Mother and Father's inattention. Stephen has suffered losses. So last Christmas morning he unwrapped what I'd thought would be a wonderful gift – a can of fixative.

As he sat dumbly holding it, rigid as a Lego chevalier, I sensed I'd gone over the line somehow. But how? I tried to dredge up enthusiasm.

"Stephen," I exclaimed, "you know how much we love your pictures. This will preserve them!"

Nothing. He set the can down on the neatly folded reindeer wrapping paper. Tucked his hands into the sleeves of his pyjamas (reindeers, too: Mother takes the festive season seriously).

I nodded at his most recent landscape. I'd hung it on the Christmas tree the night before, anticipating that he'd be eager to try out his present.

"Think of the kitchen, Stephen." Complicit noises from out there, where Mother was whipping up eggnog and waffles to justify waking Father before noon on a Holiday. Now I gestured at the blue and yellow aerosol cylinder. "The man at the store told me this will keep your colours from running even if moisture gets at them. Wouldn't that be great?"

Stephen heard me out, wide-eyed and silent. What was he thinking? Afraid of? I picked a strand of tinsel off his hair, felt him flinch and withdraw a bit.

Trespassing further, I reached for the fixative. "Just watch."

I uncapped and shook it. Then boldly sprayed his work of art where it hung: "Un, deux, trois, Voila!"

With a flourish, I let him see how natural it still looked – snow still boot-deep against the Wilson's rusted gate, ochre corn stubble bent under the white weight, sky opaque and placid as Wedgwood.

Still nothing from Stephen.

I demonstrated with my terry cloth cuff how not even rubbing would efface the pastel now. (Maybe it did look a little flat, though, on the paper.)

He cried. Covered his face and cried. Fiercely. His shoulders shaking, his legs pedalling against the floor. Maybe it was because the first gift he'd found under the tree earlier had been a five-year diary from Mother. Maybe it was because the spray smelled like death by ether. Maybe – Mother's guess – he had simply eaten too many Christmas candies before breakfast. He didn't say what upset him. Wouldn't say. Ever. Though I asked and asked him.

The can sat on his desk, unused, with the diary, for the rest of my Christmas break. It was still there when I got back in April. Victoria Day weekend, though, just in from a morning walkabout, Stephen announced that he had permanently – and conscientiously – disposed of the aerosol. Mother's hapless gift, more volatile even than fixative, evaporated about the same time.

He's long since absolved me. At least, he's never mentioned my mistake again. Nor have I. Even when a picture's been marred or rippled.

Well, this summer we're all suffering from humidity. Up

away from the water the heat can hang like a vapour, barely stirring. It saps you, you go around with your face and feet bloated, feeling pregnant with fever. The fields hum. The ditchwater stinks and disappears. The house smells of mildew. Father gets snappish and sarcastic. Stephen and I, lethargic.

But Mother, in a haze, soldiers on. Like this afternoon. It must be thirty-five in the kitchen, a steamy, sticky thirty-five, but she's got the oven preheating and the Osterizer whirling. To keep her mind off Stephen's spells. I think they terrify her.

"Aren't you worn ragged just watching? Where does he find the energy?" she asked guiltily from the doorway as she left me with him. We'd been sipping icy grape juice and trying to catch a breeze out here on the porch. It's all screens.

Where, indeed? He's still off. Head pulled down, quivering, oblivious.

I feel sorry for Mother. Her life hasn't worked out as she'd been led to expect, and she has no faith in Mystery. Here I am going into third-year Russian Literature, a choice unfathomable to her, but one she feels duty bound to defend in the face of Father's hooting; and here is Stephen. Still inexplicably rocking.

For the longest time, she kept hoping some medical wizard would unravel the enigma of his silences and dispel them. Surely he'd be scribbling his alphabet in short order when his spells stopped. I think she's losing hope now. That pathetic diary.

But to satisfy her, poor Stephen still gets carted off periodically for testing. Over the years, he's been to University Hospital in London, to McMaster in Hamilton, even, after a seventeen-month wait, to Sick Kids in Toronto. They've done CAT scans and echograms, magnetic resonance imaging and electro-myography. Monitored him waking, sleeping, talking, walking. Even half-heartedly sketching. Yet after all these years, sheer guesswork.

Because they've never caught him *listening*. Not even once. Which all the more convinces me.

No angel would be compromised like that, apprehended on

electrodes or scanners. So, of course, they abandon Stephen when he's under scrutiny. He's a shell which doesn't whisper when held to the ear. A ship standing by on radio silence. He is unflaggingly present as long as the physicians observe him. No extinguishing himself, no reverberating arc, shuttered eyes and face. Poor doctors. (No summons to the holy mountain, no unseen afterglow. Poor Stephen.)

Last time (this past June) he came back from the hospital contrite, exhausted and guileless, in clothes that smelled toxic. Still undiagnosed. Mother slumped on arrival, grey and frazzled from sleeping in armchairs, from facing incredulous specialists at yet another failed Mecca. She needed to slip, bathed, into Battenburg sheets, for a good sixteen-hour sleep. I promised to take care of things if she did. She was too worn out to argue.

Father, mercurial, headed straight for the bluffs. But not before announcing (as he booted the overnight bags down the hall): "Told us nothing we didn't already know. Do they take us for morons? Does that kid?"

He needed to stump, stew, smoke. I knew he'd slam his way back into the house late, to do some serious drinking. Understandable, I guess. Back when, he must have had visions of fishing trips and coaching his son's hockey team. Instead, humiliation and hospitals, extra billing. He gets more embittered and sullen every time he's dragged on one of these pilgrimages. (He often sleeps out here on the settee, homecoming nights, where, if the wind is up, you can hear the pounding of the lake against its moorings.) I checked to be sure the ice trays were full.

Stephen was on his rug dismantling a Lego castle. I closed the drawbridge gently and sent him for a shower. Headed for the kitchen, tripping over one of the bags Father had unceremoniously left. From the look of things, the ride home had been as much an ordeal as the medical gauntlet. So when Stephen reappeared at last in fresh pyjamas, I fed him homemade french fries and two slabs of carrot cake with praline ice cream. He said, picking at crumbs with his finger, "Do you know they make cream of carrot soup? It's gross. And watermelon Jello?"

I made a face. "Sounds awful." I twisted my neck and began to study his delicate slices of life, one at a time, to keep from quizzing him. If he had anything he needed to tell, I'd hear it in due time.

All he said was, a few minutes later, in a small voice, "I think they're really mad at me this time, Renie. They wouldn't even stop to let me use the bathroom. All the way home." He had his head in his hands.

"It's not you, Stephen. It's the doctors."

"Then how come Dad asked Mom to sell tickets next time – ringside seats –" his face was tragic, "then maybe I'd perform."

"He's just blowing off steam." My hands shaking, I grabbed the ketchup. "Better put this in the fridge before I forget. Don't want to give Mother conniptions."

I sat beside Stephen on his bed, reading Tolkien, until he was asleep. Then I retreated to my own room. My own book.

Stephen seems to be slowing a bit now, his fingers loosening. Soon he'll be back, his face and body blearily tentative as on first waking. He'll look at me with these disappointed eyes and this mouth wavering like someone had smudged it.

"Ree-nie?" he'll murmur, and I'll ache. He may let me take his hand, then. Sometimes he even lays his hot head in my lap. (His hair is dewed – smells sweet and sweaty as a toddler's, is just as fine and fair and tousled.)

We won't speak much. To soothe himself, he'll rock a bit, while the little tremors diminish. Weary as he is, he'll let me touch his cheek. And I'll do it, shyly, to feel his goodness. He has this goodness you can't get at. Sometimes I think he wraps himself in it, it's that impervious. Other times I'm impressed with the depth of it, the bottommost part of him, and the uppermost.

"Irene? Everything all right in there?" Mother. She's got the lemon simmering and the pastry shells in. The whole house shimmers with the fragrance and heat of the oven.

"We're fine." We are. Fine without her.

Yet I don't blame Mother for retreating, finding what passes for sanctuary in the mundane, in her baking and bustling. Her son's read more books than she'll ever read, but he's never signed his name to a Mother's Day card. She's had to face all those doctors and teachers. To appease Father. About his silences – what he's seeing, what he's feeling – Stephen's disclosed nothing. She's surrendered her faith in miracles. These things take their toll.

Almost time. When the angels are finished with my brother, he'll be turning shivery and walleyed toward me. If he's up to the walk later, if the sunlight is not too belligerent, a long float in the lake should cool him. Cool me, for another stint of packing.

A PROPHET IN HIS OWN COUNTRY

LORNA CROZIER

The gopher on his hind legs
trembles with holiness and fright.
A miniature prophet he knows
he could be stoned or flooded out,
an *auto-da-fé* in stubble fields,
martyr to children for a penny a tail

How can you not believe
an animal who goes down
head first into darkness, the ceaseless
pull of gravity deep beneath him?
What faith that takes, what imagination!

I come to him with questions
because I love his ears, how perfectly
they fit, how flat they lie against his head.
They hear the inner and the outer
worlds, what rain says
underground. The stone's praise
for the sparrow's ankle bone.

Little earth-otter, little dusty Lazarus,
he vanishes, he rises. He can't tell us
what he's seen.

THE MEDICINE MAN

RITA BOUVIER

We kept our distance
from the medicine man
stories of power
in his gaze
as we followed him
down the path
He carried a cane
in one hand
a medicine bag
in the other

To test him
I agreed to feign
a twisted ankle
His piercing
deep blue eyes
ran through me
as our eyes locked

He invited me
to look inside
offered me a potion
for my ailment
and a twinkle in his eye
whispered to me
"There is no cure
for your condition"

QUINCE

ANNE SZUMIGALSKI

I think of my poems as trees
remarks a self-conscious poet
who likes to talk about his work
he speaks about it often
and makes quite an impression at parties

once on TV when he is interviewed
by the farm correspondent
of a national magazine
he wants to say that he thinks
of his work as a field of wheat
but how can he explain the harvest
when the wheat is cut
and the grain threshed out?

one night a poem does grow in him
like a tree it grows in the dark
he awakes impaled on its trunk

all his entrails are wood
and his toenails take root
ah now he has to stand still
the bones of his fingers become twigs
that scratch at the inside of his flesh
write they command *spring is here*

Quince

and he can feel how the whole tree
resents him and despises him
for not becoming its glory of leaves

WILDFLOWERS

LORNA CROZIER

Wild Western Bergamot, Larkspur,
Closed Gentian near the Manitoba border,
Windflowers in the Cypress Hills.
I read the names out loud,
flip page after page as if the past were
a botanist with whom I've made a pact.
Evening Primrose, Yarrow, Wild Flax –
what would Sorrow look like, what fruit
would it bear? I have in mind no colour.
Yellow, red, or blue it would bloom
in rich abundance this July, its flowers
a burden, a fragrant heaviness,
between my fingers its leaves softly
furred, the fine hairs of a lover's wrist.
If I touched the sepals with my tongue
I'd say *anise* and then repeat it, an aftertaste,
a hint of time. Wild near the marsh
I find a kind of Rue where only yesterday
leopard-spotted frogs leapt in imitation
of the heart's strange fondness
for what is lost.

5. ADULT LANGUAGE WARNING

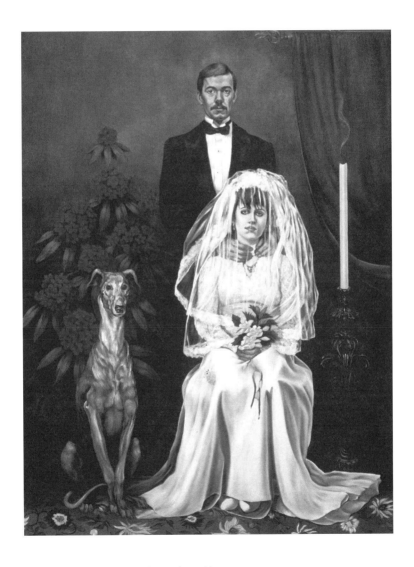

Traditional Wedding, Iris Hauser

Oil on canvas, 120.0 x 90.0 cm, 1989

Where people have power over others, there can be abuse, physical and emotional. Iris Hauser's image suggests the tension in such a relationship. As she says, here are "two people entering a doomed marriage, with an imbalance of power creating the unhealthy relationship of master and slave." Children can get caught in these situations, as Robert Currie says about his story. It "was written in an attempt to explore the mechanics of family life in an abusive relationship and particularly the problem of the child caught with torn loyalties in the conflict between his parents." In the story by Gertrude Story, a child pays a dreadful price for being caught in such a conflict. For Bill Robertson, language too has a power that needs to be considered. He says his poem "is not about swearing. It's about children growing into the language of adults in all its promise, its seeming maturity, and ultimately its pain." Connie Fife explores how the power of language can have a terrible and damaging effect, how words themselves need to be challenged. She says of her poem, "It is...my own way of breaking down or challenging stereotypes of who I am considered to be, of how history has tried to confine or restrain the truth of our reality as Native people." To resist abuse, as Judy Krause says, requires "courage and determination." And after the naming of abuse, there is much healing to be done.

ADULT LANGUAGE WARNING

WILLIAM ROBERTSON

Behind that door locked tight
with a look that says, *you
just don't understand,* my
daughter lies reading romance,
tape deck promising her love
for eternity, if she'll just
take his hand.

In the basement my son watches
a guy stiff-arm some broad
who's getting lippy and instead
of ventilating his carcass when
she has the chance
she slumps into his arms
when the cops arrive
to take him away.

I should shut all this off.
I should make lengthy explanations.
I should tell them what I learned
in Neil's Leisureland about who's
got an icebox and who puts out
and how many times you can do it
before she has to go to her mother.

I should tell them how we met
in the front seats of our fathers' cars
to exchange stories
wordlessly, both sides
too surprised to speak.

I should
but my language would be
foreign as those we spoke
in the dark
of our frightened first knowing
in these new bodies
old stories told us how
to handle.

PENCIL CRAYONS

(ROBERT CURRIE)

The Ford half-ton was moving at a good clip when they hit the tracks at the level crossing just outside of Magpie. Seated between his parents, doodling in his notebook, the boy felt the truck bounce, felt himself lifted off the seat, hovering for a second in mid-air. "Ride 'em, cowboy," his father said. "Don't be grabbing leather now." He glanced up at his father, one hand firmly turning the wheel toward town. His father was grinning, the cigarette clenched in his teeth. Even his mother seemed to be grinning. When she looked down at him, he thought she looked pretty with her town makeup thick beneath her eyes. He grinned too. It was the first time they had come to town – all three of them together – since last fall. Now that winter was on the way out, he knew things were getting better.

"Yessir!" his father said, raising both hands from the steering wheel, clapping them together. "There's nothing livelier than a six elevator town on a Saturday night!"

The boy looked beyond the blackened shell of the burnt-out CPR station at the elevators beside the track. Then at his father. At his mother. "There's only two elevators in town," he said.

The boy saw his mother turn and look at his father. "It's just an old saying," she said.

"A damn good one." His father's voice was gruff. He cranked the wheel to the left, cut across the street in front of a slow-moving red Buick, and angle-parked at McGee's Pharmacy.

"Aren't we going to the Co-op?" the boy's mother asked.

"Sure." His father's voice was light and easy now. "I'll meet you there. Got to have a word with Mac first."

His mother did not reply. She sat and watched her husband thrust open the squeaking truck door and step down onto the street. When she noticed her son looking at her, she smiled and said, "Come on, Josh. We'll see what's in the store."

The two of them were just stepping onto the sidewalk as the father swung open the door to McGee's. The boy saw him hesitate, take a step backwards, hold the door open.

"Mr. Walker, I was hoping I'd see you in town today." It was the boy's grade five teacher, Mrs. Dornan.

His father looked past her, into the store. "Hardly the place for a parent-teacher conference," he said.

The boy's mother was beside his father now. "He's not in trouble, is he, Mrs. Dornan?"

"Gracious, no." She stepped towards his father, reached for the door that he was holding open, and pushed it shut behind her. "We really shouldn't block the entrance. Mr. McGee might not approve. Perhaps, if we stepped out to the sidewalk...."

She and his mother walked out from beneath McGee's canopy into the bright March sunlight. His father stood for a moment in the shadow, glancing once more through the glass door. Then he joined the women on the sidewalk, blinking in the sunlight. The boy saw him step around Mrs. Dornan so that she was squinting up at him and at the sun.

"I sent you a note," she said. "I was hoping you'd get back to me."

The boy saw his mother turn swiftly to his father. His father kept his eyes on Mrs. Dornan. She was a big woman, round-shouldered and stout. "Looks like a pregnant cow," the boy had once heard his father say. Now he said, "Yeah, I forgot. It must've got in the pile of bills. Things are tough on the farm these days. I got crop still on the ground from last fall." He took half a step toward McGee's, but Mrs. Dornan seemed to slide sideways and was still in front of him. The boy thought for a second that the two of them looked like hockey players at a faceoff.

"What was it about, Mrs. Dornan?" It was his mother speaking, though her voice didn't sound quite right.

"Joshua," she said. "How shall I put it? The boy has a flair – a gift, a talent. Most children like to draw, but he's already good – very good in fact."

"So?" It was all his father said. The boy saw his mother throw a hard look at his father.

"Please, go on, Mrs. Dornan," she said.

His teacher, he could see, was answering his mother, but she continued to squint up at his father. "They have an artist-in-residence program in the city," she said. "Sponsored by the government. Wilber Bowen is the artist – he's rather experimental, I suppose, but a good teacher, excellent on the basics. Knows how to handle children. I've arranged for him to do a workshop at the school next Saturday. Joshua really shouldn't miss it."

His father looked down at the woman, cocked his head so that the sun was once more shining in her eyes. "How much does that set me back?"

The boy noticed a strange expression flicker over Mrs. Dornan's face. Even if he could sketch it, he wouldn't know what it meant. "You needn't worry, Mr. Walker. It's all taken care of. I've arranged that too."

"I don't need any help from you."

"Not from me." She was speaking quickly. "A grant. From the Department of Education."

Before his father could reply, the boy heard his mother say, "Thank you very much, Mrs. Dornan. What time should we have him there?"

"Nine o'clock. We'll put in a full day." She smiled down at Josh and turned to walk away.

"A full day," his father said, quietly, almost talking to himself, "starts at six a.m." Then he raised his voice. "Give my best to Mr. Dornan."

Mrs. Dornan was already walking away, but now she seemed

to do a stutter-step before continuing down the sidewalk without turning her head. When the boy looked back at his parents, he could see that his mother was furious.

"There was no call for that," she said, ice in every word.

"Wilber," his father said, "what the hell kind of name is that for a man? *Arrteest in residance.* Huh, sponsored by the government – just another kind of pogey!"

"There-was-no-call-for-that." His mother's words were even colder, and now they sent a chill down his neck.

"Mrs. Doorknob," his father said, then continued the fierce mimicry that didn't sound at all like Mrs. Dornan. "*Oi've arraanged thaat tooo.* What the hell is she – the lone arranger? Looks more like his horse."

His mother didn't smile, didn't answer.

"Damn woman ought to know her place."

"Come along, Josh," his mother said. "We'll meet your father back at the truck." When she reached for his hand, he pulled it away, but he did walk with her towards the Co-op. Behind him, he heard his father grunt, then stomp into McGee's, the board walk shaking under his feet.

Just before they entered the Co-op, he gave a tug on his mother's corduroy jacket. "What is it?" he asked. "About Mr. Dornan?"

His mother glared down at him, her eyes dark as midnight. "He moved out. Right after Christmas. You're not to tell a soul at school."

As he pushed the grocery cart down the aisle, he thought about his father in McGee's. He hoped they needed medicine, but he didn't think so.

"Mom," he asked, "what's he doing in there?"

She hesitated, a twenty-pound sack of flour in her arms, then bent and lowered it into the cart. "I guess we know," she said. She stepped around the cart to her son, put her hand firmly on his shoulder. "He tries," she said, "he really does." Her voice was just a whisper in his ear. "We don't know what it was like for him, growing up with just his uncle. That man! Raised the boy like breaking a horse."

His mother squeezed his shoulder, gave him a quick pat on the back. "Come on," she said. "We need to get some syrup."

"The boy," he thought. His father never talked about being a boy. Except that once, about slipping away from his uncle, walking in the hills of Buffalo Lake, through the blowing grass, coming upon three circles of rock. Teepee rings. The boy remembered the fire in his father's voice when he described the long afternoon, sun warm on his back as he crouched, raking his fingers through the soil, the thrill of discovery again and again, finding three Indian arrowheads, a slim flint knife.

His father had taken him there, once, when he was small, shown him the stone circles, helped him search for arrowheads. They had found nothing but a piece of dark rock, flat and sharp. "A broken scraper," his father said. "They used it for scraping buffalo hides." His father had risen from where they knelt together and stood, gazing towards the long hill across the lake. He was so still Josh felt he'd gone away. "Broken stone," he said at last, "all that's left of a broken people."

His mother was in the truck and he was tossing pebbles on the street, looping them with a splash into a pothole, when his father came out of McGee's. There was a round brown bag in his hand. He guessed he knew what that would be.

"Get in the truck," his father said.

"Aren't we going to eat at Wong's?"

"In the truck."

When he opened the door, his mother slid quickly out so that he could take the middle seat.

"I thought we were going to Wong's," he said, "for a treat."

His mother looked at his father. "No," she said, "I guess we're going home."

"Bloody rights we're going home." His father started the truck with a roar of the motor, gunned it away from the curb, spraying slush and snow onto the sidewalk. He hit the brakes while it was rolling backwards, ground the gears into low, took off with wheels spinning.

What was he so mad about? Josh wondered. Then he smelled the whisky. He could see his father's lower lip clamped between his teeth. He hoped his mother would be quiet. He looked at her, her face impassive, her eyes on the road ahead.

"Well, what did you get at the Co-op?"

"Everything on the list," she said. Her voice was quieter than his, but it sounded just as angry.

"What else?"

Josh noticed her hands clenched in her lap, one thumb rubbing against the other. She better tell the truth, he thought. "Shampoo," she said, "and hair conditioner. It was half price."

"Can't you just use soap?"

"Douglas," she said, "be reasonable."

Easy, Mom, he thought, you better watch it.

"Come on – what else?"

She glanced down at the boy before she spoke. "I bought a box of pencil crayons."

"You going to be an *arrteest* too?"

"For Josh."

"Yeah, and how much did that set us back?"

He saw his mother glance over at his father, then turn back to gaze out the front window. There was nothing to see but open road and empty fields, a few shrunken, dirty snow drifts clinging to the ditch. "Twelve ninety-eight," she said, her voice firm and clear.

"For crayons! My God, woman, that's ridiculous." The boy ducked back, closed his eyes when his father's hand moved in front of him. No, he prayed, please no. The only sound was the drone of the motor, the hum and bump of tires on the road. He opened one eye, saw his father's finger pointing, shaking at his mother. She had turned away, her head toward the side window.

"No bloody wonder we're always in the hole." But his voice was calm now, he no longer sounded angry. It was as if he'd just won something, though the boy couldn't have said what. "Let's have some music," his father said, jabbing a finger at the radio. On the remaining ten miles home they listened to the whine of country music, the chatter of the disc jockey. No one in the truck said a word.

Just before they turned off the gravel at the farm, his father began to sing along with a Garth Brooks song, changing the chorus as he sang: "I've got friends with gross faces / When they blow their nose, the snot chases / the girls away!"

When the boy grinned, his mother turned away.

He wanted to try the pencil crayons, but he thought it might be smarter to leave them in the grocery bag. From the desk where he was sketching an Indian pony he could see his father lying on the chesterfield, his head propped up on three pillows. One hand lay on the floor beside the bottle, which stood upright and uncapped, still in its brown paper bag. "Rustle us up some supper, will you, babe?" his father said.

His mother appeared in the kitchen doorway, an apron around her waist. She looked down at his father and shook her head. "I'll hop right to it," she said, her voice quiet. And sarcastic, the boy thought. She better not get that way.

"I'll set out the dishes," he said, pushing his chair back from the desk.

"You," his father said, "can come here. And bring those pencil crayons with you."

"I haven't got them," he said, too quickly he realized. His father might not be finished yet.

"Well, get them." His father didn't move on the chesterfield. "A bright boy like you – an *arrteest* – can probably figure where they are."

He hurried into the kitchen, almost bumped his mother at the sink.

"Relax," she said. "He isn't mad at you."

He already knew that. Which was why he was worried now.

She sighed and nodded at the bags on the warped plywood cutting board. "They're in the small bag."

He carried the crayons into the other room, held them out toward the chesterfield. His father raised his head to look at the package in his hand.

"How many?"

"What?" He could feel his voice quaver.

His father slowly swung his feet onto the floor, slowly raised himself into a sitting position, stared all the while at the boy. "How many in the bloody package?"

He studied the writing on the cardboard. It was shaking in his hand. He took a breath, kept his voice steady. "Ten," he said.

"Over a buck apiece," his father said. He reached out, took the package from the boy's hand.

The boy glanced past his father's shoulder, saw his mother watching from the kitchen doorway, an empty bowl dangling in her hand. He was surprised when she spoke.

"They're special," she said, talking fast. "Like watercolours, but in pencil form. I thought they'd help him at the workshop."

His father's voice was calm. "You thought," he said.

The boy was staring at his mother, watching the way she was turning the bowl around and around in her hands.

"Look at me," his father said. "What's your favourite colour?"

What was he supposed to say? "I don't know. Blue, I guess."

"You guess." His father peeled the cellophane from the package with his broad thumbnail, flipped open the lid, shook the pencils till they slipped half out of the package. He extracted one pencil, held it toward the boy. "This blue?" he asked.

"I guess so."

His father nodded at the pencil in his burly hand. "Take it," he said. "Now break it."

There was a crash, glass shattering in the kitchen doorway. His father never budged. "Sweep that up," he said, his voice rising only slightly. "Every sliver of it. We wouldn't want the boy to cut his feet when he comes down to pee." His father was smiling now. "I'll deal with you later." The boy was sure he meant his mother, but his father never took his eyes from him. "I said break it."

The boy took the blue pencil in both hands, but his hands were shaking so badly he couldn't snap the pencil.

"What a pussy," his father said. "Sit down. Here. Beside me."

The boy shrank onto the chesterfield, tried to make himself as small as possible, to keep a space between him and his father.

"Break it across your knee."

He held the pencil at each end, closed his eyes, brought the pencil sharply down on his knee. He felt his knee sting, heard the pencil crack, knew he held a piece in either hand, knew also that he was going to cry.

"Now the rest of them," his father said.

When they finished supper, pancakes again, but no sausages, his father leaned back in his chair, yawned and stretched. The boy saw his mother glance beside his plate at the bottle still inside the brown paper bag. His father, too, saw what she had looked at. "Before we're done," he said, "I'll just have me another drink." He poured amber liquid into his glass, filled it perhaps a quarter full. He lifted the glass towards the bare bulb that hung from the ceiling, gave it a little swirl, and said, "Here's to *arrteests.*" He was smiling, enjoying himself, the boy could see.

The boy's mother pushed back her chair, reached for his plate.

"You can do the dishes later," his father said. He brought the glass slowly to his lips, took a long drink, his adam's apple bobbing twice, set the glass with a snap on the table. His smile was even wider now.

The boy felt his hands begin to shake, shoved them under the table, held them still between his knees. He tried not to watch his father, but he couldn't take his eyes off him.

"Now," his father said, slowly putting both hands on the table, palms down, "I've told you before we can't afford luxuries. When you going to get that through your skull?"

The boy looked at his mother. She had her head down, staring at the floor, waiting. Please, he thought, please, don't.

His father's chair squeaked on the floor. He was standing up.

"Maybe this'll remind you."

The boy rose from his chair. "No!" he said. Loud and firm. Then his hand was at his mouth as if somehow he could stuff the word back inside.

"No?" He felt his father grab his arm above the elbow, squeeze and squeeze, lift him and shove him back into his chair. "Listen, buster, you best learn whose side you're on. And learn it fast." His father dropped him back into the chair, his arm throbbing. "Now I'm going to make a point to your mother. You got any argument with that?"

"No, sir."

"I thought not," his father said, smiling once more. His father stepped around the table, paused beside his mother who stood waiting, still holding a plate. "I said I'd deal with you later." He slowly raised his hand, the smile like a stain on his mouth, his hand open, hovering perhaps twelve inches from her face.

The boy closed his eyes, but he couldn't close his ears. He heard the sound of the slap, the sickening crack of flesh on flesh. When he looked again, his mother's head was half turned away, her eyes closed, a gob of spittle hanging at the corner of her mouth. Already on her left cheek, he could see the red outline of his father's fingers.

"I'm going into town," his father said. "I may be late. You can make my breakfast when I get up, but don't wake me. Understand?"

The boy thought he saw her head nod, but he wasn't sure.

Now his father was looking at him.

"The crayons stay in the garbage," he said. "And you leave your mother do the dishes by herself."

They heard his father start the truck and drive away, the quiet like a fog rolling slowly back around the farm. Still his mother stood motionless by the table. Finally, she gave her head a little shake and said, "I'm going to the washroom." Her voice was so quiet he could barely hear her. He thought she looked embarrassed, or maybe ashamed.

When she came out, he could see that she had washed the makeup from her face. There was the faint blue sign of an old bruise under her left eye, a red mark on her cheek, but her eyes were dry.

"I'm sorry," he said.

She stared at him a moment, her eyes steady on him as he sat huddled in the chair. "No," she said, "you've got nothing to be sorry for." She began to stack dishes from the table, set the syrup bottle on the top, turned away with the load in her hands. Paused, turned around. "I never thought he'd start on you," she said. She set the dishes back upon the table. Looked around the room. Her eyes settling on the telephone.

"Go upstairs," she said. "Fill a suitcase with your clothes. Everything you want to take."

"What?"

"You heard me. Josh," she added, her voice suddenly soft.

When he came downstairs, straining to walk straight against the weight of his suitcase, he saw his mother standing by the phone, both arms hanging at her sides. There was another suitcase by the front door. He stopped on the bottom step, watching his mother as she gazed around the room. The walls were bare except for three pictures, cheap reproductions that she had bought at Zeller's in the city. When he looked into the kitchen, he saw that she had removed his drawings from the fridge. He thought she looked incredibly sad. And somehow determined. He wished there was something he could do to help, to cheer her up.

"Mom," he said, "are you okay?"

"No. But I'm going to be." She nodded to his suitcase. "Set it beside mine." She turned slowly, her eyes going everywhere as if she were studying the room. "I phoned your grandpa. He'll be here in half an hour."

Her eyes settled on his father's homemade bookcase. It contained not books, but his father's Indian collection, a dozen arrowheads, a pair of worn and beaded buckskin moccasins, a flint knife, a stone hammer. The boy felt his lip begin to shudder, bit into it to keep from crying. But she was looking at the picture on the top shelf. Their wedding picture. Both of them so young, his big hand clasping her shoulder, a possessive smile on his face, her grinning as if the photographer had just told a joke that she didn't quite get.

She strode to the bookcase, picked up the picture, looked again around the room. Then she stepped to the table, lifted the syrup jar from the stack of dirty dishes, placed the picture face-down on the top plate, and set the syrup jar on top of it.

"Well," she said, "I've got everything I want to take." She pulled a chair away from the table and sat down to wait.

The boy wished his grandpa would hurry up. He didn't want his father coming back first. He didn't even want to think about it. He began to wander aimlessly about the room, running his fingers over the bookcase, the back of the chair, the desk where he sat to draw. Soon he was at the waste basket. His mother saw him standing there.

"If you want those pencil crayons," she said, "you'd better get them now." Her voice was dull as mud.

He pulled the package from the tin pail, began to shove the broken pencils back inside. She was so sad, he had to cheer her up. Then he knew what to do.

"Mom," he said as he held the last piece of pencil in his hand, "I can sharpen them. I'll have twenty pencils then."

When he turned to look at her, she was bent over in the chair, both fists jammed into her eyes.

HALF THE SKY

(for R.)

JUDITH KRAUSE

All she can see, with her left eye swollen shut, jaw wired. She sits on the hospital steps, trying to decide whether to spend the ten dollars in her purse on a taxi home or walk the sixteen blocks, her leg still not quite healed from the last time, ribs sore but not broken from his kicking. The cops say leave or you're dead meat, the counsellors say don't go back, but her kids want to go home. They're too old for the shelter.

Tonight her face is as mottled as the evening sky, all purple and pink, and she knows once she gets home, he'll take the ten dollars or hock her wedding ring again. He's the only man she's lived with, ever since she left home at 13 and now, at 29, her hair falling out, nails bitten to the quick, her kids won't take sides, won't even call 911 if they think she started it.

DEAR WEBSTER

Dedicated to Beth Brant

(CONNIE FIFE)

savage *(sav'ij) adj. without civilization; primitive, barbarous*
(a savage tribe) n. a member of a preliterate society having a primitive
way of life; a fierce, brutal person

i am the one who talks with the mountains
when i am not sliding down the stream of its face/
i am the one who walks the streets late at
night despite the danger
believing that this land is mine to roam freely/
i am the one who carved a mask from a thick tree
then wore it/
i am the one who raises her arms to the sun
then takes flight on winds from the east/
i am the one who says "no more"
then leaves the man whose fists have reconstructed
my bones/
i am the one who defies the narrow definition of love
and loves another woman
and heals a nation in doing so/
i am the one who meeting after meeting turns
away when men misconstrue my words
and goes on/
i am the one whose stories take our collective
pasts into the future

FIFE

Dear Webster

and guarantees that not one day is left behind/
i am the one sleeping on sidewalks
who speaks to all my relations as the masses
hear only their own silence/
i am the one who cradles close to her breasts
small children
and women who were old before they were young/
i am the one who shoots fire into the veins of those
who cannot reignite their own sparks
then gives them the responsibility of stocking
the wood/
i am the one who talks to herself and hears
others answer
then writes it down so that the words remain in
my throat/
i am the one who demonstrates against forced
relocation
and uses a shotgun to carry the message clean home/
i am the one who watched as my children's hair
was cut
and cried and wept then screamed "return them"/
i am the one struggling to find her way back
i am the one who uses brushes to paint my resistance
on a canvas
then hangs my tapestry across the horizon/
i am the one whose son died of AIDS while a piece
of myself died each day and couldn't halt either
then buried my child/
i am the one who was raped by my father then
my uncle
and spent years hiding then decided to change it all
and used all my rage to castrate my memory of them
and healed myself with love/
i am the one who late at night screams and howls
and hears voices answer/
i am the one whose death was intended
and didn't die

DAS ENGELEIN KOMMT

(GERTRUDE STORY)

When my sister Elsa was a baby she was an angel and my father called her das Engelein. At our house people never spoke in German. My mother would not allow it. Only my father ever did, and we children could hardly understand him. I should not say me. I will tell you later. It was the fury of his life having non-German children. One of the furies. He had several. The Brotherhood of Man was another. My father loved the Brotherhood of Man with an ardent, vocal passion.

He loved his daughters, too, I suppose, but they never knew it. He loved his son, and his daughters knew it. He loved him like Isaac loved Jacob or like Abraham his Isaac. My father never sacrificed his Floydie on any altar; never even tried to. But he killed his daughters a thousand times over, and this is the story of the last time he killed my sister Elsa in her snow-white Engelein gown, her wings spread and ready to soar at the church Christmas concert one year in the sandy, dry, hard farming district where we used to live.

It had to be in German. That whole church concert had to be in German. Some of the kids did OK; they had mothers who hardly spoke English. In that community the fathers went out into the world and did the business and learned to speak the language of business. The mothers stayed home and plucked geese, and made quilts and perogies and babies, and crooned them to sleep with Komm' Herr Jesu, and sent them there with a few slaps to the ear if the child went unwilling.

So it was at our house, too. Except for the German and the Jesu. My mother didn't believe in either one. She had had it different at home. Her father was just as German as anybody else in that settlement but his mind had a different order. His daughter was to go to Normal School and be a teacher but she chose Papa instead. No wonder, I suppose. Papa was tall and black and imposing and he courted every woman in the district atop his large white stallion, taking them for rides into the hills to show them the wood violets.

I think the violets stopped when my mother agreed to come into his kitchen, but his passions did not. At least I know we had violin and lots of talk and booming laughter when the neighbours came, and cold lips and steel-blue eyes when they left again.

It was a hard life in a lot of ways, but this is not that story. I tell it to you this way, though, because it is very hard, at fifty, to keep it going well. To keep the order. I've had too many other voices inside my head for so long and Papa bellering from his bed, after Mama died and the third white stallion threw him, for tea and beef broth and a pen to write his newest orders.

Papa was a difficult man. He lived for too many years. I looked after him for twenty-three of them. Mama, I think now sometimes, almost had it easy. She spoke back, you see, and the hate did not gather, black and hard and festering, around her heart as it did mine.

But I want to tell you about Elsa. I think that is what she means me to do when she comes now and stands by my side when I am writing away the blackness and drinking the coffee Papa forbade in this house because it repelled him. She has been dead thirty-eight years now, I counted it out today, and I suppose she has forgotten how to speak. On account of not knowing the sacred language, ha ha, I never believed it. Papa used to say it was all in German up there, a German preacher once told him.

For all these years I was careful not to care, but now I see that Elsa did not even go there. She couldn't have. The church says not, and they should be right on some things; it is too terrible otherwise to try to live.

But all these years I thought it was an accident and I'm sure Papa did, too. But I think now Mama knew. I do not want to do the thinking sometimes, there is a danger in it, but I think now she knew because it raised a real uproar the way she went to bed and stayed there the day it happened and wouldn't get up for the funeral.

But that's ahead of it again. I need the order. It is harder than to have it in your head and know it, this setting of it down. Once I wanted to be a writer and read King Arthur over and over until I knew the order of telling things, but now I cannot keep it straight.

It goes like this though. We always went to church. All but our mother. Papa said we had to go to church and learn the glory; it was not safe to live in this world otherwise. And the glory was only good if it came in German. It was holy that way. It was important because it had to do with Christus and the angels and your holy German soul. The words you spoke in the old tongue, he said, helped to get you the glory.

That pastor, I knew him, said so, and Papa believed him, but our mother didn't. She said it was a peasant's attitude and it was either all true in any language or it was not all true and maybe none of it true and so what, it didn't put bread on the table; but you sure couldn't break it up into German and English and French, it wasn't logical. And Papa said what was logical was if she allowed his daughters to speak German at the supper table, but the Schroeders seemed to be such English bootlickers it seemed to be more than a man could expect to have the old tongue spoken around his own fireside. And our mother said it seemed to be Schroeder money brought the coal to keep the fire going in it. And Papa said, Yes, yes, rub it in; and he took his box full of blue socialist tracts and saddled his white stallion with the red wild eyes and rode to Elmyra Bitner's to discuss the Brotherhood of Man.

And Mama would scrub hard at the fading red apples on the oilcloth on the kitchen table and make mouths at the way the corners were wearing through and she'd say, Come on girls, we'll make brown sugar fudge tonight.

And our mother made brown sugar fudge with butter and walnuts most nights he did that. And sometimes when my sister Elsa peered too long into the night from the kitchen window, straining to see his white stallion coming back out of the dark night my mother would say, Don't be silly, girl, do you think a bear will get him or something, he's only gone to get educated, come on and we'll make ourselves some popcorn.

But Elsa wouldn't. She just turned her back on our mother and went and rearranged Papa's pipes neatly beside the family picture taken when there was only Papa and our mother and Elsa and me because our sister Laura already lived just at Grampa Schroeder's, she had to, Papa said she was not his child. I hope that is the order. It seems to fit here. Laura is important; she got lost in a different way. And while Elsa looked at herself being an Engelein in the family picture on the sideboard our mother and I would pop popcorn, shelling it first, plink-plank into a pan off the cob first, and heating the heavy iron frying pan on the back of the stove while we did.

Not Floydie, though. Floydie was a boy and anyway he was young and fast asleep by that time of the night. But Elsa would only pick away at her bowlful now and again and when Mama said, Come on, eat up, it's just the way you like it, Elsa would get that tight look around her eyes and say, No, I'm saving it for Floydie. And Mama would say, He's spoiled enough, and Elsa would say, You don't like anybody, do you? And she'd go back to the window and look some more for Papa and his stallion and she only left her place when Floydie cried and then she always ran to him before Mama could go.

And yet Floydie was the reason, I don't care, why Elsa had to look out into the dark night for Papa with her pink barn-goose eyes that got teary from too much watching. And Floydie was the reason Grampa Schroeder got so mad he kept giving our mother money to buy us girls new dresses for the school picnic and the church concert. Floydie was Papa's Sunny Boy Cereal and Elsa used to be his Engelein, but now she was just a girl who had grown a long Schroeder neck and couldn't do arithmetic.

She couldn't learn her German piece, either. For the church Christmas concert you had to learn to speak a piece in German, no matter what. You had to or your folks were shamed forever. Even my mother went to the church Christmas concert. It was called the Tannenbaum and nobody missed going. It was holy, and not even the littlest ones expected to see Santa.

It was as if to say the white light of Jesus shone those nights. The church was lit with candles. Not even the coal oil lamps were lit and certainly not the gas mantel lanterns with their piercing twin eyes. Only candles were holy.

And that year, that last year, Elsa said she wanted to be an angel. An angel in German yet, and with twenty-eight lines to speak. When Pastor asked who would take the part Elsa's hand shot up and it surprised me. Elsa was not that way. She would rather not speak, even in English, and to do anything in German killed her.

Especially to speak to Papa. When you have been an Engelein and aren't any longer, to stand before Papa and say Ihr Kinderlein kommet, zur Bethlehem Stall into his pale slough-ice eyes doesn't help to make your wings grow, and if you're one to have the wings clipped you know this is the right order to say it.

Kinderlein, not Kidderlein, Papa told her. Baytlah-hem, not Bethlehem; what do you want to put a thuh in it for? The people will think you're not raised right. Now start the first verse again from the beginning and stand straight and speak it right. Twenty-eight lines only, a big girl like you, and you can't even learn it.

Hellslänzendem was the word that did it. Hellzadem, Elsa said. Who wouldn't? It's hard in German to get all the zeds and enns and urrs in, and lots of times the Germans don't even care when they talk it. But when it comes to their kids, watch out, they're supposed to all speak like preachers.

I talked German in my head all the time. Nobody knew it. One of the voices in my head was a German man and he told jokes sometimes in German on the pastor when church went on too long. Hier ist mir ein alter Fart, he'd say sometimes, and I would try not to smile; to smile was dangerous. And the voice would tell me to go look up Fart in Papa's German dictionary when we got home. But we never touched Papa's books, that was dangerous, too, and I would have if I'd wanted, but I didn't want to care about it.

Elsa cared too much. It was dangerous. Day by day she sewed on her Engelein costume, looking quite often at the picture on the sideboard. She sewed in the parlour where you weren't supposed to use thread because it worked itself into the carpet. Mama told her she could sit there when she caught her sewing at four o'clock in the morning once by the kitchen lamp. Its flame flickered pale and yellow.

Silly goose, Mama told her, it's too hard on the eyes and I could do it on the machine in a minute. But Elsa only turned her back on Mama, pretending she was looking for the scissors, and said, I want to do it. And she'd show Papa after supper how it was coming and he's say, yes, yes, yes, but you're not gonna spend your life in a dress factory, how's the piece coming? And Elsa would stand there and speak, one angel wing drooping. Bei des Lichtleins hellzadem she'd get to and Papa would look up and say, Hellslänz -, hellslänz -, put the zed in it; how come you can't remember; people will think you aren't raised right.

And then he'd call Floydie to him for a game of clap-handies and Mama would say from the parlour door, Come work in the kitchen, the light's better. But Elsa would take her piece out of her apron pocket where she kept it to learn even in the toilet, I saw her once, and her mouth made the words but she did not say them out loud and she watched Papa and Floydie whenever they laughed until Papa said, You could likely learn better in the kitchen. And then she folded her piece up and put it in her pocket and went.

And on the Tannenbaum night she spoke it pretty well, so I don't know why Papa had to do it. The candles were lit in the church and you could almost smell the glory and people shook hands with everybody they could reach even after they got sitting down in the pews, the fat ones straining hard over their chests to shake with ones sitting behind them.

Grown-ups even shook with two-year-olds, and graced each other fröhliche Weihnachts whether you were mad at each other or not. And you could smell the Jap oranges from the brown paper bags, each one packed two man's hands full of peanuts and almonds and striped Christmas candy made into curlicues almost the size and shape of Floydie's new bow tie, and each one with two Jap oranges at the bottom so that you had to dig through all the other good stuff if you wanted to eat them first. Germans never were stingy when it was nuts and candy and they had the money.

Only we were never allowed to open our bags until we got home. But that night we girls were wearing our new dresses Grampa Schroeder had given the money for and Floydie looked like a prince, true enough, like Papa said, in his royal blue breeches and snow-white shirt with the ruffles. And Mama looked nice and came along to the concert and people graced her, too, and only a few made remarks like, Well at least we see you Christmas. So it was all good, very good, for once, and Elsa spoke up, spoke right up Ihr Kinderlein kommet only with not enough zeds and enns in it. But she spoke it clear and good, her eyes shining and her hands folded and looking up into the candelabra so that her eyes became two candles, too. But the trouble was, her one wing dropped because she would not let Mama help her sew.

And Mrs. Bitner said afterwards to Papa, Now Floydie, you tell that wife of yours I got time on my hands I could help her next Chrissmas with the kids' costooms if she wants. And Mama was standing right there and Mrs. Bitner turned to her next and graced her and maybe never knew her, Mama hardly ever came to church, but Mama said later she did.

And Papa said it didn't matter, why worry about that, the point was people thought they weren't raised right, how come she let the kid show up with a costume like that, it wasn't the first time, either. We were on the way home and the horses' hooves sounded crispcrunch on the hard-packed snow of the road, and the traces jingled like bells although Papa wouldn't put brass bells on the harness like a lot of men did, he said it was frippery. And I tried to think about the Jap oranges and how they'd be when we got home and Papa let us open our bags. I had to think hard about them; to think about Elsa's drooping wing was too dangerous.

But when we got home and Papa had carried Floydie inside and us girls and Mama had our coats off and all, Elsa wouldn't even open her bag. And Mama was undressing Floydie fast asleep on the kitchen table, and Mama had one eye on Elsa sitting silent on a hard chair by the Quebec heater with her piece in her hand, and Mama looked real nice, very nice, she hardly ever dressed up.

And Papa came up behind her, his fur coat and hat still on because he still had to go out and do the horses. And he laid his hand on Mama's shoulder and said, It's always better after church. And he showed his hard white even teeth under his silky smooth moustache, he was a very good looker always. And Mama just picked Floydie up and walked out from under his hand and said over her shoulder, Elmyra Bitner has time on her hands I hear.

And Papa turned quick to the door and stepped on the paper bag with the costumes in it, I guess I should not have left it there. And he kicked at the bag and it split and the Engelein costume got tangled in his church overshoes and he grabbed it and threw it in the corner and didn't bother putting on his barn boots because he knew he wasn't going to the barn, I guess. And he drove out the yard, the harness traces clanging no rhythm, no whatsoever rhythm, because the horses were going too hard, and it was too cold for their lungs to go hard. Like Grampa Schroeder said, Papa was not much good on horses.

And Mama came out of the bedroom and picked up the Engelein costume and said, Never mind, Grampa said you looked real pretty. And Elsa grabbed the costume out of her hands and scrunchled it all up tight and held it to her and went to the window to strain her eyes into the night to see Papa going.

And there was no moon.

And that night, before Papa got home from Elmyra Bitner's, Elsa took the key to the box stall and went in to the stallion. And Papa found her when he got home. And afterwards he would not even sell the stallion.

And when we moved to town a little later because Grampa Schroeder said so, he kept it at Elmyra Bitner's and went out from town Sundays to go to German church and ride his snow white stallion.

The words are said now. They are in order I think and it does not seem too dangerous to have them down on paper. And Elsa does not speak yet, but I somehow think, now the words are all in order, if I just sit here and do not rearrange them, and think very hard on Papa, that she will nod and go.

6. A THOUSAND SUPPERLESS BABES

Indoctrination of the Natives, Celina Ritter

Mixed media, 99.0 x 122.1 cm, 1990

Although the writing in this section deals with many problems, including the central issue of racism, it is possible to find both comfort and compensation. Louise Bernice Halfe says, "When I was sent to Blue Quills Residential School, I was robbed of family. Memory and love of my grandparents have served to provide me with stories." She goes on, "For in memory, spirit lives. 'The Residential School Bus' is an important piece of recorded history. We must remember if our communities are to heal." Stories are great healers, and grandmothers are one crucial source. As Maria Campbell says, "Grandmothers are a very important part of Metis life and one can hardly tell a story without grandmother making an appearance, be it in physical or spiritual form. Grandmothers are at the heart of our families and communities." For Kim Morrissey, "If we are to continue as a nation, we must be proud of all our grandmothers, and not only allow them to speak, but be proud of their history." As SUNTEP Theatre discovered in the creation of their play, "the magic began as the students shared stories and photographs from their own families and took on the roles of their grandparents and great-grandparents." For "Stories are gifts. They last forever. They tell us who we are."

GRANNIE DUBUQUE

Excerpt from Halfbreed

(MARIA CAMPBELL)

Our new place was a big frame house with a kitchen and pantry, living room and bedroom on the main floor, and two bedrooms upstairs. It looked bare because we had nothing to put inside it. In the kitchen there was an old square table which Daddy rebuilt to accommodate all of us, a couple of benches, a cupboard, an old wood stove which never worked properly, an old washstand and woodbox. The living room had nothing except Dad's rocking chair. He made beds for all of us with old boards, and we had our mattresses from home filled with fresh straw.

Dad ploughed a big garden for me and I organized the little ones to weed and hoe. They picked berries too, and by fall I had filled every one of three hundred jars bought at an auction sale. When the berries and vegetables were finished, I canned moose meat. It was packed into jars, salted, and then boiled for three hours in the washtub.

We got a housekeeper that fall, a young Indian girl who was able to get along with and manage the little ones fairly well. School began in September and for the first time everyone had new jeans, shirts, and shoes, sent by Grannie Dubuque. She had been too ill after Momma's death to help us in any way.

School was heaven to me, at first, because I could be young for a few hours each day. I could forget the cooking and cleaning at home and there was time to read. I read everything I could find and thought about the big cities I had read about with good food and beautiful clothes, where there was no poverty and everyone was happy. I would go to these cities someday and lead a gay, rich, exciting life.

Our teacher was a young woman from a good, middle-class Christian family. She was ambitious and wanted to have a large farm and fine house, but her husband liked to drink, dance, and run around. She had different moods – sometimes she was very prim and proper, and sometimes just the opposite, and I realize now that these were often caused by personal problems.

We were the first Halfbreeds she had taught and although she tried to hide her prejudices, she was often cruel. Then she would feel guilty about her outbursts and overwhelm us with kindness. During class she would often ridicule us for mistakes. Peggie was in the first grade, a very small six-year-old, timid and shy. Because we used a mixture of Cree and English at home, her pronunciation was poor. The teacher would shake her and say to the class, "Look at her! She is so stupid she can't even say 'this,' instead of 'dis.'" She would make Peggie stand up at the front of the room for an hour, without moving. She grew so afraid of school that she would cry and wet her bed at night.

During a ten-minute health program in the mornings, one of the pupils had to check everyone for clean hands and neck, brushed teeth and so on. The student called out our names and when she said "Maria Campbell," I stood up. "Did you brush your teeth?" We never brushed our teeth, but I answered, "Yes." Robbie was always getting X's as his fingernails were never clean and his hands were chapped and dirty. One day, the teacher found his ears dirty again and told him that if he wasn't clean tomorrow, she would clean him up properly. Robbie washed well the next morning but forgot to do his ears. So she took him to the cloakroom and with a scrub brush – the kind you use on floors – started scrubbing his hands, neck and ears. We all sat still for a long time, waiting for her to finish. Soon I heard Robbie whimpering and became alarmed. He had always been a real toughie, and if he cried he was really hurt. I went into the cloakroom. She had him bent over the basin, his poor little neck was bleeding and so were his wrists. She was starting on his ears with the brush when I snatched it away and slapped her. We got into a fight and Jamie finally pulled me away and took us all home. I was so angry I would have killed her if I had found something to smash her head. Jamie went to get Daddy, as I was sure we had all been expelled, while I put salve on Robbie's scrapes. Daddy came home accompanied by Mr. Grey, and when Dad saw Robbie he got very angry. Mr. Grey told him to quieten down and that he would call a Board meeting that night. The teacher never bothered us again, and in fact, tried her best to be nice. In time my brothers and sisters forgot and even liked her, but I never forgot or became friendly.

There was no work after harvest was finished, so Daddy decided to trap until Christmas as we were getting short of everything. He left us in November with enough food to last until his return, but we ran out of flour and staples early in December. It was really cold that year and we had more snow than usual. We knew that Daddy could not be home for two or three weeks, so we decided to go to the store at our old home, twenty-five miles away, where we could buy on credit. It was an icy, snowy day. Our housekeeper was afraid that we might freeze, but we assured her that we knew what we were doing. Jamie got the team ready and, with Robbie, put the hayrack on the sleigh so that we would have plenty of room. We loaded it up with an old armchair and mattresses, then put the little ones on the chair, with hot stones wrapped in blankets at their feet. We decided to go on an old trail across country as it was shorter than the main road. (I don't know what possessed us, for we certainly knew better.) About five miles from the house, the snow started to blow and we lost the trail. Soon the horses were up to their bellies in drifts and I knew we were lost.

The children were getting cold and started to cry. I realized what could happen to us and started to panic, but Jamie remained calm and told me not to be scared or the little ones would be frightened. He finally found a fence and followed it, leading the horses back to the road. We were lucky to get home with only frozen cheeks and fingers.

So, we had nothing to eat except canned meat and berries and a little flour. Christmas was coming and we could not even bake a cake. The blizzard lasted nearly a week and we were afraid for Daddy. We did not want to go to Mr. Grey, as he might call the relief people, so whenever he stopped to see us, we told him that we were getting along fine.

Robbie caught a very bad chest cold on that trip and it grew worse each day. Finally, his fever was so high that he went completely out of his mind and could hardly breathe. I remembered that Momma and Cheechum used to make broth from bark of green poplar for colds, and that they boiled certain roots for fever. Jamie went out and got me some bark and roots and for three days we fed Robbie as much broth as he could swallow. It was bitter stuff. We bathed him with cool water and finally the fever broke; but it was awhile before he could get out of bed.

By now I was sure that we would never see Daddy again. Our food was nearly all gone, the house was drafty and cold, the younger kids were sick, and Christmas was only one day away. Jamie told me, "We're going to get ready for Christmas because Daddy will be home tonight. He always comes home on Christmas Eve." He cut a tree and we decorated it with pine cones as there was nothing else, not even crepe paper. The angel and the few ornaments which belonged to Mom were set aside for Daddy to put up. I was very depressed that whole day and evening, and worried what to tell the little ones if Daddy didn't get home. Jamie and I were still up, when shortly after midnight, Daddy came walking in. He had bags of groceries and big boxes of gifts. Later, when we were in the kitchen having tea, he handed me a small bag. Inside were two hundred and fifty dollars. He told me to buy clothes for everyone after Christmas and whatever else was needed.

Christmas was a sad time, even if Daddy was home. He tried to make us happy, but in spite of all our efforts we were a lonely family. Our people were too far away to visit and we missed the excitement and love we shared at home with them. We sat down and tried to eat Christmas dinner, but the roast beef and new toys couldn't replace what we had known. We had never eaten beef before and we found it flat and flavourless. The new toys broke the first day; we had always had handmade gifts that lasted forever. Poor Daddy, it seemed that the harder he tried, the rougher it all became.

Grannie Dubuque arrived during the holidays and we were so happy to see her. She expected us to be poor, but I don't think she expected what she saw. She cried as she kissed us all and because we were so starved for a woman's affection and love, we almost overwhelmed her.

Everything went back to its old order of peace and quiet. The little food we had tasted better, our endless sewing and mending seemed like fun; and above all, we older ones had someone who would put her arms around us close if we were hurt.

Grannie was kind and gentle like Mom, but where Mom had been quiet, she was noisy and full of fun. She would cook our dinner, then tell us that we were having chicken-à-la-king – whatever that was – and we would set the table with an old sheet taken from a bed and pretend we were rich. We would taste all the fancy salads and dishes she'd prepared, though of course they were only meat, potatoes, bannock, lard, and tea.

Grannie was a very strict Catholic and the greatest story-teller in the world. Every evening, after work was done, she made each of us a cup of cocoa and some popcorn, and then gathered us around her and told stories of the northern lights (ghost dancers), of Almighty Voice, Poundmaker, and other famous Indians. We heard many spine-chilling tales, but we asked for one story in particular over and over again.

It was about an only child whose parents were older people.

The little girl was very spoiled and was forever whining and crying. She died of a sickness when she was only six years old. A couple of days after the burial her parents discovered her hand sticking out of the grave. They went to the priest who told them that this was their punishment for spoiling her, and that if they wanted the little girl to rest in peace and go to heaven they must take a switch and whip her hand as they should have done when she was living. So each day they did this until the hand was gone. In its place was a little rosary to show that the child had gone to heaven. We were always scared and spooked when Grannie told this story. One night a figure came crashing through the window behind her chair. Glass flew everywhere as we screamed and raced from the room with Grannie right behind us. Soon we heard moaning, and Jamie peeked in. Poor Robbie was sprawled on the floor, cut and bleeding. He had slipped away from the storytelling and was trying to sneak out from the upstairs window on a rope. Somehow his pants caught and when he kicked loose, he slid down the rope too fast and hit the window. What a fright he gave us! Grannie laughed until she cried as she washed him off and I put cardboard over the window.

THE RESIDENTIAL SCHOOL BUS

LOUISE BERNICE HALFE

A yellow caterpillar,
it swallows them up.

The little brown ones their stained
faces in the windows   skinny and thick
black braids   pressing hands
grease the glass.

On its back the caterpillar
carries hand-sewn canvas bags.

Outside against the evening sun
the mothers, the fathers,
shrink.

They cannot look
at the
yellow caterpillar.

♦ ♦ ♦

The building is huge
with long white empty hallways.

A child walks softly
the echo runs ahead of her.

The smell of Lysol
and floor wax
overwhelms the memory of woodsmoke
and dirt floors.

◆ ◆ ◆

At night the little ones
press their bodies
between cold starched sheets.
Somewhere
someone
in the huge dorm
sobs quietly.

The child
clenches
two purple
suckers
underneath her pillow.

She won't eat them,
not for a
while.

◆ ◆ ◆

They line up for breakfast
and receive wonderful bowls of porridge.

She loves porridge.
Her mama always made her porridge.

She looks up and sees
her favourite brother.

Ivan's ears look like
two gliding hawks.
They've given him a crewcut.

Charlie the eldest brother
is in the big boys' room.
She doesn't see him
and doesn't care.

Her eyes linger on
Ivan. They smile.

She swallows
the porridge
that is stuck in her
throat.

✦ ✦ ✦

Geesuz
is always mad.

She sits too often
in the confessional.
She kneels too often
in front of geesuz.

✦ ✦ ✦

The vision box
collects people
and makes them dance.

She turns the buttons
and the dancing people
turn into black and white lines.

She kneels
in the corner.

The girl
with the mean stick
and fat mouth
hovers near her.
She's a
huge night moth
beating her wings
against the dance.

✦ ✦ ✦

They've arrived.
Wagonloads of
mothers, of fathers.

The children have been
berry picking.

Sister Treebow
is like that girl
with the big lips.

Sister's lips stick out
further. The arrival of
mothers, of fathers
makes her madder.

The children
stand around the corner
of the building
wondering whose
mother, whose father
was there.

She didn't want to hope.

Father Brown
in his long black dress
calls out names.

Times are scheduled.

In the bare parlour
they sit,
mother, father, Ivan
and her big brother.

Their stiff hugs,
she wants more
but can't.

The stiffness stays.

The glass between the parlour
and the hallway is marked
with grease-stained hands
and smudges of
rain.

◆ ◆ ◆

The yellow school bus
waits.

GRANDMOTHER

KIM MORRISSEY

you were born
into poplar and sand
dark dapples salt tears
in sweet autumn nights

your young girls are flushed
with the mark of spring mushrooms
rolled finger to thumb
darkening

their young men move to town
and they follow:

they learn to tell new friends they're French
bring their children at Christmas
high-cheekboned fair-haired

when you are old great-grandchildren
meet you on sidewalks
step aside pass
without speaking

Excerpt from

A THOUSAND SUPPERLESS BABES

The Story of the Metis

(SUNTEP THEATRE)

Honoré Jaxon was Louis Riel's secretary. For more than sixty years he col-lected and kept together literally tons of manuscripts and notes from Riel's life and the Metis Nation. He kept them in a New York apartment where he served as janitor until 1951 when he was evicted at the age of ninety. The documents went to the New York City dump.

INTRODUCTION

SONG: *"Honoré" by James Keelaghan (Song begins, then fade in sound of the street.)*

Honoré's huddled near East Fifty-third
His life in a pile not too far from the curb
It's come down to this place, but he's not too deterred
Honoré's huddled near East Fifty-third

Honoré sits on the Lower East Side
He's lost about everything except for his pride
A man with a vision the vision's denied
Honoré sits on the Lower East Side

They used to say Honoré wasn't all there
He'd a penchant for speeches and thousand-yard stares
They said that he'd fought when some halfbreeds rebelled
Sometimes he would weep and he'd whisper "Riel"

STREET SCENE: *Three* WORKERS *haul boxes out from backstage and stack them along the front of the stage (perhaps as the audience is being seated). This is an open stage with other actors creating the atmosphere of a New York City street by entering and exiting as hawkers, vendors, buskers, hopscotchers, and just plain passers by. Quick mini-scenes occur between them, until someone somewhere blows a whistle and they freeze.*

THE NARRATOR: It's New York City, December 13, 1951, and it's very cold. This is a brownstone building on the Lower East Side of New York City, an apartment building where the janitor has just been fired. Ninety-year-old Honoré Jaxon has been fired because he's too old to do his job. The workers that you see are hauling out all of his possessions from the basement. It's going to take them six hours to haul three tons of material out onto this sidewalk in New York City. When they're done, there will be a pile of boxes 11 meters long, 3 meters high, and 2 meters deep. In those boxes is a lifetime of work, a dream that he had, to save all that he could of the history of the Metis people. And so, over his lifetime, he collected photographs, journals, articles, anything he could find, to keep the story of the Metis alive. So it's New York City, 1951, and the old janitor is in the hospital with pneumonia while all his life's possessions are being hauled out onto the street.... And sometimes he would weep and he would whisper "Riel."

SCENE: WORKERS

WORKER #1: I didn't know anyone could have so much garbage!

WORKER #2: Yeah, I can't believe the stuff this guy had. What a bunch of junk!

WORKER #3: It's gonna take forever to get this stuff out!

WORKER #1: Well, let's go for another load. *(#1 and #2 exit. #3 opens an old trunk and finds a dusty book. #1 and #2 return with another load.)*

WORKER #1: What are you doing?

WORKER #3: I found a book.

WORKER #2: A book about nothing, I suppose!

WORKER #3: Well...let's find out.

WORKER #1: Hey guys, let's have lunch, okay?

WORKER #2: Sounds great to me. *(They sit on boxes and open their lunch kits.)*

WORKER #1: What'd you bring for lunch?

WORKER #2: Sandwiches. I think I've got a coupla boiled eggs. Wanna sniff?

WORKER #1: No way!

WORKER #2: Oh, and a can of sardines. All right!

WORKER #3: Listen to this. "It is an incredible and moving story...." *(Voice fades as Narration begins.)*

SCENE ONE

NARRATION #1: It is an incredible and continuing story...the story of the Metis. It is a story that I, Honoré Jaxon, have dedicated my life to tell...in the hope that it shall serve as an example for the downtrodden of our world...and as a lesson to the privileged and powerful, that the voices of everyday people everywhere shall not be silenced...we shall be heard!

SCENE: WORKERS

WORKER #3: "We shall be heard!" There you go. What about that!

WORKER #2: What's he talking about?

WORKER #1 Who's the "Matey"?

WORKER #2: Yeah, really...who are the "Matey"?

WORKER #3: Listen. *(Reading.)* "You may indeed ask 'Who are the Metis?'".... There you go. Maybe if you sit down and listen long enough, your questions will be answered. *(Continues.)* "It is a question many have asked...." *(Fades.)*

NARRATION #2: It is a question that many have asked...a question that continues to be asked...a question that Metis people themselves will struggle to answer...if they are ever asked!

And so I have gathered about me a lifetime of work: the notes and diaries of my life among the Metis of St. Laurent and Batoche, the minutes of meetings that I recorded when I was secretary and friend to the great Louis Riel, the photographs and interviews and memories of my visits to Canada's North-West, and the secret stories that were told to me as I prepared to tell this story. A story that must be told. And so I will begin....

SCENE: WORKERS

WORKER #3: Sounds interesting, eh?

WORKER #2: Sounds like a bunch of garbage to me!

WORKER #1: Come on, let's get back to work.

WORKER #3: You guys finished lunch already?

WORKER #2: Yeah, lets go. *(#1 and #2 get up to leave.)*

WORKER #3: Well, I'm not quite done. I haven't had a chance to eat yet. I'll be right there. *(#1 and #2 exit. #3 continues reading.)* "The Metis people were created with one, and only one purpose in mind...."

SCENE TWO

NARRATION #3: The Metis people were created with one, and only one purpose, in mind – to serve the capitalist system.

As the fur trade expanded across this continent, the wealthy merchants of England and New France needed a labour force to do all the work. They needed men who would work long hours and the longest of days...who would travel long distances away from home and family...who would be instant friends of the Indians of the North-West.... And all of this for the lowest of pay. In their own words, they needed a colony of "very...useful...hands."

And so it was a carefully calculated plan that white traders should befriend Indian women, and raise their children to serve the wealthy fur merchants of the North-West and Hudson's Bay Companies...a ready-made working class, bred and born...to be exploited by the capitalists.

Many fur traders already had families in the East or in Europe...

TABLEAU *(Trader and family, facing audience.)*

NARRATION #4: ...but they were encouraged to take wives among the Indian women of the Northwest...and to start new families.

TABLEAU *(Mother and children have their backs to the camera.)*

NARRATION #5: Of course, these new families could not be allowed in the white forts and settlements...so most traders eventually went away and left them on their own.

TABLEAU *(Only mother and children, facing audience. Trader's chair is empty.)*

NARRATION#6: And that is how the Metis were...conceived.

* * *

SCENE ELEVEN

NARRATION #31: They are a great people, the Metis...the mixed blood people of the North-West. Like other people the world over they have survived all that governments and the wealthy have thrown against them. You see, this is not a world where justice is given freely. It is a world of injustice and oppression, where "a thousand babes go supperless to bed that one monster's brat may spew on silk."

At the age of 90 years, my story is nearly over, but the story of the Metis continues on. In my lifetime, I have seen no struggle that has touched my heart and spirit like that of the Metis. Their survival, their struggle for equality gives me great hope. And so I, Honoré Jaxon, ask that this book and all of my papers and photographs be given to the Metis people that they may teach each other, and others as well...of their great history.

WORKERS: FINAL SCENE

(Workers #1 and #2 enter with the last of the boxes, just as Worker #3 closes the book.)

WORKER #1: Well, that's it. That's the last of the boxes.

WORKER #2: Good thing too! I'm tired!

WORKER #1: Well, let's call it a day. I'm going home.

WORKER #2: Me too. I've had enough.

WORKER #3: What about all this stuff? All these boxes, these books, these photographs?

WORKER #1: What about them?

WORKER #2: It's not our problem anymore. The city will take care of all this stuff.

WORKER #3: What do you mean?

WORKER #1: It's all going to the dump. Where did you think it was going?

WORKER #3: But somebody must want it. They can't just throw all this away?

WORKER #2: Why not? It's just garbage. Who would want it?

WORKER #1: Come on, let's go. Let's call it a day. *(#1 and #2 begin to exit.)* Are you coming?

WORKER #3: *(Looks at all the boxes.)* Yeah...yeah, I'm coming. I'll be right there. *(Workers #1 and #2 exit. The music begins.)*

SONG: *"Honoré"* *(Final verses. Worker #3 looks at the boxes, then at the book in her hands. She opens the book, leafs slowly through it, then closes it and places it carefully on the pile of Honoré's lifetime of work. She turns slowly away and leaves. Before she exits, she turns for one last look at the "archives" and then exits. The song fades.)*

Honoré's buried in some pauper's grave
Of his archives there wasn't much to be saved

Forty-nine boxes of books hauled away
And a deed for some land in a place called Duck Lake

Honoré was all he said so it seems
The last act of life left him far from his dreams
They took it away it can't be redeemed
Honoré was all he said so it seems

NARRATOR: The lifetime of work of Honoré Jaxon, what he had dreamed would become an archives for the Metis people, was loaded onto a truck and hauled away to the New York City dump. Jaxon died less than one month later, on January 10, 1952.

SONG: *"Honoré"* (*Final chorus*)

They used to say Honoré wasn't all there
He'd a penchant for speeches and thousand-yard stares
They said that he'd fought when some halfbreeds rebelled
Sometimes he would weep and he'd whisper "Riel"
Sometimes he would weep and he'd whisper "Riel"

VOICES *(The actors enter, one at a time, to speak out-of-role to the audience.)*

VOICE #1: We do not mourn the loss of Honoré Jaxon's lifetime of work.

VOICE #2: Instead, we celebrate both his story and the story of the Metis people.

VOICE #3: Our history does not just lie on a shelf, or in books, or in a basement full of cardboard boxes.

VOICE #4: Our history lies in the stories that are told to us by our parents and grandparents. It lies within us.

VOICE #5: Stories are gifts. They last forever. And they tell us who we are.

VOICE #6: The history of the Metis lives on in the memories of its survivors. We are those survivors.

VOICE #7: My name is Angela Johns and I am the great-great-granddaughter of Isadore and Judith Dumont. I am very proud of how my family fought for our Metis rights.

VOICE #8: My name is Janet Goller....

VOICE #9: ...and I'm Celine Mauvieux. We are the great-great-granddaughters of Christine Pilon.

VOICE #8: We are very proud to pass on her stories.

VOICE #8 & 9: Our family heritage.

VOICE #10: My name is Leanne Lasher. I am the granddaughter of Philoman Pelletier Allary. My grandmother was a great lady in her community. Unfortunately, I didn't get a chance to meet her, but I know it's not too late to know about who she was.

VOICE #11: My name is Gina. I am the great-granddaughter of Alex and Angeline Gouldhawke. I know that my grandfather would be pleased to know his Metis grandchildren no longer have to hide on either side of the aisle.

VOICE #12: My name is Tracy and it's my grandmother's story about residential schools that I told. There are many stories coming out about residential schools and the life and times back then. There are still many to tell.

VOICE #13 (NARRATOR): My name is Ben. I am a Cree Metis from northern Manitoba. The word "Metis" has come to represent mixed-blood people all across Canada. Together we have many more stories to tell.

SONG: *"When This Valley" by Don Freed (As they sing, the cast frames the screen and the final photographs of Metis men, women, children, elders. The lights gradually fade to black. During the last verse, the cast moves slowly together and joins hands across the stage.)*

When this valley's no longer a wound that won't heal
When its story is well understood
Let infinity fly where the blue of the sky

Meets the green of the river and gold of the straw
In the valley of old St. Laurent.

When this valley was young it was peaceful and free
And its citizens were friends to all
If a stranger was cold or hungry or old
They were taken well care of by an unwritten law
In the valley of old St. Laurent.

When the names of its people are held to the heart
Of a land that was built of their blood
Shamrock, thistle, oak tree, sweetgrass, fleur des lis
All entwined in a braid a hanged poet foresaw
In the valley of old St. Laurent.

GOING TO WAR

PIERRE VANDALE

(arranged by Steven Michael Berzensky)

There was one fellow
going round to dances
and things like that
and he'd tell them:
I'LL HIRE YOU

And they'd sign up
or whatever
and they ask him:
WHAT FOR?

And he said:
FOR DOING NOTHING

And naturally
he'd...get them all
to sign these papers

So a lot got involved
in going to war

And they didn't know
why they were going
or where they were going

7. THE DOUBLE-HEADED SNAKE

Daft Molly Metcalfe, Marie Elyse St. George

Acrylic on board, 17.3 x 23.0 cm, 1989

The attempt to discover what Elizabeth Brewster calls "the atmosphere" of a place is here. That "atmosphere" can be filled both with beauty and with terror, as in Eli Mandel's poem:

> we have not yet learned
> what lives north of the river
> or past those hills that look like beasts

John Newlove's narrator counts "terror and fear among the greatest beauty." That beauty and terror are clearly visible in Marie Elyse St. George's image, which she painted to commemorate the life of Molly "and the lives of all exploited children." The terror of a deadly illness, the tuberculosis epidemic, faces sixteen-year-old Sandy every day in Veronica Eddy Brock's story. She survived, but many did not. Gary Hyland commemorates his "cousin Doreen, who died of tuberculosis when she was twenty-three and I was six. Much of the poem is true. I still have the lock of hair." Perhaps in the beauty of these words and images, in art itself, as in the "sweet singing" of John V. Hicks, we can find redemption.

FROM THE NORTH SASKATCHEWAN

ELI MANDEL

when on the high bluff discovering
the river cuts below
                        send messages
we have spoken to those on the boats

I am obsessed by the berries they eat
all night odour of Saskatoon
and an unidentifiable odour
something baking
                    the sun
never reaches the lower bank

I cannot read the tree markings
today the sky is torn by wind:
a field after a long battle
strewn with corpses of cloud

give blessings to my children
speak for us to those who sent us here
say we did all that could be done
we have not learned
what lies north of the river
or past those hills that look like beasts

THE DOUBLE-HEADED SNAKE

JOHN NEWLOVE

Not to lose the feel of the mountains
while still retaining the prairies
is a difficult thing. What's lovely
is whatever makes the adrenaline run;
therefore I count terror and fear among
the greatest beauty. The greatest
beauty is to be alive, forgetting nothing,
although remembrance hurts
like a foolish act, is a foolish act.

Beauty's whatever
makes the adrenaline run. Fear
in the mountains at night-time's
not tenuous, it is not the cold
that makes me shiver, civilized man,
white, I remember
the stories of the Indians,
Sis-i-utl, the double-headed snake.

Beauty's what makes
the adrenaline run. Fear at night
on the level plains, with no horizon
and the stars too bright, wind bitter
even in June, in winter
the snow harsh and blowing,
is what makes me
shiver, not the cold air alone.

And one beauty cancels another. The plains
seem secure and comfortable
at Crow's Nest Pass; in Saskatchewan
the mountains are comforting
to think of; among
the eastwardly diminishing hills
both the flatland and the ridge
seem easy to endure.

As one beauty
cancels another, remembrance
is a foolish act, a double-headed snake
striking in both directions, but I
remember plains and mountains, places
I come from, places I adhere to and live in.

AT THE SAN

Excerpt from The Valley of Flowers

(VERONICA EDDY BROCK)

The business letter with the double red cross of Lorraine arrived on the first of June, 1944. For all the Irish premonitions she'd been weaned on by Mama, there'd been no knocks on the wall during the night, no dreams of priests, no babies crying. Not one warning of calamity. So it was with little curiosity that she tore open the flap. It changed her life in an unimaginable way.

Two days later Sandy was on the bus, her hands gripping the sides of the seat, her thoughts chasing each other around in her brain. The sun going down gave off a lemon light which made abstract shadows on the hills and valleys. Sometimes the bus stretched long and flat and hugged the ground; abruptly against the hills it grew tall and sinister.

Her head felt heavy and tense. She realized she'd tired herself pressing her feet hard against the floorboards. The letter had said, "Could you please come in for observation." Observation meant to look at a person, didn't it?

She looked okay. Oh, sure she was skinny, but there was nothing wrong with her. She could run faster than any of her brothers and sisters. When they played ball at school she could hit a home run and be around the bases before most of the city kids realized where the ball was.

Sandy and her sister Ted – her name was Evelyn but everyone called her Ted – had been light housekeeping while attending the convent school in Regina. It was "light" too, as they lived on canned soups and went to shows on the money they saved.

It meant a lot to their Mama that they could afford to go to a separate school and be taught by the nuns. Sandy had dreams of becoming Florence Nightingale and doing all sorts of brave deeds, but Ted hadn't decided what she'd like to be.

Sandy missed spring on the farm though, where small groups of crocus heads clustered together gossiping on a sunny afternoon. She missed Papa's mysterious excursions in the night, and his news of a spanking new calf the next morning; or Mama feeding a baby lamb wrapped in rags on the open oven door, the lamb gulping the milk as it poured through the nipple; or Mama and Papa both up all night to keep a mother pig from eating her little ones; and always the hurry, hurry to be the first to see the new baby whatever-it-was! Then the all-important hurry to get the crop in while the weather lasted.

The smell of hot sunlight on the new grass. Or the wind with a hint of ice in it, reminding her winter was playing a game of hide-and-seek over the hilltops and could attack at any time.

Fort Qu'Appelle was a small village sprawled in the middle of a valley, with grain elevators on one side of town and a lake on the other. A group of Indians dressed in bright colours stood idly on the sidewalk. Real live Indians! She had forgotten this had been a fort, a haven at one time for Indians and whites alike. The bus stopped; there was a cab parked outside. The driver put her suitcase in the trunk.

"Fort San!" he said, giving her a quick look. "Well, I hope you're going out there to join the staff. A pretty young thing like you."

Why did he say that? Her stomach tightened. Could he tell by the whites of her eyes? Did she look like she had it? Mama said she could tell when a girl was pregnant sometimes even before the girl knew. By her eyes.

The curves in the road and the colourful lakeshore cottages made the ride a blur of impressions. She couldn't keep her eyes off the lake. So much water in one spot. Was this what an ocean looked like?

The driver pulled up in front of a gate and Sandy reluctantly got out. He set her suitcase beside her and drove away. She took a deep breath.

Mounds and mounds of flowers lay with their eyes closed. You couldn't see where one flower left off and the other began. They looked so clean and innocent, like a baby after it had been bathed and tucked into bed for the night.

Why did she have this sinister feeling then, as if the hairs on the back of her neck were standing up? Only dogs showed fear that way; people didn't. What was frightening her? She looked around quickly. There was no one in sight.

It was the smell. It was different too. She'd smelled flowers before, but this was a sweet smell like a narcotic that would sweep into her being and she'd never be the same girl again. She felt like she was being smothered.

Now she knew what her body was remembering but her mind had forgotten. The girls at the convent said that for every flower planted here, a dead body was buried back in the hills. Their families didn't want to claim them or they'd die of the white plague too, so they got rid of them quietly.

Mother of God!

There must be thousands of people buried in the hills. She stared around her silently; the flowers lay there, petals hiding their eyes, waiting to claim their next victim.

She grabbed her suitcase, ran up the steps of the nearest building, threw open the door, and stopped short. The varnished floors were like mirrors. A lady with blue hair done in perfect waves, and wearing a white wrinkled uniform with a face to match, sat in an easy chair across from a lit fireplace. She glanced up at the interruption and scowled towards a sofa.

Chairs had been placed in a semi-circle facing the fireplace as if someone had planned a party and Sandy had stumbled onto it accidentally. She sat down. The lady was as silent as a Baptist Sunday's hush. Sandy tried to blanket her panic with sensible thoughts. Remain absolutely still. No banging your head on the floor – there was her goofy sense of humour again. Smell the burning logs and listen to the snapping and crackling, make pictures in the flames....

It seemed hours later that a short dark man in a white suit, muscles wanting to burst out of his coat, opened the door and let it slam.

"Ya got a new one here?" The woman nodded.

It was dark now and they were on a wooden sidewalk and the wheelchair ride was bumpy and long. They appeared to be going uphill past long flat buildings. She could see lights on in the rooms. So this was a TB sanatorium.

The orderly carried her up the wide front steps and passed through the foyer and hallway into a long narrow back balcony. Three beds on either side of the door faced the windows to the north. This was their bedroom, their balcony, their home.

He explained they didn't normally use this back balcony but due to the war things were more crowded than usual. Back Balcony was *dead* centre, if she'd pardon the expression.

There were balconies at each end of the hall, male at one end and female at the other. Everyone was on strict bed and that's exactly what it meant. No stretching, reaching, sitting, moving – lie as still as possible unless told otherwise by your doctor. Rest, rest, and more rest, if you ever had a hope in hell of getting out of this place.

The space on each side of the door contained barely enough room for three beds with lockers squeezed between them. By stretching a little, the inhabitants could pass things to each other. The walls were a beige colour but there wasn't much of them.

This balcony hung onto the north side of the building, dark

and depressing. The sun never got around far enough to give them any direct sunshine; the hills, trees, and buildings got in the way. It seemed they were in a twilight zone, neither heaven nor hell – more of a purgatory. They could go no lower except to die. If they went higher, they would be moved to a pavilion with exercise.

For the first few months in the Infirmary, the nights were a nightmare. From far down the hall came a cough, dry and rattling, like the dried rattle of a rattlesnake her brothers had "borrowed" from a suitcase of a rodeo rider on the run. Another cough was nearer, gurgling and strangling, leaving the cougher gasping and struggling for breath.

Then from the men's room farther down came a harsh deep cough. Then nearer yet, right across the hall it seemed, someone (maybe it was Mary Donovan whose voice was just a whisper) would begin to wheeze and cough desperately. Sandy would lie still as a piece of petrified wood, as if the gods might notice her moving and force her to join the struggle.

Involuntarily she'd try and breathe for the others. Gradually the time came when she didn't hear them anymore and slept through it all.

Below them was the morgue. They were the first to know when someone died. They'd sit up and watch the hearse being loaded and Sandy would wave goodbye.

The hearse was there often; the change of seasons and death went hand in hand. Patients would endure the long cold winter only to die in the spring, or live through the summer and die in the fall. The girls hadn't been touched closely by death, so there was no reality to it.

The undertaker's name was Mr. Stiff. He was mentioned in the *Believe It or Not* column by Bob Ripley. Mr. Stiff had a daughter he named Mary Rose. It broke the girls up to say Mary Rose Stiff. There was a seamstress whose name was Nellie Hook and a gardener who was called Mr. Gardiner.

When Elizabeth would catch sight of Mr. Stiff in her mirror, she'd say, "He looked me right in the eye today. I'm sure I'm being measured for a coffin." They'd all laugh at that too.

When the girls got their sputum results back and they were positive, they'd say quite cheerfully that they'd "killed the guinea pig." When Sandy asked how they'd done this, old Gimlet Eye, one of the Infirmary nurses, would explain: "The guinea pig is very susceptible to TB, so one bacillus taken from sputum injected into a pig could cause the disease. After a waiting period of two months, they kill the pig and examine it for the presence of disease."

It was strange to have anyone so close to her. Sandy was dumped unceremoniously in the middle bed on the left side of the balcony, Elizabeth to the right of her and Nina on the left.

Elizabeth had high cheekbones, flawless skin, and a long sad face like a horse. She wore her brown hair braided and wrapped around her head. She was quiet, read constantly, and seldom smiled – just came out periodically with cryptic remarks like, "Mother, pin a rose on me, everything else has been pinned on."

Elizabeth had been a sergeant in the Canadian army and was putting her group through the TB unit when someone suggested she have an X-ray. Why not? The doctors found large cavities in both lungs. She had the yellow fingers of a recent smoker, still indulged occasionally, but never complained. Her mother, who had a broad Scottish accent, visited her every Sunday, and Sandy (who pretended to be reading) loved to listen to their conversations. Elizabeth also had two sisters who visited only once or twice a year.

Nina had a round Eaton's doll face, red curly hair and large green eyes. She was a city kid, well filled out and short in stature, Sandy's age. She had a stream of visitors all summer long, plus her Mom and dear old Dad on weekends. Her city classmates spent the summer at the Qu'Appelle lakes. Five or six of them came trooping in every day – braided, blond, bronze-skinned gods and goddesses in bathing suits and bare feet, scattering sand everywhere they walked. They spoke with a flippancy Sandy resented, as if she knew the life they represented would never exist for her and had no right to thrust itself in here. She hated them in their carefree freedom to swim or sail or race or party, but she missed them when the summer was over, as if suddenly the stage had emptied and all the actors had gone home.

Sandy was the only one who didn't cough or have positive sputum. The gurgling choking sounds of the other five hacking and spitting made her want to vomit, but she became inured to it. She worried that if she stayed here any length of time, she could easily be infected on the balcony of this snuffling, snorting, spitting chorus. She still didn't believe she had TB. Every time the other girls flipped open their wax sputum cups, she could visualize this vast army of grey germs all in battledress marching out and heading for her unprotected nose or mouth.

Amy, Pauline, and Beatrice were the girls in the other three beds.

Amy had a wide brow over steel grey eyes and brown hair parted in the centre. She looked to be in her thirties and lived in the Queen City of Regina, like Elizabeth and Nina.

Amy had had an important job with the government – at least she gave the impression it was important. She spoke very precisely and at the slightest provocation would whip out her dictionary and correctly enunciate the word, carefully, distinctly, and properly.

No one ever caught her unprepared; she was in complete control at all times. Sandy was sure she'd walked out of the womb with a dictionary in one hand and a typewriter in the other.

If one of the girls was careless enough to let an oath escape her lips, Amy would clear her throat loudly until they felt like runny-nosed brats back in grade two. She read only psychology and wrote long instructive letters to her mother.

She never even broke a rule unless she had the doctor's written permission and she seldom had visitors. She swore she would never marry because she couldn't expose herself to a male person. She sat on the bed with the sheet pulled over her head when changing her clothes so her balcony mates didn't get a glimpse of that precious body.

Pauline was a shy, smiling, round-faced, dark, kinky-haired girl, married to a big Ukrainian twice her size. His name was John, and they had a farm up in the north. Pauline looked about twenty years old, and had no family.

Beatrice, in the next bed, was a small, blue-eyed blond girl, with a tiny face and thin body. She was married to a farmer, and her home was in the rolling hills of the southwest cattle country. She had two small children, aged seven and nine.

Beatrice was a diabetic, besides having TB. If her insulin wasn't given on time or her diet was inadequate, she'd go into a drunken state and finally a coma. The girls weren't long in finding out that she would answer any question they asked her and have no memory of it afterwards. They'd question her up until she went into a coma and then start yelling for the nurse. They found out her husband was sleeping with the hired girl and wanted a divorce. Embarrassed gasps came from the girls; they hadn't bargained on this!

Each girl had a different horror story to tell Sandy about pneumo before the big day arrived, so she was wheeled down the hall to the operating room feeling she should have written her last will and testament.

Three stretchers were lined up in the hallway ahead of her. Two male patients and one female eyed her critically.

The first open doorway was Mary Donovan's. Sandy glanced in and saw Mary lying in bed. Then she looked up at the squares of soundproofing on the ceiling. Was that put there so other patients couldn't hear her scream? Maybe she should've sent for the priest. She wished she could make herself invisible.

Soon she was in the operating room and the ether smells or alcohol or whatever were making her sick. A white-sheeted nurse helped her from the stretcher to a table and her accordion-suited doctor was ready to perform the operation. He was in a bank robber disguise but she recognized the suit.

"Turn on your right side, Alexandra, and raise both arms above your head." He pushed her pyjama top up around her neck. Gad, these doctors could get away with anything!

"Don't move." His fingers were feeling for a spot between her ribs and, when he found it, the nurse split the skin with a jab. That hurt! Then she felt another needle digging in her side. It was uncomfortable. She kept her body rigid waiting for the Big Hurt, but it never came. The doctor pushed her pyjama top down. Holy Mother in Heaven, was that all there was to it? Those despicable girls, making her worry all night.

"When we insert air in between the lung and the pleura lining, that forces the lung to rest," Dr. Schmitt said, "so we hope this hurries your cure."

Some of the doctors were a bit rougher than others or maybe they were klutzes. The patients named them "the vets." Occasionally the doctors hit a nerve or punctured the lung or put air in a vein, but as much as she worried about it, it never happened to her.

After the pneumo injection of air, the orderly pushed her into a small dark room known as the fluoroscope room. Doctor Eden was in charge here. He was short, stocky, and wore a leather apron. His fingers were burnt off to the first knuckle. The patients said it was the rays going through the fluoroscope, and he never wore gloves for protection.

"Sit up, cross your legs and face me." He moved a flat plate into position under her chin, and a light came on through the plate to gauge how much her lung had collapsed.

Twice a week she had pneumo. If it wasn't for getting out of the room and seeing the other patients she could have gladly given it up. From the waist up to the neck she was exposed to the same rays as the doctor's fingers. Probably one of these days her head would come off at the neck. Wouldn't she look odd walking around with her head tucked underneath her arm, just like in the song George Formby used to sing.

FIRST DEATH
for Doreen Bastedo

GARY HYLAND

I found it in a green velvet case
in the grey light of a failing winter.

A coil of pale blonde hair.

Gathered with a faded ribbon
and clipped to a letter.

A doctor writing
my aunt from the sanatorium
that my cousin was dead.

Her lungs surrendered
and someone, my mother most likely,
who would have done her hair,
saved these strands.

First death resurrected after
so many others.

First Death

Winter has been long and harsh
gouging with burrs of ice,
jagged gusts,
two more deaths.
I want it in its grave –
nothing clipped from it
nothing saved.

I want a wide-striding summer
its farthest foot in November.

I want death human,
wealthy, winter-spent
and sailing to a distant season.

WHERE YOU BEGIN LIKE RIVERS

JOHN V. HICKS

Where you begin like rivers
I hear a sweet singing;
the little stones have voices.
I and the flood tide
are one; we gather and rush on together
under the steepled mountain; we are flying
horses that leap and thunder and are thrown
over a brink and far
out, far down, far on
into a tranquillity of waters;
and faint through the ensuing silence I
hear again the small rock voices,
the sweet singing,
where you begin like rivers.

WHERE I COME FROM

ELIZABETH BREWSTER

People are made of places. They carry with them
hints of jungles or mountains, a tropic grace
or the cool eyes of sea-gazers. Atmosphere of cities
how different drops from them, like the smell of smog
or the almost-not-smell of tulips in the spring,
nature tidily plotted in little squares
with a fountain in the centre; museum smell,
art also tidily plotted with a guidebook;
or the smell of work, glue factories maybe,
chromium-plated offices; smell of subways
crowded at rush hours.

                        Where I come from, people
carry woods in their minds, acres of pine woods;
blueberry patches in the burned-out bush;
wooden farmhouses, old, in need of paint,
with yards where hens and chickens circle about,
clucking aimlessly; battered schoolhouses
behind which violets grow. Spring and winter
are the mind's chief seasons: ice and the breaking of ice.

A door in the mind blows open, and there blows
a frosty wind from fields of snow.

8. EDITING THE PRAIRIE

Modern Farming 1, Laureen Marchand

Oil on canvas, 101.6 x 127 cm, 1985 , CARCC

Saskatchewan people have choices to make: in farming, in cultural relations, in the very way we consider the land itself. Lois Ross helps us to understand one of those choices, as she "delves into the historical and contemporary uses of farm chemicals, as well as...the thoughts of those who use and sell farm chemicals." Those choices can separate us or, as Doug Cuthand says of his tale about a moose, "I told this story to bring people together on the day for the elimination of racial discrimination. It's a timeless and universal theme." On the prairies, as Wallace Stegner says, the landscapes makes us "very acutely aware" of ourselves. As we develop that awareness, we are taking the first step on a journey of understanding. Understanding the place itself, as Randy Lundy has tried to do in his poems, making "an attempt at a translation. As one might translate a poem from Cree into English, I have attempted to translate the Moon's own songs into the language I write in, which happens to be English." And understanding our relationship to this place, its people, and its history. Perhaps, as Don Kerr suggests in his humorous response to an imaginary editor of this place, we need to "edit" our way of looking at the prairie, rather than try to "edit" the prairie itself.

THE NATURAL OR CHEMICAL WAY?

LOIS ROSS

Towards the end of May the wheat plant enters what is commonly referred to as the four-leaf stage. The local chemical dealer is well prepared for the event. This is the time when the majority of prairie farmers begin spraying to rid their field of wild oats. For several months television advertisements have been priming farmers, using key words like deaden, kill, attack. Now the time has come to get the weeds.

It's Saturday morning at the chemical dealer's warehouse. Half-ton trucks back in and out. Sometimes their boxes are completely filled with five-gallon pails. Other times the farmers are more judicious, perhaps only buying five or ten. As they pick up their orders, some linger to chat about the latest techniques, auction sales, equipment prices, or the weather. Shop talk. Buying chemicals is occasion for an ad hoc special gathering.

As one farmer prepares to leave with his gallons I ask him jokingly, "So, how much did you empty your pockets of this time around?"

"Boy, it sure doesn't take long, that's for sure," he says, barely breaking step towards his truck. "Would you believe this is twenty-five hundred dollars' worth and it's not over yet?"

I follow him out to the truck. "Well, it must be worth it...if the stuff works. Does it?"

"I don't know," he says, pausing by the truck's cab. "It seems that every year there are more and more weeds and they seem to be getting tougher and tougher to get rid of. But what else is there to do? You can't let them take over your crop."

A lot of farmers aren't sure whether agricultural chemicals are performing the job. Others are convinced they are. But in an economic climate where one bad crop can cause the downfall of generations of work, few are prepared to risk throwing out the sprayer. In fact, most farmers are using more chemicals than ever.

The use of agricultural chemicals has increased five-fold since 1940. For every North American four pounds of agricultural chemicals are used in the growing of food. In Saskatchewan nine pounds of herbicides are used for each individual. There are five million gallons spread over Saskatchewan annually. On the prairies 80 percent of cropland is sprayed with 2,4-D or its derivatives. An additional 40 percent is sprayed with wild oat killers.

Often when a farmer has a problem with an unusual or a recurring weed, a local representative from Agriculture Canada is called in for advice. Once I sat at a kitchen table and listened to the Ag Rep and farmer discuss solutions. The Ag Rep suggested using a specific chemical. The farmer asked if there was another way, perhaps a less expensive way such as cultivation, to deal with the problem. The Rep appeared to find this question a little beyond the realm of possibility. "No, the chemical is definitely the quickest, surest way to kill that weed." The more money farmers owe, the less time there is to experiment and the more locked in they are to using the surest, fastest method: chemicals.

Prairie farmers are caught in a twisted, environmentally damaging, and expensive form of agriculture. They keep trying to soften the blow of low commodity prices by expanding their operations, taking on more and larger equipment, producing more and increasing supply, which in turns lowers the price of their product. As their farms get larger, they also have to face the problem of trying to juggle the additional workload. In an effort to increase volume, farmers have bought more and more artificial fertilizers and agricultural chemicals.

Meanwhile, while most scientists agree that it's impossible to determine the tolerance of the environment to chemicals, many believe we've reached the limit. The question remains: how much damage have we done? The monitoring of Saskatchewan water basins has proved that they contain residues of 2,4-D, 2,4,5-T, and other agricultural chemical products.

At the same time soil fertility is dropping. Scientists attribute the decline to a decrease in organic matter and nitrogen levels due to improper agricultural practices. In the last 70 years nitrogen levels in the soil have dropped by 50 percent. In Alberta, seven times more nitrogen fertilizer is used than in 1970, yet it is estimated that by 1985 an average acre will produce 20 percent less yield. Six million acres, an estimated 4 percent of crop land in Alberta and Saskatchewan, are saline, or turning into salt, a condition caused by erosion or water drainage problems that allow once subsurface salts and minerals to rise to ground level. That figure is estimated to rise by 10 percent every year. By the year 2000 topsoil will have blown or washed away to the tune of $8 billion worth of potential production. In the face of all of this it's wise to remember that to begin with, only 13 percent of land in Canada is suited to agriculture and less than 5 percent is prime agricultural soil.

And if all that is not enough, plants and insects are becoming resistant to the chemical controls that cost prairie farmers more than $250 million to purchase annually. A six-year study completed in 1983 by University of Saskatchewan biologist Dr. Jim Naylor shows that wild oats, the major weed problem on the prairies, is becoming increasingly resistant to the two most popular forms of chemical controls, Avadex and Treflan. Naylor's study shows that in some fields, following four years of use, double and triple the amount of chemical was necessary to control wild oats. There is also evidence to suggest that wild oats, which is thus becoming resistant to common products, may also be developing a parallel tolerance to other chemicals. Naylor's findings on the prairies are consistent with studies from the United Nations Environment Program, which reports growing resistance to chemicals in hundreds of pests and plants around the world.

Perhaps the most troubling point is that it is impossible to assess the human cost of living in a sea of chemicals. In recent years a new disease called "ecological illness" has been recognized. Essentially this disease is a series of chemical allergies that often forces its sufferers to seek out food which has not been contaminated by chemicals in growth, processing, or packaging.

Even the concern of doctors, long known to be a fairly conservative group when it comes to ringing alarm bells, became evident in 1982 when the Canadian Medical Association passed a resolution on hazardous wastes, stating that both levels of government should promote policies to reduce dependency on potentially hazardous chemicals. The association resolution included a call to "prohibit the manufacture or sale of potentially hazardous chemicals that cannot be recycled or disposed of harmlessly."

Meanwhile, the Canadian Agricultural Chemical Association (CACA), which represents 53 Canadian chemical manufacturers, including Dow and Monsanto, increased its advertising and public relations campaign in 1982 to counteract the bad publicity. In doing so, the association admitted, albeit silently, a threat to their industry. The CACA has often been quoted as saying that agricultural chemicals are only hazardous if they are misused by farmers. "Read the label" is its common suggestion.

Industry spokespeople are quick to reassure farmers that chemicals are indeed necessary and that the industry has a financial commitment to food production. The research and testing of a new chemical costs about $25 million. The industry expects that global sales of each chemical will last for nine years at an annual return on investment of about 40 percent for each chemical.

In March 1983 a spokesperson for CACA revealed that the global market for agricultural chemicals is $10 billion to $12 billion a year. The association is fond of saying that the Canadian market of $450 million to $550 million a year, most of it on the prairies, is a drop in the international bucket. Yet, when tackling environmental issues, past-president of CACA, A.D. St. Clair was quoted as saying that concerned environmentalists are "underinformed activists" with "an unreasoning prejudice against the chemical industry." The association has also stated that chemical technology is a reality of food production and saves farmers from losing 30 per cent of their crops.

But research studies and experts have estimated crop loss would only be between 1 and 15 per cent if herbicides, which are 85 percent of the Canadian agricultural chemical market, were not used.

Most farmers now say they are concerned about chemical hazards. After all, many handle the sprayers themselves and believe their health could suffer from the volatile substances. These days, however, there is an increasing trend among farmers to hire outside help when it comes to chemical applications.

The fear of chemicals is real, but no more real than the economic reality that spirals the need for production, expansion, and chemical use.

MOON-SONGS

(RANDY LUNDY)

Kise-pisim
The Great Moon of Returning Hope (January)

the stars are tiny, scattered seeds
sending forth tendrils of light

you are the single, white blossom
vitrifying the land with your gaze

snow-laden branches
bend into shrines

where the winds circle
chanting softly

where small birds have left
three-toed offerings

Mikisiwi-pisim
The Eagle Moon (February)

eagle-mother stares beyond
the long curve of the earth

deep into the reach of shadow
where purification is taking place

where sun lies drowsing
serpent in a bed of roots and stones

dreaming broad, strong wings
to lift sky from earth

Niski-pisim
The Goose Moon (March)

tonight sun comes mounted
upon the backs of snow geese

riding up from a land without light
to admire moon's blooming face

the river waxes full
preparing to shed a heavy skin

moon dreams her own image
reflected in a slow flow of water

Ayiki-pisim
The Frog Moon (April)

these voices rise with the moon
waxing and waning in their throats

bright stone from the centre of the earth
rising through branches and bones

she is the song they sing
moon-song, song of slow light

pale asphodel
blooming in the night

Sakipakawi-pisim
The Budding Moon (May)

translucent husk of seed
thin bone of sacrifice

your fragrant light opens
the dark cavern of night

slender eyes on the branches of trees
wake slowly, soundlessly from sleep

your song brings a festival
green hands and feet

Paskowihowi-pisim
The Hatching Moon (June)

moon shakes her cloak
and climbs
into a new body of light

you gather an offering of feathers
a bundle of blackened blossoms
plant them in the earth

later, in someone's dream
moon-stones grow
round and white as eggs

in the heat of a fire
they tremble and crack
releasing the voices of birds

Paskowi-pisim
The Moulting Moon (July)

moon digs a grave
deep in the shadow of the earth

her light
a thin sybilline voice
wanes
slowly into silence

whispers in hidden ears

you must fall
you must fall

birds shed feathers of grief
into the black hole of night

Ohpahowi-pisim
The Flying-up Moon (August)
(for debbie s.)

my heart flies up with the moon
small hand-drum in the night sky

skin scraped thin
tanned white
stretched tight
over bone

slow-beating song
at the centre of night

this is my gift to you
an offering of light

this sudden blossom
this unfolding of wings

Nocihitowi-pisim
The Mating Moon (September)

moon is in full bloom
yellow disc with six white petals

dressed in the plumage of love
she garners a last glance

as sun passes without a word
beyond the edge of the light

soon she will wander naked
giving birth again and again
to absence

Pinaskowi-pisim
The Migrating Moon (October)

it is a lie to say
the wind worships nothing
but emptiness

tonight
the wind is a lonely animal
raising a howl from the highest hill

searching the valley for moon's hidden face
buried in a bed of roots and leaves

overhead
the voices of eight ancestor-geese
trail the sun's southern journey

Ihkowi-pisim
The Frost Moon (November)

moon's face has been veiled
three days and three nights

tonight
a slender splinter of hunger
remembering sun's far light

she is an owl made of snow
perched among frosted branches

dreaming
a thin blade of bone

a pool of blood
spilled on an altar of stone

Pawacakinasisi-pisim
The Frost-Exploding Moon (December)

i would like to say

nothing is forgotten
because nothing moves

then moon moves from behind
a heavy bank of snowclouds

the frozen landscape explodes
into light and silence

the green branches of a pine
the only voice in the night

THE QUESTION MARK
IN THE CIRCLE

WALLACE STEGNER

I have sometimes been tempted to believe that I grew up on a gun-toting frontier. This temptation I trace to a stagecoach ride in the spring of 1914, and to a cowpuncher named Buck Murphy.

The stagecoach ran from Gull Lake, Saskatchewan, on the main line of the Canadian Pacific, to the town I shall call Whitemud, sixty miles southwest in the valley of the Whitemud or Frenchman River. The grade from Moose Jaw already reached to Whitemud, and steel was being laid, but no trains were yet running when the stage brought in my mother, my brother, and myself, plus a red-faced cowpuncher with a painful deference to ladies and a great affection for little children. I rode the sixty miles on Buck Murphy's lap, half anaesthetized by his whisky breath, and during the ride I confounded both my mother and Murphy by fishing from under his coat a six-shooter half as big as I was.

A little later Murphy was shot and killed by a Mountie in the streets of Shaunavon, up the line. As I heard, the Mountie was scared and trigger-happy, and would have been in real trouble for an un-Mountie-like killing if Murphy had not been carrying a gun. But instead of visualizing it as it probably was – Murphy coming down the street in a buckboard, the Mountie on the corner, bad blood between them, a suspicious move, a shot, a scared team, a crowd collecting – I have been led by a lifetime of horse opera to imagine that death in standard walk-down detail. For years, growing up in more civilized places, I got a comfortable sense of status out of recalling that in my youth I had been a friend of bad men and an eye witness to gunfights in wide streets between false-fronted saloons. Not even the streets and saloons, now that I test them, were authentic, for I don't think I was ever in Shaunavon in my boyhood, and I could not have reconstructed an image from Whitemud's streets because at the time of Murphy's death Whitemud didn't have any. It hardly even had houses: we ourselves were living in a derailed dining car.

Actually Murphy was an amiable, drunken, sentimental, perhaps dishonest, and generally harmless Montana cowboy like dozens of others. He may have been in Canada for reasons that would have interested Montana sheriffs, but more likely not; and if he had been, so were plenty of others who never thought of themselves as badmen. The Cypress Hills had always made a comfortable retiring place just a good day's ride north of the Line. Murphy would have carried a six-shooter mainly for reasons of brag; he would have worn it inside his coat because Canadian law forbade the carrying of side arms. When Montana cattle outfits worked across the Line they learned to leave their guns in their bedrolls. In the American West men came before law, but in Saskatchewan, the law was there before settlers, before even cattlemen, and not merely law but law enforcement. It was not characteristic that Buck Murphy should die in a gun-fight, but if he had to die by violence it was entirely characteristic that he should be shot by a policeman.

The first settlement in the Cypress Hills country was a vil-lage of Metis winterers, the second was a short-lived Hudson's Bay Company post on Chimney Coulee, the third was the Mounted Police headquarters at Fort Walsh, the fourth was a Mountie outpost erected on the site of the burned Hudson's Bay Company buildings to keep an eye on Sitting Bull and other Indians who congregated in that country in alarming numbers after the big troubles of the 1870's. The Mountie post on Chimney Coulee, later moved down onto the river, was the predecessor of the town of Whitemud. The overgrown foundation stones of its cabins remind a historian why there were no Boot Hills along the Frenchman. The place was too well policed.

So as I have learned more I have had to give up the illusion of a romantic gun-toting past, and it is hardly glamour that brings me back, a middle-aged pilgrim, to the village I last saw in 1920. Neither do I come back with the expectation of returning to a childhood wonderland – or I don't think I do. By most estimates, including most of the estimates of memory, Saskatchewan can be a pretty depressing country.

The Frenchman, a river more American than Canadian since it flows into the Milk and thence into the Missouri, has changed its name since my time to conform with American maps. We always called it the Whitemud, from the stratum of pure white kaolin exposed along its valley. Whitemud or Frenchman, the river is important in my memory, for it conditioned and contained the town. But memory, though vivid, is imprecise, without sure dimensions, and it is as much to test memory against adult observation as for any other reason that I return. What I remember are low bars overgrown with wild roses, cutbank bends, secret paths through the willows, fords across the shallows, swallows in the clay banks, days of indolence and adventure where space was as flexible as the mind's cunning and where time did not exist. That was at the heart of it, the sunken and sanctuary river valley. Out around, stretching in all directions from the benches to become co-extensive with the disc of the world, went the uninterrupted prairie.

The geologist who surveyed southern Saskatchewan in the 1870's called it one of the most desolate and forbidding regions on earth. I can remember plenty of times when it seemed so to me and my family. Yet as I poke the car tentatively eastward into it from Medicine Hat, returning to my childhood through a green June, I look for desolation and can find none.

The plain spreads southward below the Trans-Canada Highway, an ocean of wind-troubled grass and grain. It has its remembered textures: winter wheat heavily headed, scoured and shadowed as if schools of fish move in it; spring wheat with its young seed-rows as precise as combings in a boy's wet hair; grey-brown summer fallow with the weeds disked under; and grass, the marvelous curly prairie wool tight to the earth's skin, straining the wind as the wheat does, but in its own way, secretly.

Prairie wool blue-green, spring wheat bright as new lawn, winter wheat grey-green at rest and slaty when the wind flaws it, roadside primroses as shy as prairie flowers are supposed to be, and as gentle to the eye as when in my boyhood we used to call them wild tulips, and by their coming date the beginning of summer.

On that monotonous surface with its occasional ship-like farm, its atolls of shelter-belt trees, its level ring of horizon, there is little to interrupt the eye. Roads run straight between parallel lines of fence until they intersect the circle of the horizon. It is landscape of circles, radii, perspective exercises – a country of geometry.

Across its empty miles pours the pushing and shouldering wind, a thing you tighten into as a trout tightens into fast water. It is a grassy, clean, exciting wind, with the smell of distance in it, and in its search for whatever it is looking for it turns over every wheat blade and head, every pale primrose, even the ground-hugging grass. It blows yellow-headed blackbirds and hawks and prairie sparrows around the air and ruffles the short tails of meadowlarks on fence posts. In collaboration with the light, it makes lovely and changeful what might otherwise be characterless.

It is a long way from characterless; "overpowering" would be a better word. For over the segmented circle of earth is domed the biggest sky anywhere, which on days like this sheds down on range and wheat and summerfallow a light to set a painter wild, a light pure, glareless, and transparent. There is no haze, neither the woolly grey of humid countries, nor the blue atmosphere of the mountain West. Across the immense sky move navies of cumuli, fair-weathered clouds, their bottoms as even as if they had scraped themselves flat against the flat earth.

The drama of this landscape is in the sky, pouring with light and always moving. The earth is passive. And yet the beauty I am struck by, both as present fact and as revived memory, is a fusion: this sky would not be so spectacular without this earth to change and glow and darken under it. And whatever the sky may do, however the earth is shaken or darkened, the Euclidean perfection abides. The very scale, the hugeness of simple forms, emphasized stability. It is not hills and mountains which we should call eternal. Nature abhors an elevation as much as it abhors a vacuum; a hill is no sooner elevated than the forces of erosion begin tearing it down. These prairies are quiescent, close to static; looked at for any length of time, they begin to impose their awful perfection on the observer's mind. Eternity is a peneplain.

In a wet spring such as this, there is almost as much sky on the ground as in the air. The country is dotted with sloughs, every depression is full of water, the roadside ditches are canals. Grass and wheat grow to the water's edge and under it; they seem to grow right under the edges of the sky. In deep sloughs tules have rooted, and every such pond is dignified with mating mallards and the dark little automata that glide after them as if on strings.

The nesting mallards move in my memory, too, pulling after them shadowy, long-forgotten images. The picture of a drake standing on his head with his curly tailfeathers sticking up from a sheet of wind-flawed slough is tangled in my remembering senses with the feel of the grassy wind, the weight of the sun, the look of the sky with its level-floored clouds made for the penetration of miraculous Beanstalks.

Desolate? Forbidding? There was never a country that in its good moments was more beautiful. Even in drought or dust storm or blizzard it is the reverse of monotonous, once you have submitted to it with all the senses. You don't get out of the wind, but learn to lean and squint against it. You don't escape sky and sun, but wear them in your eyeballs and on your back. You become very acutely aware of yourself. The world is very large, the sky even larger, and you are very small. But also the world is flat, empty, nearly abstract, and in its flatness you are a challenging upright thing, as sudden as an exclamation mark, as enigmatic as a question mark.

It is a country to breed mystical people, egocentric people, perhaps poetic people. But not humble ones. At noon the total sun pours on your single head; at sunrise or sunset you throw a shadow a hundred yards long. It was not prairie dwellers who invented the indifferent universe or impotent man. Puny you may feel there, and vulnerable, but not unnoticed. This is a land to mark the sparrow's fall.

MOOSE TALE

(DOUG CUTHAND)

Indian teachings are couched in humour and tradition, and are often conveyed through stories that tell of momentous events.

Many stories centre around the creation of the earth and its creatures. The world was created by an emissary sent to earth by the "Almighty" or "Manitou." This emissary was called Wesake-chak and his duty was to create the land and animals, thus preparing an earth for the people.

All the animals were considered gifts from the Almighty to the people. There are many stories about how the animals got their uniqueness, and the story of the moose is one of those. When Wesakechak had finished creating the animals, he discovered he had some spare parts left over. He had a huge dark robe that was much too big for the other animals, two big funny-looking flat antlers and a huge round nose. Wesakechak put these parts together, along with several other odds and ends. He came up with this large, ungainly animal.

The moose was very proud of himself and strutted around with pride and confidence. Wesakechak introduced him to the other animals, but they broke out in laughter because he was so funny looking.

The poor moose was heartbroken and told Wesakechak that he would forever live by himself in damp, lonely places.

And so, today, moose do not associate with each other in herds. Instead, they live deep in the forest by themselves.

The Cree word for bachelor literally translates to mean "a

man that lives like a moose."

But this story has a moral. Children are told this story as a way of teaching kindness and tolerance of others.

If you make fun of someone, then that person will be very hurt and may suffer the hurt for a long time.

The message may be told in a First Nations context, but it is timeless and universal. All the world's religions stress kindness and love of our fellow humans.

But history has shown this message has been lost or swept aside time after time as nations, religions, and races go after each other.

The message of brotherly love is bent and perverted to meet secular ends. Too often, we see only the extremists – the Ernst Zundels and David Dukes of this world.

But they exist only because they have supporters and sympathizers who condone their message of hate.

Racism is something that exists within our society at various point of the spectrum. It's not black and white, there are many shades of grey.

The first step is to look into our own hearts and examine our attitudes toward others. How do we see others? Do we fear them? Are we uncomfortable in the presence of others? Have we told a racist joke recently?

Then we must look around at our friends and relatives and see what level of intolerance exists there. Something as simple as racist jokes may at first seem funny, but the laugh is at the expense of others.

Tearing people down is no way to build a positive, multicultural society. In Canada, we are fortunate to live in a land that is home to a wide variety of cultures. We must celebrate our cultures and build on what's good about us.

As First Nations people, we have seen too much racial intolerance. But our elders tell us to look the other way because those who want to hurt us have their own problems and are in pain and suffering.

March 21st has been designated as the day for the elimination of racial discrimination. I don't think racial discrimination will be eliminated in one day, but the designation will at least bring the issue to the public's attention.

Every journey begins with a single step, and awareness is the first step.

LOUIS RIEL

STEVEN MICHAEL BERZENSKY

Afterwards
his child takes
the hangman's noose

turns it back
into a ball of yarn
and gives away
the threads

These are
the loose ends
of the rainbow
he says

EDITING THE PRAIRIE

(DON KERR)

Well, it's too long for one thing
and very repetitive.
Remove half the fields.
Then there are far too many fences
interrupting the narrative flow.
Get some cattlemen to cut down those fences.
There's not enough incident either,
this story is very flat.
Can't you write in a mountain
or at least a decent-sized hill?
And why set it in winter
as if the prairie can grow nothing
but snow.   I like the pubic bush
but there's too much even of that,
and the empty sky filling all the silences
between paragraphs is really boring.
I think on due consideration
we'll have to return your prairie.
Try us again in a year
with a mountain or a sea or a city.

AUTHOR BIOGRAPHIES AND STATEMENTS

Janice Acoose

Born in Broadview, Saskatchewan, Janice Acoose's roots stem from the Sakimay (Saulteaux) First Nation and the Marival Metis Community. As an Associate Professor with the Saskatchewan Indian Federated College and a student of Indigenous literature, she aspires to empower Indigenous peoples through critical reading and writing English, while simultaneously advocating for retention of Indigenous languages. She was Saskatchewan's first Native Affairs Columnist for the *Saskatoon StarPhoenix* and has regularly contributed to the *Regina Leader-Post*, the *Prince Albert Herald*, *Aboriginal Voices*, *New Breed*, and *Windspeaker*. Janice Acoose's first book, *Iskwewak Kah Ki Yaw Ni Wahkomakanak*, was published in 1995.

Author's Statement: "In Memory of my Koochum, Madelaine O'Soup Acoose"
"Inspired by the time I was fortunate to make connections with my Koochum Madelaine, I honour her memory by writing about her. She was not only my Koochum (paternal grandmother), she was my teacher and my role model. When she was a baby, she was uprooted from her homeland in Ireland and placed in the care of a loving 'Indian' family on the Cowessis Reserve. A white-skinned, red-haired beauty, she was constantly reminded of her difference amidst a community of brown-skinned, dark-haired people. Me, I was uprooted and placed in an 'Indian' boarding school at five years old; later, because my father was banished from the reserve, I was uprooted and schooled in an all-white community. Blocking out the memories of years of abuse, loneliness, and racism, I too have gaping holes in my memory. And, like my Koochum, I too cannot claim to be 'purely' anything! Neither of us fit those neat little boxes we place people in to try to understand them."

Marie Annharte Baker

Annharte began her writing career during the years she lived in Saskatchewan. She now lives in Vancouver and is a Carnegie Writers' Group member. As a "cybergran," she's learning multi-media/video poem production. Her published poetry works are *Coyote Columbus Café* and *Being on the Moon*.

Author's Statement: "Put on My Mask for a Change"
"The ritual art of South American Indigenous people bonds mothers and daughters. Instead of the proverbial 'walk a moccasin mile,' the poet asks the readers to take off their false fronts or masked selves and cleanse or apply a healing mask of appreciation for the beauty and self worth of another person."

Steven Michael Berzensky

Born in California, Stephen Michael Berzensky moved to Canada in 1965 and to Saskatchewan in 1973. In 1985, he was appointed writer-in-residence in Yorkton and has lived there ever since. A poet, songwriter, creative-writing teacher, and editor, he has five book publications and numerous self-published chapbooks to his credit. *Variations on the Birth of Jacob* received the Saskatchewan Poetry Award for 1998.

Author's Statement: "Louis Riel"
"Louis Riel is probably the most written-about figure in Saskatchewan's history, so the challenge was to compose a different kind of poem about him. Visualizing the eldest of his children, I asked myself, 'How would you feel if you found out your father had been executed?' I wanted to say something simple but stark about the child's loss. I wanted the images to allow each reader his or her own interpretation. It must touch many people deeply, because it's my most reprinted poem."

Rita Bouvier

Born and raised in Île à la Crosse, Rita Bouvier works in Saskatoon for the Saskatchewan Teachers' Federation. Previous occupations include dishwasher, restaurant hostess, classroom teacher, administrator for an Aboriginal teacher-education program, curriculum developer, and sessional lecturer at the University of Saskatchewan. Rita Bouvier holds B.Ed. and M.Ed. degrees from the University of Saskatchewan. She co-edited a book on the urban experiences of Aboriginal people, *Resting on Mother Earth*, and her first collection of poetry, *Blueberry Clouds*, was published in the fall of 1999.

Author's Statement: "Medicine Man"
"I wrote 'Medicine Man' as part of a university assignment many years ago. 'Medicine Man' is a piece remembering an old man in my community who

was recognized as knowledgeable about medicinal properties of various plants. With his medicines in hand, he often made home visits to his patients. As children, we were warned he also had powers to transform our physical characteristics if we misbehaved. Curious, we often followed several paces behind as he made his rounds in the community. While we tried our best to conceal our secretive operation, hiding behind buildings, grass, and whatever else might be in our path, he often responded by chasing us, which only reinforced the possibility of the extended powers granted to him through story. On one of those days, he caught me."

Elizabeth Brewster

Elizabeth Brewster was born in Chipman, New Brunswick. She grew up there, but since 1972 has lived in Saskatoon, where she is now Professor Emeritus at the University of Saskatchewan. She has published over twenty books of poetry, including *Footnotes to the Book of Job*, which was a finalist for the Governor General's Award for Poetry in 1996, and *Spring Again*, which was a finalist for the Pat Lowther Award. Other awards include the E.J. Pratt Award for Poetry, the President's Medal and Award from the University of Western Ontario, and the Lifetime Award for Excellence in the Arts from the Saskatchewan Arts Board.

Author's Statement: "Parallel Lives"
"A Saskatoon friend asked if I knew a memoir written by a holocaust survivor with a name very similar to mine – Eva Brewster. When I looked up the book, *Progeny of Light / Vanished in Darkness*, I discovered that Eva was born in the same year I was. She had gone through the horrifying wartime experience while I was finishing high school and attending university in comparatively peaceful New Brunswick. I wrote her, we exchanged letters and phone calls, and I was moved to write the poem. She saw the several drafts of the poem, and the final words are hers. Her life is the important one here, and the few details of my life (the Fredericton elms and willows) are mainly presented as contrast."

Author's Statement: "Where I Come From"
"This is a poem I wrote over forty years ago, when I was a graduate student at Indiana University. There were many students there from other parts of the world, who carried with them, I thought, the atmosphere of those dif-

ferent places suggested in the early part of the poem. I might have said that the title applied only to the backwoods New Brunswick represented in the later part of the poem, with the pine woods, blueberry patches, and old wooden farmhouses – the location of many of my earliest memories. However, when I showed the poem to a young poet from India, Ramanujan, with whom I was friendly at the time I wrote it, he suggested that those of us who move from place to place may be 'from' several places, and I might be from several cities hinted at in the earlier section of the poem (London, Boston, Ottawa) where I encountered smog, the smell of subways at rush hour, the 'tidily plotted' squares and crescents of part of London, the 'almost-not-smell of tulips' in an Ottawa spring. Maybe I should write a new 'where I come from' poem, and include Victoria, Edmonton, and Saskatoon."

Veronica Eddy Brock

Veronica Eddy Brock was born on the Saskatchewan-Montana border and attended school at Round Grove, Moose Jaw's Sion Academy, and Regina. From ages sixteen to twenty-one, she lived at the Fort San sanatorium near Fort Qu'Appelle. She left behind the disease, but also a lung and seven ribs. Told never to marry, she nevertheless married a farmer from McTaggart, and has five children and thirteen grandchildren.

Author's statement: "At the San," an excerpt from The Valley of Flowers
"I was interested in writing about my five-year experience at Fort San. This is my story, with 'Sandy' as a pseudonym. Whenever I would be recounting some experience, my youngest child would say 'What's a sand, Mom?' The present generation is in the same situation. They don't know what tuberculosis is and they don't realize what an epidemic it is."

Sharon Butala

Sharon Butala was born in Nipawin, Saskatchewan, and has lived in this province nearly all her life, in Saskatoon and, for the last twenty-five years, on her husband's ranch in the southwest of the province. She is the author of six novels, two short-story collections, and three works of non-fiction, including *The Perfection of the Morning* and *Wild Stone Heart: An Apprentice in the Fields.*

Author's Statement: "Home"
"I am not one of those who thinks Nature should be roped off from

humanity. When talking about human beings' need for Nature, I would be just talking pie-in-the-sky without talking about rural agricultural people and their fate. People do live on the land, and have a right to, and their needs must be considered in any discussion about preserving Nature."

Maria Campbell

Maria Campbell is a writer, storyteller, and teacher. Born in northern Saskatchewan, she makes her home at Gabriel's Crossing in Batoche. In 2000-2001 she was the Stanley Knowles Distinguished Visiting Professor at Brandon University, Brandon, Manitoba. Her best known work is the autobiographical novel *Halfbreed*, first published in 1972. She is the author of half a dozen other books, many of them for young readers, and has written film scripts and dramatic works as well.

Author's Statement: "Grannie Dubuque," an excerpt from Halfbreed
"Grandmothers are a very important part of Metis life and one can hardly tell a story without Grandmother making an appearance, be it in physical or spiritual form. Grandmothers are at the heart of our families and communities."

David Carpenter

David Carpenter was conceived in Saskatoon, but born and raised in Edmonton. He returned to Saskatoon in 1975, where he writes full time. He has also lived in Oregon, Winnipeg, Toronto, and Victoria, and spent many summers working in Banff. He has published three short-fiction collections, *Jewels, Jokes for the Apocalypse,* and *God's Bedfellows*. His first novel, *Banjo Lessons*, received the City of Edmonton book award. His non-fiction publications include the essay collections *Courting Saskatchewan* and *Writing Home* and a book on trout fishing in western Canada. (See also Editor Biographies.)

Author's Statement: "Turkle"
"I grew up on wilderness stories and this is one of them. It's a tall tale about a terrible storm that has some basis in fact. I got the inspiration for the story one warm October day while taking a drive along the North Saskatchewan River with my family. 'Turkle' is the fastest short story I ever wrote; it took only four or five days. I wrote the second draft of this story in an attempt to re-examine some of the convictions of the old prairie

patriarchs who believed that men ran things and women existed to serve. Watch out for baby imagery. Check some of the names in the story. Above all, read this story in winter, but read it in a warm and cosy place."

Lorna Crozier

Born in Swift Current, Lorna Crozier lived in Winnipeg, Regina, and Saskatoon before moving to Victoria in 1991. She has published a dozen books of poetry, including the 1992 Governor General's Award winner, *Inventing the Hawk*. Among her editing credits is the influential anthology *A Sudden Radiance*, an anthology of Saskatchewan poetry.

Author's Statement: "A Prophet in His Own Country"
"When people's thoughts turn to the sacred, many think of what lies above us. They look at the sky. Instead I want to honour what's under our noses, under our feet, the common but holy inhabitants of our world. The gopher is one of the most cursed animal characters on the prairies, but even he knows things we don't know. His understanding of the earth – its darkness, its roots, its pathways to the light – goes much deeper than ours."

Author's Statement: "Wildflowers"
"We've named every flower and categorized it by shape and colour, but what of the other things that matter just as much? Brown-eyed Susans are yellow with a dark centre. What colour is sorrow? Bull thistles are a bristly, vibrant purple. What colour is grief? Words, classifications, lists, don't help to identify the feelings that are part of being human. This poem is one that loves names but recognizes their inadequacies. No words can come close to naming the things we lose."

Robert Currie

Born in Lloydminster, Robert Currie lives in Moose Jaw, where he taught for three decades and where he and his wife raised two children. He received the Joseph Duffy Memorial Award for excellence in the teaching of language arts. A poet and fiction writer, Robert Currie has published four books of poetry and two short-story collections, and his work has appeared in more than forty anthologies. He is a founding member of Coteau Books and has also received a Founder's Award from the Saskatchewan Writers Guild.

Author's Statement: "Pencil Crayons"

"This story was written in an attempt to explore the mechanics of family life in an abusive relationship and particularly the problem of the child caught with torn loyalties in the conflict between his parents. The story is set during bad times on the farm, which exacerbate a trying situation. Its inspiration was partly the result of wondering what kind of man a school-yard bully might grow up to be."

Doug Cuthand

Doug Cuthand was born in La Ronge and moved to southern Alberta with his family at age fourteen. After attending Simon Fraser University during the 1960s, he took a job as editor of *The Native Newspaper* in Edmonton. He then moved back to Saskatchewan to become editor of *The Saskatchewan Indian* and later the director of the communications program for the Federation of Saskatchewan Indian Nations. He now operates his own video-production company and writes a weekly newspaper column for the *Regina Leader-Post* and the *Saskatoon StarPhoenix*. He lives in Saskatoon with his wife and three children.

Author's Statement: "Native People Finally Claim Their Future"

"This column is a short history of Saskatchewan First Nations. I looked at the 20th century and what it meant for our people and what direction we would be going in the 21st century. I don't like to rant about the past, pre-ferring to emphasize positive changes, but sometimes we must remind the public where our roots lie and that the mistakes of the past are the reason for our present situation. When a people are treated as if they have a past that's not worth saving, a present that doesn't include them, and no future, the results are devastating. But in spite of this, our people have survived and are now taking their rightful place within the Canadian mosaic."

Author's statement: "Moose Tale"

"I remember once I asked my father a simple question and his answer was, 'In 1922 your grandfather....' I settled in for a long answer. Traditional Indian people didn't lecture their children. They told stories that got around to the point in sensitive and creative ways. The stories of the creation of the earth are such examples. The earth's creatures were created by Wesakechak, the Almighty's emissary on earth. Therefore, we can make fun and tell humorous stories without offending the Almighty. Wesakechak is the trickster and full of funny stories. The creation of the moose and his subsequent tragic end is a story that tells of human nature and its hurtful consequences. It also tells young people about present-day moose and where they can be found. I told this story to bring people together on the day for the elimination of racial discrimination. It's a timeless and universal theme."

Rex Deverell

Rex Deverell was resident playwright for Regina's Globe Theatre from 1971-1990. His plays range from documentaries on Saskatchewan history to whimsical works for young audiences. His work has a reputation for social commentary. Currently he lives in Toronto, where he continues to write on topical themes. A play for young audiences about refugees and war has just been translated into Italian. Recent productions include a docudrama about auto workers and in progress is a work about slaves who escaped from the South via the "underground railroad."

Author's Statement: An excerpt from Black Powder
"The Great Depression was just beginning. In the Saskatchewan coalfields surrounding Bienfait and Estevan, pay and working conditions had deteriorated to the point of desperation. Workers and their families tried to survive in ramshackle company houses and truly 'owed their soul to the company store.' In September, 1931, they went out on strike. On Tuesday the 9th, they marched into Estevan to hold a demonstration. Several of the workers were shot by police, three of them fatally. Annie Buller was a leftist leader who came to Saskatchewan in support of the miners. This speech, reconstructed from newspaper reports, led to a charge of inciting a riot and nine months of hard labour in the Prince Albert Penitentiary."

John G. Diefenbaker

Born in Ontario in 1895, John Diefenbaker moved west with his family in 1903. Educated in one-room country schools and at the Saskatoon Collegiate Institute and the University of Saskatchewan, John Diefenbaker determined at an early age that politics held his destiny. After serving in the First World War and practising law in Wakaw, he moved, in 1924, to Prince Albert. Finally elected to the House of Commons in 1940 after several defeats, he was re-elected in 1949, but redistribution eliminated his constituency. However, in 1957, the Conservative Party, under his leadership, scored an electoral upset, ending twenty-two years of Liberal rule. His next electoral triumph in 1958, the largest ever accorded any political leader in Canada's history, led to much progressive legislation, including the creation of The Canadian Bill of Rights. John Diefenbaker died in 1979.

Connie Fife

Originally from Saskatchewan, Connie Fife is a Cree writer and editor. She was was the recipient of the Prince and Princess Edward Prize for Aboriginal Literature in 1999. The author of *Beneath the Naked Sun* and *Speaking Through Jagged Rock*, she is the editor of *The Colour of Resistance: A Contemporary Collection of Native Women's Writings* and several other publications. Her work has also appeared in numerous anthologies and periodicals around the world. She lives in British Columbia.

Author's Statement: "Dear Webster"
"'Dear Webster' is a piece born after my having dug into the dictionary for the definition of 'savage.' Each line represents a person who is either a friend or someone I encountered who offered me their story or their secrets. It is also my own way of breaking down or challenging stereotypes of who I am considered to be, of how history has tried to confine or restrain the truth of our reality as Native people. This poem is my attempt to honour those whose lives shaped this particular piece and is a reflection of the impact they have made on my own life."

Joanne Gerber

Joanne Gerber grew up in Toronto but now makes her home in Regina. The mother of two sons, she writes, teaches, and works as an editorial assistant. Her first book, *In the Misleading Absence of Light*, received three Saskatchewan Book Awards and the Jubilee Award for Short Fiction from the Canadian Authors Association, and was a finalist for the Danuta Gleed national short fiction award and the City of Toronto Book Award. She has also co-written an opera, *Sea Change*, with composer David L. McIntyre.

Author's Statement: "Listening to the Angels"
"I think 'Angels' is a story about our need for Mystery, our need to believe that there is meaning shimmering just behind the mundane veil of events.

It's a story about looking at the world through different eyes, listening through attentive ears. This story was a kind of gift – though I had to work hard to unwrap it. I was in the shower when this line shot into my head: 'Stephen is listening to the angels again.' I thought, which angels? Who is Stephen? As I hurried to my study, I suddenly pictured this frail boy, curled into a bow, clutching his hair, rocking. Starting with the line I'd been 'given,' I began to write, draft after draft, until I discovered Stephen's story. I grew to love him and his fiercely tender sister Irene in the process."

Louise Bernice Halfe

Louise Bernice Halfe, also known as Sky Dancer, is a Cree mother, wife, and grandmother. Her original home is Saddle Lake First Nations Reserve in Alberta, although she has lived in Saskatchewan for twenty years with her family. She is fluent in Cree and considers this her first language and her first love. Not only a writer, she holds a degree in Social Work and facilitates workshops in drug and alcohol abuse prevention training. Louise Bernice Halfe made her debut as a published poet in *Writing the Circle: Native Women of Western Canada*. Her journal writing then led to the birth of her first collection, *Bear Bones and Feathers*, which received the People's Poet Award for 1994. Her understanding of the need to preserve story and to promote Native history in both communities – mainstream and Native – led to her second poetry collection, *Blue Marrow*.

Author's Statement: "Nohkom, Medicine Bear"
"'Nohkom, Medicine Bear' is a tribute to my grandmother, Adeliene Halfe. However, the word 'Kokhom' implies that Kokhom is also the reader's grandmother. 'Nohkom' is the correct identification for 'My Grandmother.' My grandmother was a medicine woman who ran her own sweat lodge. My grandfather, William Halfe, provided service for this lodge. Together they worked in harmony. I was raised by these grandparents for three years while my mother convalesced in the TB sanatorium. When I was sent to Blue Quills Residential School, I was robbed of family. Memory and love of my grandparents have served to provide me with stories."

Author's Statement: "The Residential School Bus"
"The residential school bus is one that I, and many other children, boarded. The extended stays in residential school brought loneliness, confusion, and

bitterness. Parents missed their children, cried for them. The children became lost. Rules and regulations imposed by the government and the schools' religious orders forced out the children's Spiritual practices. Child-rearing became confused. Parents forgot about their responsibilities. Shame became ingrained in our lives. However, in the midst of this crazy-making, memory surfaced as the people fought destruction. For in memory, spirit lives. 'The Residential School Bus' is an important piece of recorded history. We must remember if our communities are to heal. Dance and song, ceremony and feasting, are part of this memory."

John V. Hicks

John Hicks was born in London, England, came to Canada as a child, and lived in several parts of the country before settling in Prince Albert. He worked as an accountant, a civil servant, a church organist, and a choir-master. A children's writer as well as a poet, he was widely anthologized and had many of his works broadcast on CBC Radio. In 1978, the City of Prince Albert named him poet laureate for the city, and the University of Saskatchewan awarded him an honorary Doctorate of Literature in 1987. He received the Lifetime Award for Excellence in the Arts from the Saskatchewan Arts Board in 1990, and the Saskatchewan Order of Merit in 1992. His dozen book publications, most of them poetry collections, include *Now Is a Far Country*, *Winter Your Sleep*, *Silence Like the Sun*, and *Fives & Sixes*. John V. Hicks died in 1999.

Gary Hyland

Gary Hyland is a Moose Jaw writer, columnist, editor, and arts activist, and an occasional lecturer at the University of Regina. A former high school English teacher, he has served on the Board of SaskFilm, and was a founding member of Coteau Books, the Sage Hill Writing Experience, ArtSchool Saskatchewan, the Saskatchewan Festival of Words, and Moose Jaw Arts in Motion. Gary Hyland has published four books of poetry, including *Just Off Main*, *Street of Dreams*, *After Atlantis*, and *White Crane Spreads Wings*.

Author's Statement: "Local News"
"On a warm April day in the late 1970s, I was teaching poetry to a Grade Twelve class. Things were going fine, although more than the usual number of eyes were, from time to time, straying to the window. Then it was

lunch. I used to stay in my room to work, this day on my income tax. Halfway through a sandwich, the idea for the poem jumped into my head, probably an escape mechanism from the dreaded income-tax chore. I began to write the first draft of this poem. At that time, all car licence registrations also had to be renewed in April."

Author's Statement: "First Death"
"Maybe some day my feelings and my thoughts about death will coincide. Intellectually, I know death is inevitable, a natural phenomenon. Emotionally, I have never been able to accept it. The year I began this poem, my father and two other people I cared about died. I was sick to death of death. I went back to the first death I could remember, though vaguely, that of my cousin Doreen, who died of tuberculosis when she was twenty-three and I was six. Much of the poem is true. I still have the lock of hair."

Don Kerr

Don Kerr has published five books of poetry, the most recent being *Autodidactic*. He has also had more than half a dozen of his plays professionally produced, and one of them, *Talking Back: The Birth of the* ccf, has also been published. His short stories have appeared in literary periodicals across Canada, and were collected in *Love & the Bottle*. An architectural heritage buff, Don Kerr was born in Saskatoon and continues to make his home there. He teaches in the English Department at the University of Saskatchewan.

Author's statement: "Editing the Prairie"
"I had recently completed the editing on a book of poems. I was travelling by car to Regina, and thought of 'editing the prairie.' I was lucky with this poem – it came on the first try."

Judith Krause

Judith Krause is a Regina writer, editor, and teacher who has three collections of poetry, *Silk Routes of the Body*, *Half the Sky*, and *What We Bring Home*. (See also Editor Biographies.)

Author's Statement: "Half the Sky"
"'Half the Sky' is dedicated to a former student whose violent home life made it extremely difficult for her to attend classes on a regular basis. I

admired her courage and determination to build a better life for herself and her children."

Lea Littlewolfe

Lea Littlewolfe is from Onion Lake Cree Nation on the Alberta-Saskatchewan border. Her tribal affiliations are Abenaki and Odawa, while her European heritage is "mixed" as well. She has taught secondary school subjects in public schools, band schools, and Metis education programs since 1973. She started out busking her poetry and stories on street corners, mostly in Victoria, British Columbia, and began publishing in literary periodicals and other magazines in 1995.

Author's Statement: "swap"
"'swap' began at a 1985 gathering at Fort Pitt near Onion Lake to commemorate the 1885 Resistance and to recall the signing of Treaty Six. The occasion was an exercise in romanticizing history. Modern powwow dancers strutted in feathers and buckskin, actor fur traders swaggered in beards and buckskin, amateur rodeo performers struggled with wagons and horseflesh, Indian and white politicians bragged up the benefits of assimilation. My perceptions of childhood experience on Alexis, Alexander, and Hobbema reserves, and of my adult experience on Sturgeon River, Sunset House, and Onion Lake reserves, clashed with the tone of the festivities on a beribboned stage in a grassy field. My sarcastic poet's mind provided the commentary."

Randy Lundy

Randy Lundy is a member of the Barren Lands First Nation, based near Brochet, Manitoba. Born in Thompson, Manitoba, he lived in Quesnel, British Columbia, and Hudson Bay, Saskatchewan, before moving to Saskatoon in 1987 and Regina, where he currently lives, in 1999. He has an Honours English Degree from the University of Saskatchewan. He has worked as a sessional lecturer at the Saskatoon campus of the Saskatchewan Indian Federated College and as writer-in-residence at the Regina campus of SIFC. Randy Lundy has published poems and essays in a number of literary periodicals and scholarly journals. His first book is the poetry collection *Under the Night Sun*.

Author's Statement: "Moon-Songs"
"The 'Moon-Songs' are sung both to the Moon and, in another sense, by

the Moon. The Moon has her own voice and language: she sings her own songs, articulates her own dreams, desires, joys, and sorrows. These poems, then, are an attempt at a translation. As one might translate a poem from Cree into English, I have attempted to translate the Moon's own songs into the language I write in, which happens to be English. This is not to suggest that the Moon's voice doesn't have its own legitimacy; I believe it does, and my attempt at a translation is a gesture of respect toward that voice and an invitation to the reader to listen for the original language. In the final poem, 'Pawacakinasisi-pisim,' the poet's voice is eclipsed."

Eli Mandel

Elias Wolf Mandel, poet, critic, editor, anthologist, and teacher, was born in Estevan. He attended school in Regina, served in World War II, and took his post-secondary education at the Universities of Saskatchewan and Toronto. He taught at the University of Alberta and York University. Eli Mandel was a prominent figure among Canadian writers and critics. His first poems appeared in the 1950s, and he produced ten volumes of poetry between 1954 and 1981. His fourth collection, *An Idiot Joy*, shared the 1967 Governor General's Award for Poetry. Eli Mandel died in 1992.

Ken Mitchell

Born in Moose Jaw, Ken Mitchell has at times worked as a writer, dramatist, and actor. He is currently Professor of English at the University of Regina and was recently appointed to the Order of Canada for his work as a "literary ambassador" across Canada and beyond. Ken Mitchell has published novels, short stories, poetry, and plays, and is perhaps best known, internationally, for his various works on Dr. Norman Bethune, including the play *Gone the Burning Sun*. (See also Editor Biographies.)

Author's Statement: An excerpt from Gone the Burning Sun
"In China, Dr. Norman Bethune is still revered sixty years after his death, as a doctor and healer who gave his life for the Chinese struggle against Japan. Living in China in 1980, I became acutely aware of his status and fame when people mistook me on the street for the legendary 'doctor without borders.' I travelled throughout China visiting Bethune locations, and on a train wrote the first draft of a one-man play that dramatized the man's life and times. It was intended to be performed in China but, to my sur-

prise, became a Canadian success. It premiered at the Guelph Spring Festival in 1984, and won the Canadian Author's Association award for 'Best Canadian Drama' that year. Later, the play went on to tour Canada, China, and many other countries."

Author's Statement: "Mouseland," an excerpt from That'll Be the Day!
"This legendary parable was created by Saskatchewan's great orator and politician, T.C. 'Tommy' Douglas, premier of the province from 1944 to 1962. Of all his well-remembered anecdotes and jokes, this fable of the mouse with an idea – a socialist idea – has assumed the status of a folk tale in Saskatchewan. This version, adapted from a recording Tommy did for CBC Radio in the mid-1950s, appeared in a scene from my play about the life of Douglas, *That'll Be the Day!* It was first presented at the T.C. Douglas Performance Centre in Weyburn in 1996. The action of the play occurs during the evening of June, 1962, with Douglas defending Medicare on the night of his first defeat in federal politics."

Kim Morrissey

Saskatchewan born, Kim Morrissey was educated at the University of Saskatchewan and lived in Saskatoon for many years. Her latest book is the play *Clever as Paint: The Rosettis in Love.* Her black comedy about Freud, *Dora: A Case of Hysteria,* is a suggested text for the United Kingdom's Open University. She has published two books of poetry: *Batoche* is taught in schools and universities, and five poems from her book *Poems for Men Who Dream of Lolita* have been reprinted in the Open University textbook anthology for Women and Gender Studies. Her work has been broadcast on CBC and BBC radio and the BBC World Service.

Author's Statement: "Grandmother"
"Some poems provide questions rather than answers. 'Grandmother' is from my book *Batoche,* a series of poems about the 1885 battle and its aftermath, written from various points of view. For many generations after the defeat, members of the community were considered 'rebels' and 'troublemakers.' This poem is about the desire to blend in with what is perceived as a predominantly White Anglo-Saxon Protestant culture, and invites a discussion about multiculturalism. If we are to continue as a nation, we must be proud of all our grandmothers, and not only allow them to speak, but be proud of their history."

Greg Nelson

Greg Nelson writes for both stage and radio. Stage plays professionally produced include *Spirit Wrestler*, *Castrato*, *The Cure*, and *Slow Zoom*. *Castrato* won Edmonton's Sterling Award for Best New Play, an Alberta book award, and first prize in the Canadian National Playwriting Competition. His adaptation of *Castrato* for CBC Radio's Monday Night Playhouse was nominated for a Gabriel Award. His other radio plays include *The Burning*, which is also based on Doukhobor history. Born and raised in Central Canada, Greg Nelson received an MFA degree in Playwriting from the University of Alberta. A former playwright-in-residence at the University of Saskatchewan, he currently lives in Calgary.

Author's Statement: An excerpt from Spirit Wrestler
"I set out to write a play about Doukhobors. In the process, I found myself writing about my own non-Doukhobor history, about the experience of coming (as most of us have) to this country, and this society, from somewhere else. I became fascinated by the idea that the 'paradise' described by Nikolai in this scene was, for many immigrants, a difficult one. And that in the process of claiming it, we have, all of us, paid a significant price."

John Newlove

John Newlove was born in Regina and raised in a variety of Saskatchewan towns and villages (he remembers, in rough chronological order, St. Brieux, Ituna, Yellow Grass, Lloydminster, Grenfell, and Verigin) by a peripatetic mother-teacher; he calls Kamsack home although he currently lives in Ottawa. The author of many poetry collections, he received the 1972 Governor General's Award for Poetry for the book *Lies*.

Author's statement: "Doukhobor"
"Doukhobor was written in the early 1960s. I had many Doukhobor friends in Verigin and Kamsack, highly interesting people. 'Doukhobor' is, of course, an elegy for a way of life, not merely for one man alone."

Author's statement: "The Double-Headed Snake"
"This poem was also written in the early 1960s. The First People (a designation I find more attractive, capitalized, than Aboriginals) appear briefly in 'Doukhobor' at one point. I am not sure how and when I absorbed an

overwhelming prejudice against them (it's hard to like, respect, or forgive people you have harmed), which took me years to rid myself of. One of the ways of ridding myself of these racial and cultural blinkers was to find out as much about the People as I could, and one result was things such as 'The Double-Headed Snake.'"

Louis Riel

Louis Riel, a leader of his people in their resistance against the Canadian government in the Canadian Northwest, was born in the Red River Settlement (in what is now Manitoba) in 1844. Ambitious, well-educated and bilingual, Riel quickly emerged as a leader among the Metis of the Red River. In 1869-1870, he headed a provisional government, which would eventually negotiate the Manitoba Act with the Canadian government, establishing Manitoba as a province and providing some protection for French language rights. Although chosen for a seat in the House of Commons on three occasions, he was unable to take his seat in the house. In 1875, Louis Riel's role in Manitoba resulted in his exile from Canada. In 1884, while teaching in Montana at a Jesuit mission, he was asked by a delegation from the community of Metis from the south branch of the Saskatchewan River to present their grievances to the Canadian government. Despite Riel's efforts, the federal government ignored Metis concerns. In March of 1885, a provisional government was declared. On May 15, shortly after the fall of Batoche, following a number of battles with Canadian forces led by General Middleton, he surrendered to Canadian forces and was taken to Regina to stand trial for treason. On August 1, 1885, a jury of six English-speaking Protestants found Louis Riel guilty but recommended mercy. Judge Hugh Richardson sentenced him to death. He was hanged in Regina on November 16, 1885.

William Robertson

William Robertson is a poet, university English instructor, and freelance writer, reviewer, and broadcaster. He has published three collections of poems, the most recent of which is *Somewhere Else*, and a biography of singer k.d. lang. Born in Tokyo, Bill Robertson has lived in various places in Japan and Canada, including Ontario, British Columbia, and Saskatchewan. Educated at the University of Saskatchewan, he served on the board of *NeWest Review* for ten years. He reviews books and plays for

CBC Radio, and writes book and music reviews for the *Saskatoon StarPhoenix*.

Author's Statement: "Adult Language Warning"
"'Adult Language Warning,' which is the title of a whole collection of my poems, is not about swearing. It's about children growing into the language of adults in all its promise, its seeming maturity, and ultimately its pain. The motivation to write this poem came from a bad time I was going through with my stepdaughter. She was about fourteen and seemed to hate everything, mostly, it would seem, me. But, of course, who she hated most of all was herself. She just took it out on the rest of us because she didn't know what was happening to her. She thought all her problems would be solved if she could move to Vancouver or L.A., if she got a guitar, different hair, different face. I saw my son in the basement watching violent movies where problems are solved with a gun and I knew that method was just as unreal as hers."

Lois Ross

Lois Ross is a native of Gravelbourg, Saskatchewan, and was raised on a farm there. She is the author of three non-fiction books, including *Prairie Lives: The Changing Face of Farming*. Her journalistic writing has been published in various newspapers and magazines both nationally and internationally. She also does some fiction writing, particularly short stories. These days she makes her home in Ottawa, with her husband, Rolando, and their son, Decio. In between working full time in communications, she continues to pursue her love of photography and writing.

Author's Statement: "Farming: The Natural or the Chemical Way?"
"My book, *Prairie Lives: The Changing Face of Farming*, was created in an effort to let farmers speak for themselves regarding the trends in agriculture and the future of the family farm. Each chapter explores a key aspect of agrarian prairie society. In that same vein, the chapter entitled 'Farming: The Natural or Chemical Way?' delves into the historical and contemporary uses of farm chemicals, as well as exploring the thoughts of those who use and sell farm chemicals. While a later chapter deals with farmers who are convinced that chemicals are damaging to human health and the environment, this chapter provides a forum for those

farmers who either accept, are beginning to question, or prefer to justify, the use of agricultural chemicals. It provides a glimpse into the reasoning of those who continue, despite risking personal and public health, to apply these poisons."

Barbara Sapergia

Barbara Sapergia writes fiction and drama for stage, film, television, and radio. Her fiction includes *Foreigners, South Hill Girls*, and *Secrets in Water*. Seven of her stage plays have been professionally produced, including *Roundup*. Her radio plays have been aired nationally on CBC programs including "Morningside" and by the Australian Broadcasting Corporation. She is a co-creator and co-writer of the nationally broadcast children's television series *Prairie Berry Pie* and is writing a screenplay based on *Foreigners* for Saskatchewan's Minds Eye Pictures. Barbara Sapergia was born in Moose Jaw and now lives in Saskatoon.

Author's Statement: An excerpt from Roundup
"*Roundup* was inspired by the droughts of the 1980s. Unfortunately, its concerns are even more urgent today. As a child visiting my relatives' ranch near Old Wives Lake, I grew to love the grass and the hills and the sky that seemed always in motion. Then I thought the life there would go on forever; later I learned how fragile that life was. We've had so many farm crises that sometimes it seems people have stopped listening. The questions still remain. Why can't people who grow something as necessary and precious as food make a living? How can they get more control over their lives? Can the dream of a people-centred rural life survive when so many farm families have already left for good?"

Stephen Scriver

Stephen Scriver was born and raised in Wolseley, Saskatchewan. His father ran the local newspaper, and Stephen's writing career began when he was appointed obituaries editor for the paper at the age of ten. He has taught school for thirty years and in addition has been a hockey-league executive, published four books of poetry and three plays, and had a hand in the production of ten documentary films. He and his wife, a midwife, live in Edmonton but long to return to Saskatchewan.

Author's Statement: "Marty Coulda Made'r"
"As a hockey player, I was a 'never was,' so I wasn't burdened with the title of 'prospect' or 'gonna be' or, in the end, a 'shoulda been' like Marty. Over the years I have met, played with, observed, taught, and coached kids who have had great hopes riding on them, hopes that are usually not fulfilled for a multitude of reasons. Consider that only one in 100,000 kids who starts playing hockey ever makes a living at it, and most of them for just a short time."

Author's Statement: "Stanislowski vs. Grenfell"
"This poem resulted from a staff-room argument while I was teaching at Grenfell High School. I refused to buy a ticket to see this violinist, arguing that, first, there was a local hockey game on the same night, and, second, I had doubts about this guy's credentials. Let's face it – you never saw the Stanley Cup champs play in Grenfell, so he wasn't likely to be that world famous either. After the poem was published, I was berated by an anthropology professor who said that I had erred in stating that there was little or no culture in Saskatchewan. What he missed was the capital letter on 'Culture,' my meaning being that a European violinist playing European music may be admirable, but it's not Canadian, while Paul Henderson's last goal against the Russians in 1972 is one of the great moments in a Canadian culture in its infancy. And by the way, the elevator agent's name really was Art!"

Wallace Stegner

Wallace Stegner was born in Lake Mills, Iowa, but spent some of his childhood in southwestern Saskatchewan. Over a sixty-year career, he wrote thirty books. Among the novels are *The Big Rock Candy Mountain, Joe Hill, All the Little Live Things* (Commonwealth Club Gold Medal), *Angle of Repose* (Pulitzer Prize), *The Spectator Bird* (National Book Award), *Recapitulation, Collected Stories,* and *Crossing to Safety.* The non-fiction includes *Beyond the Hundredth Meridian, Wolf Willow (A History, A Story, and a Memory of the Last Plains Frontier), The Sound of Mountain Water,* and *Where the Bluebird Sings to the Lemonade Springs: Living and Writing in the West,* a collection of essays that earned him a nomination for the United States National Book Critics Circle award. *Wolf Willow* is based largely on Stegner's boyhood life in Eastend. Wallace Stegner died in 1993.

Sheila Stevenson

Born near Fort Qu'Appelle, Sheila Stevenson attended university in Regina and Saskatoon, and now teaches in her home town. She has written a film script and several short stories, and contributes articles to several Aboriginal newspapers.

Author's Statement: "David Goes to the Reserve"
"This story is based on a real incident that I described in a conversation several years ago. I wrote this story as an experiment; I was curious to know if my writing could be published, what details I could include to make the characters and the setting seem real, and what choices I could make in the structure and timing of the story without losing my readers. I hope this story raises awareness of how fear prevents us from transcending borders of race and culture, and how the anger and humiliation common to our experiences can be channelled into a specific triumph, a unique form of expression leading towards healing."

Gertrude Story

Born in Saskatchewan, Gertrude Story began working as a freelance writer and broadcaster in the 1950s, and started publishing books in the early 1980s. Her ten books of fiction, poetry, and essays include the "German quartet" of short stories – *The Way to Always Dance, It Never Pays to Laugh Too Much, The Need of Wanting Always,* and *Black Swan*. Gertrude Story has led many writers' workshops and classroom sessions, and has been writer-in-residence for various Saskatchewan Writers Guild and Canada Council programs. She received her B.A. in English, with the President's Medal and the Arts Prize, from the University of Saskatchewan in 1981.

Author's Statement: "Das Engelein Kommt"
"This story, and all the stories in those first four short-story collections, were, in fact, simply dictated to me. Interior voices came to me and said they were teachers of mine, and if I would just take down the dictation of these life lessons in the form of stories, then publication would follow, and also my family would be looked after. And this is exactly what has happened."

Andrew Suknaski

Andrew Suknaski was born near Wood Mountain, Saskatchewan. Over the years he worked at a number of jobs, including farm hand, night watchman, editor and writer-in-residence. He has published half-a-dozen books of poetry, the best-known of which is *Wood Mountain Poems.*

Author's Statement: "Estevan Saskatchewan Transportation Company Bus Stop"
"I rode the bus a lot back then, in the late 70s, early 80s. I was a hunter. A hunter of poems. I wanted to write about the three men killed in the Estevan riot. Because I was writing poems with a documentary flavour, I wanted authentic details. There's a lot of poetry in reality, but it takes a poet to see it. Back then, I was writing poems everywhere – on the bus, the street corner, cars, bars, trains, you name it. A lot of those poems never got published. They ended up with my other papers in the University of Manitoba archives, sold for only $5,000, like the way my father sold the farm for too little."

SUNTEP *Theatre*

SUNTEP Theatre is a troupe of students and staff of the Saskatchewan Urban Native Teacher Education Program in Prince Albert. SUNTEP is a teacher education program affiliated with the University of Saskatchewan. The students are Metis and First Nations, from all over northern Saskatchewan. With Lon Borgerson as teacher-director, SUNTEP Theatre has created numerous collective creations. The plays grow out of discussion and improvisation and are essentially scriptless in the conventional sense. Instead, much of the script is oral, and changes from performance to performance. The work of SUNTEP Theatre is therefore an extension of the storytelling and oral traditions of Metis and First Nations people.

A Note on Process: A Thousand Supperless Babes
"*A Thousand Supperless Babes* grew out of a desire by SUNTEP students to tell the story of the Metis. Research began with archival and textual material, but the magic began as the students shared stories and photographs from their own families and took on the roles of their grandparents and great-grandparents. A remarkable local hero, Honoré Jaxon, provided the perfect narration for the play. With photographs as a backdrop and with dance, drama, and two songs written by Don Freed, *A Thousand Supperless Babes* became a multi-media presentation that delighted local, provincial, and international audiences. It was performed at the 1996 World

Indigenous Peoples Conference on Education in Albuquerque, New Mexico."

Anne Szumigalski

Anne Szumigalski was born in London, England, and immigrated to Saskatoon in 1951. She played a vital role in the development of Saskatchewan's writing community. She was a founding member of the Saskatchewan Writers Guild, Saskatchewan Writers and Artists Colonies, Saskatoon's AKA Artist Run Centre, and *Grain* magazine. Anne Szumigalski's several collections of poetry include *Woman Reading in Bath*, *Doctrine of Signatures*, *Rapture of the Deep*, and *Voice*. *The Word, The Voice, The Text: The Life of a Writer* is a memoir in which Szumigalski recounts her unusual childhood and her development as a writer. Her play about her experience in World War II concentration camps, *Z: A Meditation on Oppression, Desire and Freedom*, was produced at Saskatoon's Twenty-Fifth Street Theatre. She won the 1995 Governor General's Award for Poetry for the collection *Voice*. Anne Szumigalski died in 1999.

Pierre Vandale

Pierre Vandale was a bilingual Metis. He worked as a farm labourer and a wood cutter in north-western Saskatchewan for most of his life, around Meadow Lake, Leoville, Duck Lake and Green Lake. He contracted tuber-culosis as a school-aged boy and recovered from the disease at a nearby sana-torium. His poem "Going to War" comes to us as a "found poem," extracted from the transcript of an interview that was done with Mr. Vandale in 1973. The poet/editor was Stephen Michael Berzensky. It discusses the not uncommon practice, during WWI, of tricking uneducated Metis men into enlisting for the armed forces by buying them drinks and getting them to sign induction papers under the deception that they were being given a job.

Guy Vanderhaeghe

Guy Vanderhaeghe is the author of three collections of short stories, three novels, and two plays. His short story collection *Man Descending* won the 1982 Governor-General's Award for Fiction and the Geoffrey Faber Memorial Prize in Great Britain. His novel *Homesick* was the winner of the City of Toronto Book Award. His novel *The Englishman's Boy* won the Governor General's Award for Fiction in 1996, the 1996 Saskatchewan

Fiction Award and Book of the Year Award at the Saskatchewan Book Awards, and was a finalist for the 1996 Giller Prize and the 1998 International IMPAC Dublin Literary Award.

Author's statement: "Home Place"
"To my mind, this story is about obsession, and about how obsessions are likely to blind us to what is really important. Gil MacLean is prepared to sacrifice his son for the sake of the land, and Ronald is ready to despoil the land as a way of injuring his father. The 'home place' is no home at all."

Brenda Zeman
Brenda Zeman is a Saskatoon anthropologist, author, and former competitive athlete. She has had fiction, non-fiction, and drama published in anthologies and produced for radio, but is now primarily a fiction writer. Her book publications are a sports history *Hockey Heritage: 88 Years of Puck-Chasing in Saskatchewan*, and the collection of sports profiles *To Run With Longboat*.

Author's Statement: "The Reluctant Black Hawk"
"The question is, why did Freddie Sasakamoose only last eleven games in the NHL? Because there is no easy answer – no omnipotent Truth – I have disrupted the linear storyline, made several switches in first-person narrative, and stressed the actual speech of the characters, with Freddie as the repeating voice. All in an effort to engage the reader and, I hope, to reveal several small truths."

ARTIST BIOGRAPHIES AND STATEMENTS

Dennis Bruce
Dennis M. Bruce was born in Lestock, Saskatchewan, to the Muskowekwan Band (Saulteaux). He was a self-taught artist who ventured beyond his people's traditional artistic styles to find himself on the leading edge in contemporary Canadian Aboriginal art. Using traditional symbols such as the eagle, the buffalo, the warrior, and the mother and child, he stayed true to his heritage. However, his use of colour and line was masterfully unique. As well as a solo exhibition of his work at the Nunavut Gallery in Regina, Dennis Bruce's work was part of a number of group exhibitions in

Saskatoon. He created commissioned murals for, among other places, the Muskowekwan Band Hall and the Natural History Museum in Regina. Dennis Bruce died in 2000.

Don Hall

Born in Humboldt, Don Hall took his artistic/photographic training at the then Regina Campus of the University of Saskatchewan and at the Northern Alberta Institute of Technology in Edmonton. He has been employed since 1975 as a photographer and sessional lecturer in Photography in the Faculty of Fine Arts at the University of Regina. Don Hall has shown his work in galleries and exhibitions across the country and has work in many public and private collections.

Artist's Statement: "Near Big Muddy"
"Landscape has always been at the core of my photography. I have always been interested in the landscape of southern Saskatchewan – the expansiveness and amazing light. What interested me about this scene was the humour of the playing card images – the uncertainty, the 'gambling,' of trying to make a living from the land."

Iris Hauser

Iris Hauser is a well-known Saskatoon painter who utilizes classical painting techniques to create dramatic narrative paintings, richly layered with symbolic meaning. After having studied art at the Nova Scotia School of Art and Design, she continued to develop her art through independent study, including a stay in Kassel, Germany. Best known for her painting of human figures, Iris Hauser has had numerous solo and group exhibitions of her work, and has pieces in both private collections and those of the Saskatchewan Arts Board, Saskatchewan Government Insurance, the Mendel Art Gallery, the University of Regina, and the Canada Council Art Bank. Her work has also been used on numerous Canadian book covers.

Artist's Statement: "Traditional Wedding"
"'Traditional Wedding' is a painting that represents a narrative in the form of a play. On the surface is the cautionary tale of two people entering a doomed marriage, with an imbalance of power creating the unhealthy relationship of master and slave. Beneath this tableau lies a second story; just

as an actor brings his own personality and emotion to playing a character, so too the 'Man in the Suit' from this series of paintings tells the story of an individual who is alienated from society, unhappy, angry, and self-destructive. In this way, the truth about an individual's struggle with depression and low self-esteem is expressed within a constructed fable ."

Molly Lenhardt

Celebrated Saskatchewan folk artist Molly Lenhardt was born Sefanka Molly Bassaraba, either in Ukraine or on a farm near Lake Winnipegosis. Her parents supported both her education and her interest in art, unusual attitudes for the time. She graduated from Grade Ten, but illness prevented her from furthering her schooling. She married and spent the rest of her life running the Fairway Confectionery in Melville, taking up painting classes and a painting career after her children had grown. Molly Lenhardt's first solo exhibition was organized by the Dunlop Art Gallery in Regina in 1990. By then she had appeared in several important group exhibitions: From the Heart: Folk Art in Canada, by the National Museum of Civilization, and Grassroots Saskatchewan at the Norman Mackenzie Art Gallery. Collections that contain her work include the Ukrainian Museum of Canada, the Saskatchewan Arts Board, and the Ukrainian Cultural and Educational Centre in Winnipeg. Molly Lenhardt died in 1995.

Laureen Marchand

Laureen Marchand has a B.F.A. from the University of Alberta and her M.F.A. from the University of Saskatchewan. She also has a Library Science degree from the University of Western Ontario in London and has worked in a number of library positions in addition to her art work. She has exhibited throughout Western Canada and was one of the artists chosen to paint one of the Duck Lake Murals. Laureen Marchand's work is in many public collections, including Saskatchewan Government Insurance, Saskatchewan Arts Board, City of Moose Jaw, and Grant McEwan Community College in Edmonton. Her work has also been used on a number of Canadian book covers.

Artist's Statement: "Modern Farming 1"
"'Modern Farming 1' is one of three paintings in a series created to recognize Canada's farm crisis. It shows a man and a woman posed in front of their combine. Behind them, in a place they apparently don't see, are two policemen

in dress uniform. Are the officials there to protect the farmers or to take possession of their farm? Although the Modern Farming series was made in the mid-1980s, it seems as though the situation has not changed much today."

Celina Ritter

A Chipewyan born at Cold Lake, Alberta, Celina Ritter received her B.F.A. from the Alberta College of Art in Calgary and her M.F.A. from the Fine Arts Program at the University of Regina. She lived in Regina for a time, but currently lives in Calgary, Alberta. Her work has explored most visual arts genres, from oil and acrylic painting to collage, sculpture, and printmaking. Celina Ritter's creations have appeared in several group exhibitions, including ones in Prince Albert, Regina, Saskatoon, and Calgary.

Artist's Statement: "Indoctrination of the Natives"
"It was the search for Identity that led me to return to my childhood, to write about my experiences as a child, and to paint and collage the Residential School series. The impact on my life of that childhood realm has much to do with the personality I now have – the negative as well as positive experiences were all embedded in my way of thinking and doing things. The art of survival that the negative inspired me to do, the positive that one day I would no longer have to be there, were the 'light at the end of the tunnel' for me. The work itself is collaged on a white church, with pictures of Grey Nuns in the windows. There are also portions of text from the Bible which warn of heaven/hell situations that I felt were brainwashed into me. On one level the nuns taught us kindness, etc., from the Bible. On the other hand, they were going against their own teaching by the abuse we suffered. It was my intent to convey this message by collage rather than paint, as it represented the piece by piece gluing, as parts of memory ingrained into myself to make a part of my personality and way of thinking. I learned to forgive, in a sense, but the memory is still embossed in my subconscious. Maybe one day I will forget, but it is unlikely."

Marie Elyse St. George

Marie Elyse St. George was born in Ontario and has lived in Saskatoon since the mid-1970s. She has worked and studied in Canada, England, and the United States, where she has exhibited her visual art in major galleries and in art and literary publications. Her work has also been used on a number of Canadian book covers. Her book of poems, etchings, and paintings, *White Lions in the Afternoon,* was published in 1987. A collaborative exhibition with Anne Szumigalski at the Susan Whitney Gallery in Regina in 1993 led to a major exhibition at the Mendel Gallery in Saskatoon in 1995, and the book *Voice,* for which Anne Szumigalski received the Governor General's Award for Poetry.

Artist's Statement: "Daft Molly Metcalfe"
"I've always made art from life, prose, and poetry that has moved me. I try to avoid simple reportage and instead use imagination and insight to work with art elements like colour, line, and composition, pushing the drawing just a little into the surreal to make it mine. 'Daft Molly' is a true story told by Yorkshire folksinger Jake Thackery. She was a foundling born in the early 1900s who was sent at age eight to mind sheep on the moors. She went mad from the isolation and died at twenty-eight, caught in a sudden blizzard. Because I've experienced the moors and have always been moved by lost childhood, I painted 'Daft Molly Metcalfe' to commemorate her life and the lives of all exploited children."

Allen Sapp

Allen Sapp has lived and worked on the Red Pheasant Reserve near North Battleford all his life. His work has been characterized by realistic portrayals of the daily life of his people in the 1930s and 1940s. His paintings have been collected and exhibited around the world and sold in galleries in Toronto, Regina, and a gallery named after him in North Battleford. Allen Sapp has received the National Aboriginal Award for Lifetime Achievement, the Order of Canada, the Saskatchewan Order of Merit, and the Saskatchewan Arts Board's Lifetime Award for Excellence in the Arts.

Artist's Statement: "The Hockey Game"
"Sometimes we would play hockey on a slough behind my old home. There would always be a few boys who would like playing out in the open. Many times we didn't have skates, but that didn't stop us from playing. When I paint the pictures of kids playing, I will sometimes dream about having real hockey nets just like we would see in the movies. The painting would always be happy scenes that I would remember from playing with my friends on the reserve."

GENERAL EDITOR AND CONSULTING EDITOR BIOGRAPHIES

Larry Warwaruk (General Editor)

Larry Warwaruk received his B.ED. at the University of Regina and M.ED at the University of Oregon. He then taught English and Drama and worked as a principal in central Saskatchewan for many years, recently retiring from teaching. He is the author of two novels, *Rope of Time*, and *The Ukrainian Wedding*, for which he won the Saskatchewan Book Award for Fiction. His short stories have been published in *Grain*, *NeWest Review*, and elsewhere, and have been heard on CBC Radio. He is also active in community theatre – he helped found the Snakebite Players in Beechy, and has received several Best Director awards in Saskatchewan Community Theatre Festivals.

David Carpenter (Fiction)

David Carpenter began his professional life as a high school teacher in Edmonton. He left teaching to do a Master's degree in English at the University of Oregon, a PH.D. at the University of Alberta, and a post-doctoral fellowship at the University of Manitoba. He was a Professor of English at the University of Saskatchewan for many years, but has taken early retirement to be a full-time writer.

Margo Day (Drama)

Margo Day is a teacher of drama, a director of plays, and an occasional actor. Recently she wrote the Drama strand of the Arts Education Curriculum for Saskatchewan Education. She currently fills her working life as a teacher for the Prairie West Regional College and a lecturer in Drama Education at the University of Saskatchewan. Raised as an "airforce brat," Margo Day completed her formal education at Acadia University in Wolfville, Nova Scotia, and at the University of Saskatchewan, where she met her husband. They live on their farm in West Central Saskatchewan.

Heather Hodgson (First Nations/Metis Literature)

Heather Hodgson is a lecturer in the English Department of the Saskatchewan Indian Federated College, University of Regina. She has been teaching at SIFC in the departments of Science and English since 1994.

She has a B.A. from the University of Saskatchewan and an M.SC. in Administration from Central Michigan University. She is presently completing an M.A. degree in English Literature at the University of Regina. She worked as an associate producer and arts co-host on CBC radio's "Morning Edition," and as the Program Manager of Family and Lifestyles programming for the Saskatchewan Communications Network. She edited an anthology of contemporary aboriginal writing, *Seventh Generation*, published by Theytus Books. Heather Hodgson is of Cree and English descent.

Judith Krause (Poetry)

Judith Krause is an award-winning Regina poet, editor, and teacher. She has studied languages, literature, and writing in Saskatchewan, France, Switzerland, and the United States, earning a bilingual B.A. (University of Regina), a B. OF VOC/TECH ED, and an M.F.A. in Creative Writing (Warren Wilson College, North Carolina). She is the co-editor of *Out of Place*, an anthology of stories and poems, and has served as poetry editor of *Windscript* and *Grain* magazines. A past president of the Saskatchewan Writers Guild, Judith Krause has worked as Literary Arts Consultant to the Saskatchewan Arts Board, co-ordinated the Creative Writing Program at the Saskatchewan School of the Arts, and has taught Creative Writing at the School as well as through the University of Saskatchewan Extension Division and at the Sage Hill Writing Experience. She currently teaches in an adult-education program in Regina.

Ken Mitchell (Non-fiction)

The author or editor of over twenty books, Ken Mitchell has been teaching at the English Department of the University of Regina, where he is now a Professor of English, for more than thirty years. His latest publication is a novel, *Stones of the Dalai Lama*. He is also the author of several dozen screenplays, stage dramas, and radio dramas, most notably *The Hounds of Notre Dame* (Genie nomination for Best Screenplay) and *Cruel Tears*, the country opera which has gone on to international acclaim. In 1999 he received the Order of Canada for his work as a "literary ambassador," teaching and promoting Canadian literature to India, Russia, Greece, and elsewhere, most notably for two years in China.

TITLE INDEX

AUTHOR/ARTIST INDEX

GENRE INDEX

Poetry

Short Stories

Introduction to

UNIT AND THEMATIC INDEXES

These several indexes provide ideas for some ways that material from *Sundog Highway* could be used in classrooms. Certainly, teachers will have many other ideas of their own. Educators are encouraged to choose suitable titles for as many curricula and teaching situations as are appropriate in helping them meet the particular needs and interests of their students. Of course, titles should be chosen in accordance with each individual school division's selection policy.

Teachers should note that this anthology has been custom-designed to support the English Language Arts A30 and Canadian Studies 30 curricula.

ENGLISH LANGUAGE ARTS A30 THEMATIC INDEX

Aboriginal Voices

Batoche; PAINTING; *Lenhardt*; frontispiece
David Goes to the Reserve; SHORT STORY; *Stevenson*; p. 126
Dear Webster; POETRY; *Fife*; p. 193
Going To War; POETRY; *Vandale*; p. 229
Grandmother; POETRY; *Morrissey*; p. 219
Grannie Dubuque; SHORT STORY; *Campbell*; p. 207
The Hockey Game; PAINTING; *Sapp*; p. 95
Indoctrination of the Natives; COLLAGE; *Ritter*; p. 205
In Memory of My Koochum, Madelaine O'Soup Acoose; ESSAY; *Acoose*; p. 40
Louis Riel; POETRY; *Berzensky*; p. 272
The Medicine Man; POETRY; *Bouvier*; p. 170
Moon-Songs; POETRY; *Lundy*; p. 256
Moose Tale; ESSAY; *Cuthand*; p. 269
Native People Finally Claim Their Future; ESSAY; *Cuthand*; p. 17
Nôhkom, Medicine Bear; POETRY; *Halfe*; p. 152
Put on My Mask for a Change; POETRY; *Baker*; p. 154
The Reluctant Black Hawk; ESSAY; *Zeman*; p. 98
The Residential School Bus; POETRY; *Halfe*; p. 213

Marginalized Voices

Multicultural Voices

Nature and Seasons

Personalities and Values

CANADIAN STUDIES 30 UNIT INDEX

HISTORY 30

Unit 5 – Challenges and Opportunities

Home; ESSAY; *Butala*; p. 3
Modern Farming I; PAINTING; *Marchand*; p. 249
Moose Tale; ESSAY; *Cuthand*; p. 269
The Natural or Chemical Way?; ESSAY; *Ross*; p. 251
Roundup; PLAY; *Sapergia*; p. 32

SOCIAL STUDIES 30

Unit 1 – Change

Home; ESSAY; *Butala*; p. 3
Indoctrination of the Natives; COLLAGE; *Ritter*; p. 205
Modern Farming I; PAINTING; *Marchand*; p. 249
Near Big Muddy; PHOTOGRAPH; *Hall*; p. 1
Roundup; PLAY; *Sapergia*; p. 32
Things to Come; PAINTING; *Bruce*; p. 149

Unit 2 – Economic

Black Powder; PLAY; *Deverell*; p. 73
Coal Miners; PHOTOGRAPH; *Saskatchewan Archives*; p. 45
Estevan, Saskatchewan Transportation Company Bus Stop; POETRY;
    Suknaski; p. 77
Modern Farming I; PAINTING; *Marchand*; p. 249
The Natural or Chemical Way?; ESSAY; *Ross*; p. 251

Unit 3 – Culture

Doukhobor; POETRY; *Newlove*; p. 61
In Memory of My Koochum, Madelaine O'Soup Acoose; ESSAY; *Acoose*; p. 40
Moose Tale; ESSAY; *Cuthand*; p. 269
Native People Finally Claim Their Future; ESSAY; *Cuthand*; p. 17
The Residential School Bus; POETRY; *Halfe*; p. 213
Spirit Wrestler; PLAY; *Nelson*; p. 63
swap; POETRY; *Littlewolfe*; p. 30

NATIVE STUDIES 30

Unit 5: Social Development

ACKNOWLEDGEMENTS

Coteau Books would like to acknowledge the assistance of the Department of Education, and many hard-working people in the Curriculum and Instruction Branch and elsewhere, in the development of *Sundog Highway*.

Coteau Books would also like to acknowledge the financial assistance of the SaskTel Pioneers organization in producing the book.

CONTRIBUTOR ACKNOWLEDGEMENTS

Janice Acoose – "In Memory of My Koochum, Madelaine O'Soup Acoose" is reprinted from *Canadian Women's Studies, Volume* 12, No. 2. Reprinted by permission of the author.

Annharte (Marie Annharte Baker) – "Put On My Mask For a Change" is reprinted from *Coyote Columbus Café*, Moonprint Press. Reprinted by permission of the author.

Steven Michael Berzensky – "Louis Riel" is reprinted from *A Sudden Radiance*, Coteau Books. Reprinted by permission of the author.

Rita Bouvier – "The Medicine Man" is reprinted from *Cloudberries*, Thistledown Press. Reprinted by permission of the publisher.

Elizabeth Brewster – "Parallel Lives" is reprinted from *Burning Bush*, Oberon Press. Reprinted by permission of the publisher. "Where I Come From" is reprinted from *Selected Poems Volume 1*, Oberon Press. Reprinted by permission of the publisher.

Veronica Eddy Brock – "At the San" is an excerpt reprinted from *The Valley of Flowers*, Coteau Books.

Dennis Bruce – "Things To Come" is reproduced from the Permanent Collection of the Saskatchewan Arts Board. Reproduced by permission of the artist's estate.

Sharon Butala – "Home" is a chapter reprinted from *The Perfection of the Morning*, by Sharon Butala. A Phyllis Bruce Book, HarperPerennial Canada. Copyright © 1994 by Sharon Butala. All rights reserved. Reprinted by permission of the publisher.

Maria Campbell – "Grannie Dubuque" is a chapter reprinted from *Halfbreed*, by Maria Campbell, McClelland and Stewart, the Canadian Publisher. Reprinted by permission of the publisher.

David Carpenter – "Turkle" is reprinted from *Due West*, Coteau Books, NeWest Press, and Turnstone Press. Reprinted by permission of the author.

Lorna Crozier – "A Prophet in His Own Country" is reprinted from *Grain*, Vol 26, No. 4. Reprinted by permission of the author. "Wildflowers" is reprinted from *What the Living Won't Let Go*, by Lorna Crozier, McClelland and Stewart, the Canadian Publisher. Reprinted by permission of the publisher.

Robert Currie – "Pencil Crayons" is reprinted from *Things You Don't Forget*, Coteau Books.

Doug Cuthand – "Moose Tale" is reprinted from the *Regina Leader-Post*. Reprinted by permission of the author. "Native People Finally Claim Their Future" is reprinted from the *Saskatoon StarPhoenix*. Reprinted by permission of the author

Rex Deverell – "Black Powder" is an excerpt reprinted from *Black Powder*, Coteau Books. Reprinted by permission of the author.

John Diefenbaker – "Human Rights" is an excerpt of a speech given in the House of Commons on July 1, 1960.

Connie Fife – "Dear Webster" is reprinted from *Reinventing the Enemy's Language*, Norton. Reprinted by permission of the author.

Joanne Gerber – "Listening To the Angels" is reprinted from *In the Misleading Absence of Light*, Coteau Books.

Don Hall – "Near Big Muddy" is reproduced from the Permanent Collection of the Saskatchewan Arts Board. Reproduced by permission of the artist.

Louise Bernice Halfe – "Nôhkom, Medicine Bear" and "The Residential School Bus" are reprinted from *Bear Bones and Feathers*, Coteau Books

Iris Hauser – "Traditional Wedding" is reproduced by permission of the artist.

John V. Hicks – "Where You Begin Like Rivers" is reprinted from *Now is a Far Country*, Thistledown Press. Reprinted by permission of the publisher.

Gary Hyland – "First Death" is reprinted from *White Crane Spreads Wings*, Coteau Books. "Local News" is reprinted from *Just Off Main*, Thistledown Press. Reprinted by permission of the publisher.

Don Kerr – "Editing the Prairie" is reprinted from *In the City of Our Fathers*, Coteau Books

Judith Krause – "Half the Sky" is reprinted from *Half the Sky*, Coteau Books

Molly Lenhardt – "Batoche" is reproduced from the Permanent Collection of the Saskatchewan Arts Board. Reproduced by permission of the artist's estate.

Lea Littlewolfe – "swap" is a previously unpublished work, published by permission of the author.

Randy Lundy – "Moon-Songs" is reprinted from *Under the Night Sun,* Coteau Books.

Eli Mandel – "From the North Saskatchewan" is reprinted from *The Other Harmony,* Canadian Plains Research Center. Reprinted by permission of the author's estate.

Laureen Marchand – "Modern Farming 1" is reproduced by permission of the artist.

Courtney Milne – "Aegean Grass Sea ; camera motion on windswept grass, near Central Butte, Saskatchewan, 1983" (cover image), is reproduced by permission of the artist.

Ken Mitchell – "Gone the Burning Sun" is an excerpt reprinted from *Gone the Burning Sun,* Playwrights Canada Press. Reprinted by permission of the author. "Mouseland" is an excerpt from a previously unpublished work, *That'll Be the Day.* Reprinted by permission of the author.

Kim Morrissey – "Grandmother" is reprinted from *Batoche,* Coteau Books.

National Archives of Canada – "Louis Riel addressing the jury", photo #c-00 1879

Greg Nelson – "Spirit Wrestler" is an excerpt reprinted from *Spirit Wrestler,* Coteau Books.

John Newlove – "The Double-Headed Snake" and "Doukhobor" are reprinted from *Apology for Absence,* The Porcupine's Quill. Reprinted by permission of the publisher.

Celina Ritter – "Indoctrination of the Natives" is reproduced from the Permanent Collection of the Saskatchewan Arts Board. Reproduced by permission of the artist.

William Robertson – "Adult Language Warning" is reprinted from *Adult Language Warning,* Brick Books. Reprinted by permission of the publisher.

Louis Riel – "The Testimony of Louis Riel" is an excerpt from the transcript of the trial, *The Queen vs Louis Riel,* Canada, Sessional Papers, 1886, #43. Vol. xix, Number 12.

Lois Ross – "The Natural or Chemical Way?" is reprinted from *Prairie Lives: The Changing Face of Farming,* Between the Lines Press. Reprinted by permission of the author.

Marie Elyse St. George – "Daft Molly Metcalfe" is reproduced by permission of the artist.

Barbara Sapergia – "Roundup" is an excerpt reprinted from *Roundup,* Coteau Books

Allen Sapp – "The Hockey Game" is reproduced from the Permanent Collection of the Saskatchewan Arts Board. Reproduced by permission of the artist.

Saskatchewan Archives Board – "Coal Miners," photo #R-A 5996-2

"John George Diefenbaker," photo #R-B 1 133 1.

"T.C. Douglas," photo #R-A 5739- 1.

Stephen Scriver – "Marty Coulda Made'r" and "Stanislowski vs. Grenfell" are reprinted from *More All Star Poet*, Coteau Books.

Wallace Stegner – "The Question Mark in the Circle" is an excerpt reprinted from *Wolf Willow*, by Wallace Stegner. Copyright © 1955, 1957, 1958, 1959, 1962 by Wallace Stegner. Reprinted by permission of Brandt & Brandt Literary Agents, Inc.

Sheila Stevenson – "David Goes to the Reserve" is reprinted from *Due West*, Coteau Books, NeWest Press, and Turnstone Press. Reprinted by permission of the author.

Gertrude Story – "Das Engelein Kommt" is reprinted from *Black Swan*, Thistledown Press. Reprinted by permission of the author.

Andrew Suknaski – "Estevan, Saskatchewan Transportation Company Bus Stop" is reprinted from *In the Name of Narid*, The Porcupine's Quill. Reprinted by permission of the author.

SUNTEP Theatre – "A Thousand Supperless Babes" is an excerpt from a previously unpublished work *A Thousand Supperless Babes*. Reprinted by permission of SUNTEP Theatre. Lyrics for the song "Honoré" reprinted by permission of James Keelaghan. Lyrics for the song "When This Valley," Scratchatune Publishing, reprinted by permission of Don Freed.

Anne Szumigalski – "The Elect" and "Quince" are reprinted from *On Glassy Wings: Poems New and Selected*, Coteau Books.

Pierre Vandale – "Going To War" is a found poem reprinted from *Towards a New Past, Vol. II - Found Poems of the Metis People*, Saskatchewan Department of Culture and Youth

Guy Vanderhaeghe – "Home Place" is reprinted from *Things as They Are?*, by Guy Vanderhaeghe, McClelland and Stewart, The Canadian Publisher. Reprinted by permission of the publisher.

Brenda Zeman – "The Reluctant Black Hawk" is reprinted from *To Run With Longboat*, GMS2 Ventures. Reprinted by permission of the author.